WEB OF LIES

CHRISTINA JAMES

This is a work of fiction. Names, characters, places and incidents are either the product of the author's imagination or are used fictitiously. Any resemblance to actual persons living or dead, business establishments, events, or locales, is entirely coincidental.

Web of Lies

Published by Valerie Harris

Copyright 2012 by Valerie Harris

Cover by Angela Anderson, Angela Anderson Design

ISBN: 978-0-9851596-7-2 (Amazon)

978-0-9851596-8-9 (Barnes & Noble)

978-1-938799-12-9 (Apple)

978-1-938799-05-1 (print)

To my children, Courtney and Scott,
for being my world
and always believing in their Mom.

CHAPTER 1

"We are following Breaking News out of New York City," the reporter blurted out on live television as she sat at the news desk trying to be calm in explaining the developing situation. "As you can see from video at the scene, plumes of thick smoke billow from the ambulance bay at New York General Hospital in what is believed to be another horrible act of violence in a healthcare setting. Our very own Channel Nine, Beth Davies, was one of the first reporters on the scene. Tell us what you know so far, Beth, about this very sad event."

The camera zeroed in on the slender brunette as she turned from the camera to the hospital behind her and back to the camera. "Well, Candace, as you can see, the scene is very chaotic. The hospital declared a disaster and is in lockdown mode, not allowing anyone to enter. The few people who have streamed out described a scene from hell. Smoke filling the corridors, people screaming, hospital staff running in every direction, injured people lying on the floor crying."

Candace shook her head in disgust. "Beth, has a suspect been apprehended?"

"Suspects you mean—this wasn't the act of just one person. An unidentified hospital security guard reported to me that they believe multiple people were involved in order to pull off an attack of this magnitude since the explosions rocked four different areas, centering around the Emergency Room located on the southwest side of the building. Speculation at this point is that the suspects wanted to cripple the emergency services this hospital provides. No one knows why yet, but Saudi Prince Jamal Al-Hussein is confirmed as a patient here. One theory then is that this was an assassination attempt on the prince. A New York City policeman also told me the police haven't yet determined that this was not an act of terrorism so they have not asked for a change in the national terror alert status but will, if they deem necessary."

"Beth, have you heard what types of injuries are being treated?" Candace asked.

"Yes. There were a number of smoke related issues. The explosions, which were minor but numerous, had created a toxic cloud of choking smoke that has irritated those patients with respiratory problems. The Emergency Room is reported to be under immense strain attempting to treat so many patients especially when they were at maximum capacity before the attack. I'm also told some nurses were injured, adding to the problem. Hospital administration is assuring us they are handling the situation since this is what their disaster plan deals with and that they have re-assigned staff from other floors to where they are needed at this critical moment. Non-critical patients are being prepped for transport to other area hospitals as well."

Beth turned her attention to a stream of black vehicles

entering the hospital parking lot, blue and white lights flashing in their front grills. Men dressed in dark suits jumped out and secured the perimeter of the hospital, pushing crowds back. Guns drawn. Eyes scanning the crowds. Stern faces daring anyone to cross their paths.

Candace yelled to get the other woman's attention as Beth whirled around to assess the new development. "Beth, can you find out what is going on?"

A hospital spokesperson walked toward the reporters assembling on the sidewalk outside the hospital. The man dressed in a tan suit stepped into the circle of reporters and held his hands up as microphones were thrust into his face and questions hurled at him.

"A statement. I'd like to make a statement, if you would please allow me to do so."

The crowd immediately stilled. All eyes were fixed on the man as he spoke slowly and methodically.

"The Blue Diamond, a treasured heirloom of Prince Jamal Al-Hussein, has been stolen while he is here at New York General Hospital for treatment of a rare genetic disorder. The Blue Diamond, considered priceless, has been in the Saudi Royal Family for over five hundred years and believed to protect from harm those who possess it. Given the Saudi Prince's deep familial traditions, it's no surprise he brought the diamond with him to New York while seeking special medical treatment. The thieves shot and killed three members of the prince's security detail. Behind me, the Secret Service has arrived to assist in the investigation of this mega-theft. The New York Police are investigating the homicides. The hospital remains in lockdown until further notice and is cooperating fully with all authorities."

The reporters rammed him with questions again.

The man sighed and held his palms out. "I will take no

questions at this time. Prince Al-Hussein wishes for me to convey a statement from him though. The prince is, understandably, immensely upset by the theft of such a prized family heirloom and promises that, if the thief returns the diamond, no questions will be asked. All he wishes is to recover his diamond. Anyone with information is urged to contact their local police department as all law enforcement agencies are diligently working on this case. That'll be all for now."

"How was the Blue Diamond stolen?"

"What about charges for the explosions? If the thief turns in the diamond, will he or she still face charges for the explosions?"

"Was the prince's security force disabled during the theft?"

"Was this an assassination attempt against the prince?"

The questions hurled relentlessly at the retreating form of the spokesman.

Beth faced the camera again. "Candace, the developments in this situation keep coming with one mystery after another rearing its ugly head. Who stole the famed Blue Diamond from the powerful prince and how did they defeat the prince's security team to do so? There are a lot of questions to be answered and I'll try to get our viewers some more information. For now, though, back to you, Candace."

Candace swiveled in her chair. "Well, folks, as you heard, we have a lot of Breaking News here at the Channel Nine News Desk. Imagine the poor people who thought they'd be safe at a hospital only to be caught in a violent attack. We'll take a short break now. Stay tuned for more details of the explosion at New York General Hospital and the theft of the priceless Blue Diamond," Candace announced before going to a commercial.

"Son of a bitch!" Derek Norris exclaimed, slamming his beer against his partner's, before sucking it down in one gulp.

"They think we're still inside the fucking hospital. Morons—we're in our hotel room," he yelled at the television. "Shit on you, boys." He laughed and paced the floor.

"Don't get too cocky, asshole. We're still on the run," Carlos warned.

"Come on, Carlos, you big bad ex-Special Ops soldier. You can't tell me you're not beaming with pride that our plan went off without a goddamn hitch."

"I never said that. I just don't like cockiness, especially from someone like you who thinks a few months of training makes him a tough guy."

Derek snarled. "No, it made me a fucking hit man, asshole. You know, Carlos, I didn't need you on this job as much as you like to think I did. I took out those soldiers before they could even fire a shot at me."

Carlos laughed as he stood, his large body barely fitting in the chair. "That was a horseshoe up your ass. Just remember, kid, I may have taught you everything you know, but you'll never be better than me. One fucking successful heist doesn't make you a bad ass. When I was in the military, Special Ops guys fell from a bullet just like anyone else. So don't ever forget you're not invincible."

Derek was no one's fool. He had gone to jail for his boss, Bones—took the fall for the mobster—and knew from the moment Bones had him trained as a hit man that his life was on a ticking clock. Bones thought he was fooled.

For years, Derek had been waiting and training for just the right circumstances to prove his worth and become rich. He knew everyone thought he was a pea-brained thug, but he could protect his own ass.

With the size of this job, Derek knew that once he handed over the Blue Diamond to Bones he was a dead man. Without a doubt, Bones would find him disposable and a loose end to tie up. Derek's loyalty wouldn't mean shit to the mobster in the face of a multi-million dollar windfall.

"Just so you remember, Carlos, it was *me* who stole the Blue Diamond and not your fat ass," Derek said as he tugged the Blue Diamond from his pants pocket and gripped it hard in his palm. He wasn't about to give it up and then lose his life. *Hell no!*

"Fuck off," Carlos grumbled. "Without me planning the theft, right down to every friggin' detail, you wouldn't have gotten your snaky fingers around it. Remember, it was me who got you past the prince's soldiers. They're some of the best-trained military men in the world. Hell, even I'm smart enough to know we had a good dose of sheer luck today. If those explosions we had set in the ER hadn't been such a great diversion during their morning prayer time, you would've had more than three armed men to deal with."

Derek grinned when he remembered the chaos that had ensued after the first explosion rocked the building and fire alarms sounded. "Man, when them access-controlled doors were automatically dismantled from the fire alarm system, I'd never felt such a rush of adrenaline in my life."

The images of the morning ran through his mind. Lurking in the stairwell, he had quickly entered the floor where the prince recuperated. Dressed in those stupid hospital scrubs, he blended in enough to skirt by the panicked staff without being questioned. Timing proved the most important part of their success. It had been brilliant to hit when the prince's security team had the least number of soldiers in the room due their obligatory prayer time.

Derek beamed, pride consuming him. "I'll give you

credit for the planning. But it was my ass that had to get onto the floor. That nurse is damn fucking lucky she didn't lie to us about where the Blue Diamond was."

While the staff ran around scared to death, Derek had eased into the prince's room pretending he was there to assist the trio of alert soldiers. When he pulled out his pistol with the silencer, the three men lay dead in four seconds.

"Pretty hard to lie when your family's lives are at stake," Carlos said. "If she didn't help us the right way, then Bones would've blown her family's heads off—including her kids."

Derek shook his palm holding the Blue Diamond in the air and yelled, "I don't give a fuck about how many nurses you got to help us get onto the right floor or share the soldier's routine. What it comes down to is that I was the one to do it."

"Oh, Christ, kid. Fine. You need a fucking at-a-boy pat on your back then fine. I got you onto the floor but *you* were the one to steal it. Now come on, Bones said we need to get out of the city," Carlos injected, his eyes watching the door.

"Yeah, well, Bones isn't running this show, Carlos. Okay? I say when we leave. The police aren't looking for us. They're running around the city with their heads up their asses."

Carlos stared at him. "What's gotten into you, Derek? Bones would slit your throat if he heard you talking shit like that. He's the boss."

Derek's smile creased his lips slowly. "Like he doesn't plan on offing me once he gets his slimy paws on the diamond? Hell, he's probably already arranged for you to do the dirty deed, you prick. What the fuck—do I look that stupid? Bones ain't gonna do shit to me. I'm gonna be a friggin' millionaire. Way richer than him."

Carlos faced him with his arms across his chest looking down at Derek. "Man, I don't like this kind of talk."

"Good thing I don't plan on talking much more to you," Derek said, pulling a knife. "In fact, I'm done talking."

Carlos jumped back, cornered. "What the fuck are you doing?" Automatically, he reached for the gun at his side.

Derek kicked the gun clear of his grip. They should never have trained him to be a killer. "Just getting rid of witnesses."

Carlos struggled, out of breath. "I'm your goddamn partner. You wouldn't have scored that diamond if it weren't for me figuring out it was here in the first place."

"Then let me say thank you before I kill you."

"Bones will find you. If you double-cross the Mob, your life won't be worth shit."

"Once I sell this Blue Diamond, my life will be worth more than Bones could ever dream of. Nighty night, Carlos."

Derek raised the knife high and swung fast. Carlos' fat body hindered his defense. Gone was the elite Special Ops man he had once been, replaced by an awkward overweight man too slow to defend himself. Easily, Derek sliced Carlos, the blade sliding into his skin like a knife through butter. When Carlos sagged against the blood stained wall, Derek smiled and stuffed a washcloth into Carlos' mouth to keep him quiet. He only wished he could stick around and watch him suffer before he finally croaked.

"Won't be long before you bleed out, my friend," Derek sneered, packing the Blue Diamond in his jean's pocket and walking to the door. "And I never needed your help, Carlos. I heard about the Blue Diamond and its value years ago and tracked it ever since. It's the one reason I agreed to work for a prick like Bones these past years. Just needed my chance."

Laughing, he stepped into the hallway, closing the door

behind him, never looking back at a dying Carlos. Stepping onto the crowded New York street, Derek blended in with the thousands of people rushing somewhere.

Derek was in no hurry. He'd go into hiding until he could figure out his next step. Just how the hell would he sell the Blue Diamond? Bones had the connections, not him. But screwing over Bones was the right thing to do. Derek was the one who followed the Blue Diamond's every movement through snitches. Why should Bones profit for doing nothing? Derek had risked his life not to mention would have had his probation revoked if caught. No way in hell would he ever go back to jail.

Derek walked into the subway and into obscurity, smiling, remembering how easy it was to silently gun down the three-man security detail for the Blue Diamond as they foolishly looked out the small window watching the explosions, their fellow soldiers the next floor down in the hospital meditation room...praying. Serves the foolish prince right to lose it. The fool actually believed the dark gem could aid him in his pathetic medical treatment.

The only mystical power it had was to disrupt the busiest city in America when a no-name thug like Derek claimed it as his.

∿

"I don't care what it takes to recover my Blue Diamond. Just do it!" Prince Jamal Al-Hussein yelled, his fists clenched while he sat in his private New York hospital room, throngs of press mulling about outside the building.

"Please do not upset yourself," his wife insisted. "Doctor said no good for your recovery."

"How can I not be upset? Am I to go down in Saudi

history as a laughing stock? As a fool because I lost the most valuable heirloom of my family's history? All because I allowed most of my security force to perform their morning prayers?"

"No, my dearest. Your men will recover the Blue Diamond. Just give it time and please rest."

He kissed her hand. "Please leave me now. I await my men. We have urgent business."

"Yes, my dear," she said, obediently leaving the room.

Within minutes, the general of the Royal Soldiers entered. "Your Highness. If I may have a word with you?"

"Start talking, General Khalid. What have you found out?"

"We believe the theft was orchestrated by an organized crime family. We will find out more."

The prince pounded the bed. "You damn well better. When we find the thief, and we will, I will personally carve out his heart."

"Yes, sir."

"You are to stay with a team in New York, General Khalid. I want to know when the dirty thief is found. Then I will kill him, along with anyone who stands in my way of retrieving what is mine. So whether child, friend, woman, I don't care. They will all face my wrath."

With a quick wave of his hand, he dismissed the general who turned and left immediately.

"Crazy American bastards. Whoever you thieves are, you and all you love will suffer for the shame you have brought on my family." The prince pounded his hand into his palm, the oath heard only by him.

CHAPTER 2

Three months later

Amber Norris wondered just what the hell she ever saw in the man standing before her, attempting to force his way into her apartment. Young and dumb that's what she had been when she first met Derek Norris. At the naïve age of eighteen, she thought the twenty-one-year-old was a God—handsome, sexy, charming, with his shaved head, twinkling brown eyes, and rebellious attitude.

Now eight years later, Derek was anything but that, standing at her door disheveled like he hadn't bathed in a week. And smelling like it too, although he usually stank of booze and cigarettes instead of BO. He still shaved his head, but his once fascinating eyes lacked the luster that first mesmerized her young heart.

Between them stood the only link they still had, their seven-year-old daughter, Jenna. With shoulder-length light brown hair in pigtails and her curious hazel eyes wide, Jenna danced in place. In her small arms, she clutched the doll Derek had surprised her with when she had opened the door. Amber tried to instill in her young daughter the need to let only Mommy open the door when someone knocked, but Jenna hadn't remembered that once she recognized her daddy standing on the other side of the thin slab of wood that offered the only protection against the deranged man.

"Don't tell me, Derek, that you came all the way here just to give Jenna a doll. What are you up to?" Amber asked, refusing to let him past the doorway, using her body to block his entrance, but knowing he could easily push past her. They stood in the small entranceway, neither budging.

Derek's eyes bounced around the room like he expected a ghost to jump out and holler *boo*. "She's my daughter too, Amber, and if I want to give her a present, I can."

Amber huffed a breath, nausea settling deep in her gut, a normal reaction whenever she was around this pathetic excuse for a man. "That's bull and you know it. You've never done anything for either one of us so why start now? You just want something, that's the only time you ever show your face." She kept her chin up, knowing if he saw her fright he'd take full advantage of the weakness and then God knows what trouble he would cause.

Derek's bloodshot eyes drooped. "I didn't come here to argue. Just take care of the doll, Jenna. Daddy saw it and immediately thought of you. I remember how much you like to play with dolls."

Amber bit her tongue to keep from lashing out any more in front of Jenna. He couldn't remember anything about Jenna since he had rarely been home and was high those few times he had been. "Fine. You did your good deed for the decade. Now leave, Derek."

He stepped closer so they were nose-to-nose, but she stood her ground. "I was hoping to crash here tonight. Been on the road and am a little short on cash."

She laughed, but there was no humor in it. "I knew it. No way. I want you out of here right now. Jenna, please go to your room," Amber calmly instructed without taking her eyes off of Derek.

Jenna leapt onto her father's legs with a big hug, but he didn't put his arms around her to accept it. "Thank you for the doll, Daddy. She's beautiful."

"Just as pretty as you, sweetie," he said softly, leaning down to kiss the top of her head, the effort more rehearsed than meaningful. Once Jenna was out of the room, he turned back to Amber. "Don't be a fucking bitch. I'm staying here tonight." Gone was the fake tender voice he had used with his daughter. In its place was the harsh tone of a monster Amber remembered all too well.

Amber crossed her arms, keeping her eyes on his. "Don't you talk to me like you did when we were married. I'm no longer afraid of you." Out of instinct, she stepped back on trembling knees.

He stepped closer, his breath sour and suffocating her. "Yeah? Maybe you should be."

"Get out now."

"Let me at least take a fucking shower."

Her chin shot up. "There's a hose outside. Use that. Now get the hell out of here before I call the police."

His eyes were menacing. "Go ahead and try that, bitch. I guarantee I'll break your hand before you can dial."

Swallowing the hard lump in her throat, she continued the eye contact, the wild look in those lifeless depths disturbing. "What, Derek? Did your latest stint in jail for that armed robbery charge make you a tough guy? Get the hell out and don't come back. I won't allow you the chance to destroy me and Jenna again."

"Fuck you. I didn't destroy shit." His voice rose as it usually did when she didn't please him.

But she was no longer that trapped and frightened young girl he had married. She stared at him. "You forget we lost our house because of you being sent to jail."

His voice thundered, his beady eyes pierced hers. "Then you fucking divorced me. Do you know what that was like... sitting in jail and being served divorce papers by my ungrateful whore of a wife?"

She raised her voice to compete with his. She refused to show how frightened she felt. If she allowed him to walk all over her, he would. "Do you know what it was like worrying if I could feed our daughter? Thank God I found a job to support us since you couldn't."

"Just because I ran into some bad luck was no excuse to abandon me, you ungrateful bitch."

Her jaw dropped. "Abandon you? Bad luck? You robbed a bank, for Christ's sake. You're a criminal. Look at you. You're a mess. Are you on drugs again?"

"None of your business what the fuck I do."

"It is when you come around my house. You're not making any sense either. You never bought a damn thing for your daughter. Why start now?"

He bared his teeth like the animal he was. "Maybe I'm trying to make up for past mistakes. Daddy's little girl deserves pretty toys."

She stood with her arms crossed. "Well, that takes a lot more than a doll, Derek. You should've thought of this before you ruined our lives. Don't even think that you're going to start playing daddy now after all these years. She doesn't know what you're all about, Derek. But if you start coming around now, she's old enough to figure out that her daddy isn't a very nice man and she won't be giving you hugs so easily. The best thing you can do for her is to stay the hell away."

"I don't need any shit from you, Amber. I have enough problems to deal with."

She stepped around him, hoping to edge him back out the door. "And you're my biggest problem. Bringing a gift for Jenna isn't going to help you sweet talk me. Now leave."

"No. I said I'm staying here, damnit."

The thought of him being in the same house with her precious little girl sent her over the edge like never before. "Get the hell out!" she screamed, her heart pounding, expecting the first blow from his fists to strike at any second. Most of his abuse had been out of reflex, the need to control her with brute force.

His teeth clenched. "Fine. But I'll be back to see my daughter." His voice was raw, mean and promising.

Neighbors had watched the scene unfold from the outside, some stood on porches and others on the sidewalk. Great, just what she needed when she had always kept a low profile to protect Jenna from the scandal known as her father. And, God forbid, any of the nosy people call the police to help her when the man on her doorstep harassed her.

Amber's newfound temper exploded. She pointed her finger into his face. "You stay the hell away from Jenna, or so help me God, I will kill you, Derek. You've damaged her life enough. Come near us again and you'll regret it, you bastard!"

She slammed the door and locked it, sagging against it, sucking in great gulps of air to calm her shaking nerves. She refused to cry, remembering her oath years earlier to never again waste a tear on a shit-bum like Derek Norris.

She allowed herself a few minutes to pace the parlor to

regain her composure so as not to frighten her daughter. Poor Jenna was so innocent and such a good child no matter how bad her father was. Now that she was alone again, Amber's temper deflated.

Walking quickly to Jenna's room in the back of the apartment, Amber was glad to see her daughter wasn't upset, obviously missing the argument between her parents. Her little angel played with the new doll, hugging it and singing lull-a-byes.

Jenna smiled wide when she noticed Amber watching her from the doorway. "Mommy, isn't she beautiful? Why did Daddy give her to me? It's not my birthday yet."

"I don't know, honey. But I'm glad you like her."

"I love her! She's going to sleep with me and go everywhere I go." Jenna hugged the doll fiercely and jumped up and down.

"Well, right now it's bath time. She can sleep on the counter while you soak in bubbles," Amber told her with a smile. Amber promised herself a nice long bubble bath later too, once Jenna was asleep.

Jenna obeyed Amber who settled her into a bath filled with her favorite bath toys.

"Mommy, why doesn't Daddy live with us?"

Amber stared at the child not sure where to begin to answer such a question, knowing there was no simple answer. "Well...it has nothing to do with you, honey. When you were a baby, Daddy got into some trouble and Mommy thought it would be better for me and you if we didn't live together anymore."

"Did he go to jail?"

Shock settled deep into Amber's belly. "Jenna, where did you hear that?"

Jenna fussed with her bubbles and avoided eye contact.

"Paula from school teased me before, but I didn't care. I told her that all I needed was you."

Amber smiled. "Yes, Daddy went to jail for a while. Sometimes kids hear things from their parents and then repeat them when they really shouldn't. Next time, you come to me right away to let me know. Okay?"

"Okay." Jenna's innocent eyes focused on her mother. "I'm glad Daddy doesn't live here because he looked scary. But I'm glad he gave me the doll."

"I know, honey. Now scrub up and you can play with her." She left Jenna to bathe.

Amber sighed with relief when she peaked through the parlor window to see no trace of Derek. He wouldn't stick around. He never did, even when they were married. Never stayed long when there was nothing he could get from it. Bitter memories surfaced, but she refused to dwell on them. The past was the past and that's where Derek belonged.

DEREK WALKED AWAY from Amber's apartment only because he didn't want to draw any unnecessary attention to himself. Not because she told him to leave.

Who the hell does she think she is anyways, ordering me around? A good smack upside her head would remind her who she was talking to. But then the bitch would call the cops and the wrong people could find out he was back in town.

He walked quickly with his face down and his ears listening for any sign of trouble. He had covered his tracks really well these past months knowing Bones had every available man looking for him. And not just the ones who worked for him. Every loser who wanted a big payday would no doubt be on the lookout for Derek, hoping to cash-in by bringing him to Bones.

Like Derek would ever allow that to happen. He'd been patient this long, awaiting his own payday. Just a little longer was all he needed.

His fucking stupid bitch of an ex-wife should've just let him crash there for the night. What harm would it have done? He could've cleaned up, ate and slept.

He walked into the small diner a few blocks from Amber's house and sat at the far end of the lunch counter. This way he could see the door and, more importantly, who came in it.

"Coffee and a grilled cheese," Derek told the waitress. His last five dollars would barely cover that.

He grinned at the irony of having a fifty-million dollar diamond in his possession and yet not be able to afford a decent meal. This wasn't how it was supposed to be. He was starving when he should be surrounded by a feast.

Soon. Very soon.

As Derek waited for his sandwich, his stomach growled loudly. The smell from the meatloaf dinner the guy next to him ate was almost too much to bear. His mouth watered as he watched the man lift a large chunk of the meat, dripping with brown gravy, to his mouth and chew. Derek wanted to stab the man just for eating in front of him.

Where the fuck is my goddamn grilled cheese? How long does it take to slap a few slices of cheese between bread and grill it? As if she read his thoughts, the waitress placed his sandwich and coffee in front of him and approached another customer for their order.

Eagerly, Derek chewed the first half of the measly sandwich washing it down with the coffee. The T.V. caught his attention as the nightly news came on.

"Still months after the incredible attack at New York General Hospital, the Blue Diamond is still missing," the reporter announced. "Today, confirming what had been widely speculated, the Secret Service has finally declared that the attack was meant to look like an assassination attempt on Prince Jamal Al-Hussein to distract authorities from the theft in process. The finely tuned scheme to steal the Blue Diamond even turned out to be no match for the prince's elite soldiers. With explosions riveting the rest of the hospital, the three Saudi soldiers guarding the Blue Diamond were shot and killed by a thief who managed to bypass extremely tight security and disappear with a price-less heirloom in mere minutes. Many have criticized the prince for authorizing time-off for four of his seven-member security detail to perform their morning prayers. It is widely debated that hospital staff may have alerted the thieves to the soldiers' prayer routine, therefore, aiding the thieves in their ability to catch the three remaining soldiers off-guard."

Another reporter continued. "Prince Jamal Al-Hussein has remained in seclusion, no doubt suffering quite a bit of embarrassment for his poor decision. Some critics taunt that he practically handed the thieves the diamond. The Saudi Royal family has demanded the safe return of the diamond with no questions asked. But there have been no sightings of the magnificent stone. We'll keep you updated as developments continue to come in. Now to today's other news events—"

Derek tuned out the rest of the reporter's words. He smiled as he finished the last bite of his dinner, the sand-wich suddenly tasting like the finest filet mignon.

Damn right. No one is better than me. Fucking no one.

CHAPTER 3

Two days later
Amber opened the door to find three police officers—two in uniform and one in plain clothes, holding out his badge for her examination. During her marriage, she'd grown accustomed to seeing the men in blue on her doorstep inquiring about Derek's latest wrongdoing. But now that she'd been divorced for five years, she hadn't a clue as to what they'd want, other than to track down her wayward ex.

"Mrs. Norris?" the tall, plain-clothed officer asked, his voice deep and serious.

"Ms. Norris now. I'm divorced. What do you need, officer?"

"I'm Detective Maguire. Officers Stevens and Heaton. May we come in?" he asked, shoving his credentials into the back pocket of his jeans.

A sigh escaped her lips. "Sure, if you must." She stepped aside and allowed them entry. "Let me guess. My ex-husband has gone and committed another crime and you think he's here. Well, feel free to search the place because he's not." She crossed her arms and resisted the urge to scream.

"Here's a search warrant, ma'am," Detective Maguire said, handing her a folded piece of paper much like the ones she'd seen before.

She accepted the paper without looking at it. Detective Maguire motioned for the other two men to begin their search. They moved around the apartment cautiously, hands on their guns. Thank God Jenna was at a play date. Amber returned her attention to the detective when he started to speak again.

"When did you last see your ex-husband, ma'am?" The man was tall, about six-feet-two, lean and toned. Not a bad package if he weren't looking at her as if she was lower than something on the bottom of his shoe. Still, with his short black hair and screaming bright blue eyes on a freshly shaven face, he could've passed for a model instead of a cop. He looked so out of place standing in her small parlor, too handsome to be single yet wearing no wedding ring.

Amber watched him with her arms crossed, the search warrant held tightly in her hand when she really wanted to burn it. "It's Amber; ma'am is reserved for my mother. I kicked Derek's sorry ass out of here two days ago when he showed up unexpectedly to see my daughter. I wasn't pleased."

"Is she his daughter, too?" That voice was smooth like molasses and just as sweet. Sharp contrast to the determined look in his eyes as he studied her with each answer she gave.

Heat pricked her cheeks, humiliation nothing new to her. "Yes. Unfortunately, Jenna got stuck having a loser for a dad. I try to make it up to her since it was my bad decision to be with him in the first place."

"How long were you married, Amber?" Her name rolled off his lips, as if he enjoyed saying it. What the hell had gotten into her? He was here to interrogate her, not to pay a social visit.

"We began dating when I was eighteen. Got married at nineteen. Had Jenna a few months later. I divorced him five years ago, when I was twenty-one, because he went to prison for armed robbery." She hated having to relive the bad memories of her teenage years.

The detective studied a small notebook, flipping the pages. "Yes, he has a lengthy record. Someone close to him should've known what he was up to." His tone was accusatory, but that was nothing new either. She had lived the last few years of her life distancing herself from her ex-husband's reputation without much luck. His gaze held steady.

Her chin shot up and she held his stare. "I don't like your tone, Officer. Or your insinuations."

The corners of his mouth twitched like they begged to smile. Something he probably never did, except when he looked at himself in the mirror. The jerk! "It's Detective Maguire, not officer. Why don't you explain to me how, as his wife, you didn't have any idea of where your husband made his money?"

Her cheeks grew hotter with embarrassment. "Because I was young and dumb, *Detective* Maguire," she said, drawing out his name. "I believed every word Derek told me...up until the police raided our house and forced me onto the floor with him, handcuffed me and almost charged me with conspiracy to armed robbery—all while my baby cried and I couldn't hold her." She stopped abruptly, closed her eyes and forced the tears not to fall. Slowly, she opened her eyes to find him still watching her without any change in his stern expression. "They thought I helped him rob that bank because there was a female driver in the get-away car."

"Since you weren't thrown in jail and have no criminal record—"

Cutting him off, she spoke not caring if sarcasm dripped from her words. "Ah, so you've already checked into my past."

"Wouldn't be doing my job if I didn't."

Amber hated being questioned for things that had nothing to do with her. Damn! "There was a female get-away driver, but it wasn't me. It was Derek's whore, something else I was too naïve to realize he was doing behind my back." She stepped closer to him. "I've worked hard to start my life over and raise my daughter. Now, Detective Maguire, is there a reason you're here—other than to humiliate me by reminding me of my past and how foolish I was? If it's Derek you're looking for, you won't find him here. And don't even bother to ask me where he could be. I stopped keeping tabs on him years ago."

"Unfortunately, yes there is." He spoke gently but firmly, his gaze glued to her face. "Derek Norris was found murdered last night."

Words that she had always expected to hear finally came, but she was still shocked.

Derek. Dead. Wow.

"What? How? Oh my God."

Those blue eyes studied her patiently, as if he was a human lie detector or something. "You tell me, Amber. Where were you last night around ten o'clock?"

Her eyes widened. "Are you serious? I was home here with my daughter."

"Any adults see you here?" Scribbling something in his small notebook, he didn't look at her.

"Of course not, it's only Jenna and me here. What are you getting at, Detective?" She swallowed hard, her throat dry.

His eyes caught hers again. "Neighbors claim you argued with your ex two days ago."

"Again that was nothing unusual. So, yes, I did argue with him and then kicked his ass out of here. I didn't want him here, but I already told you that. Look in your notebook." The urge to stomp her foot was suddenly overwhelming.

He stood staring down at her, arms folded, pen in one hand, notepad in the other. "True. But you failed to mention you threatened to kill him."

Now she had to laugh. This nightmare called Derek Norris continued to grow even when he was dead. "At the time, it didn't seem important to mention it, especially since I've threatened that before. Too many times to count."

"So you admit you wanted him dead?"

More than he would ever know. "I wanted him dead years ago. He's...was an evil person. And I'll tell you right now, I regret I wasn't the one to kill the bastard. If I wouldn't have left my daughter an orphan then there's a good chance I would've killed him. Years ago."

He walked around her small parlor. There really wasn't much to look at but it was clean and hers.

"Wait a minute," she said, getting his attention. She waited until he faced her to speak again. "The search warrant. It's not to look for Derek, is it?" she asked as she quickly unfolded the legal document with trembling hands.

"No, Amber. I know where Derek is."

She ignored his sarcasm as she scanned the paper. "This is to search my house for evidence in the death of Derek Norris." Why she read it out loud when he obviously knew what it said, she didn't know. Maybe hearing it would help her fathom just what the hell was going on.

"Yes," Detective Maguire answered while looking around the room again. "It'd be in your best interest to cooperate fully with us. If there's anything here that has a connection to Derek Norris, then I suggest you speak up and save yourself a lot of grief in the long run."

She stepped closer to him and spoke coolly. "The only connection here to that bastard is many bad memories and my precious little girl who, despite her father's blood in her veins, is truly a wonderful child. Believe me, Detective, I've already been through my fair share of grief. Nothing surprises me anymore when it comes to Derek. Nothing."

He was silent for a minute as he contemplated his next move. His voice remained professional when he finally spoke again. "I appreciate your honesty, Amber. But it's not helping to rule you out as a suspect. We could do a polygraph if I get a warrant approved by the judge. Maybe that makes you nervous."

"Of course not. I have nothing to hide." She had passed them before, numerous times, when she had been falsely accused of being a part in one of Derek's scams or thefts.

The detective faced her with a grim look. "Nothing to hide? Really? Well, now that brings me to my next question. When Derek came by to see you two days ago, did he happen to give you any jewelry?"

Laughter exploded from her. Was there a hidden television crew waiting to pop out of their hiding spot and tell her she was on candid camera because this had to be some kind of joke. "Are you crazy? He's never given me a piece of jewelry in my life. For a wedding ring, he used a twisted paperclip."

He almost smirked, the corner of his mouth lifting

before he clamped those stern lips steady. "Look, Amber, I'm sure being married to him wasn't all glamorous, but cut the crap. I know he gave you the Blue Diamond to hide until he could fence it and make a hefty sum of money for both of you."

Blue diamond? Derek make money for her?

Now that was even funnier. "Detective, I hate to contradict your vivid imagination, but Derek gave me nothing but heartache. I wouldn't have taken anything from him, especially knowing it would definitely have been received through illegal means. Search my house if you don't believe me. I'm hiding nothing. Oh, wait. You're already searching my house," she said sarcastically, glancing behind her at the other officers walking in and out of rooms then looking back to him. "It doesn't look like your men are having any luck. No diamonds. No murder weapons. I'll hold the 'I told you so' until they're completely finished. But you are definitely wasting taxpayer's money here."

She stopped to take a breath. "You know, Detective, if you even bothered to check with my neighbors you would find that I never even allowed him in the house. We could have saved a whole lot of time and effort here."

He frowned, the damn expression only adding to his sexiness.

Where did that come from? Amber shook her head. The man definitely reeked of sex appeal, but she wanted to kick herself for even having a thought of attraction for the cop who thought she was a murderer.

"Do you have a passport?" he demanded, tapping his pen on his notepad.

"No. Why? Do I need one?"

"Only to surrender it. I'm advising you not to leave the state of Massachusetts or the country, until I tell you otherwise. You're the primary suspect in a homicide investigation. I suggest you seek legal counsel immediately."

Her world shattered. *Primary suspect?*

"What in the hell are you talking about? I didn't kill him. Oh God. Am I under arrest?" Her belly revolted, only a second away from heaving the sandwich she ate for lunch on the floor by his feet. *What would happen to Jenna?*

"No. The investigation is only in the preliminary stages. If I had planned to arrest you, I would've read you your rights by now, before questioning you." His stare pinned her.

Humpf. "Like I have any rights after being married to that loser." If he thought those bright blue eyes could shake her, he was so mistaken. After living with Derek's mean glares, Detective Maguire's were anything but.

"I haven't arrested you because I don't have sufficient evidence yet. *Yet.* But I will very soon. Get a lawyer. Here's my card and cell number in case you remember anything that may be helpful in this investigation." Did his expression just soften a little bit or were her eyes playing tricks on her?

She grabbed the card and shoved it in her pocket. It'd be a cold day in hell before she called Detective Maguire for anything. "If I had anything helpful, I would've told you. Or your amazing police officers would have found it."

He ignored her as the other officers joined them. "Nothing found, sir."

"Told you that you'd find nothing," she sneered, her innocence finally proven.

Detective Maguire offered her a mocking grin. "Only means you and Derek are good at hiding things. I'll be in touch." He motioned for the other officers to leave, stopping at the door to face her again. "Word of warning. The police are not the only ones looking for this missing diamond. It seems the Mob hired your ex-husband to steal it from a Saudi prince."

She couldn't help but gasp. *Stupid, stupid Derek.*

"And they are all looking for it. The Mob. The prince. The police. The hit men. Word on the street is that you have it. Watch your back, Amber Norris." He turned and walked down the stairs.

She yelled after him. "How dare you come in my house and accuse me of a crime? And how dare you leave me with the bit of knowledge that my life is in danger? You're the police. Thought you were supposed to protect people."

He stared at the ground for a minute before looking back up at her. "I can't help you if you won't help yourself, Amber. Come clean with what you know and I assure you I'll do whatever I can to keep you safe."

Her stomach twisted into violent knots while she did everything in her power to remain upright. "I know nothing. How am I supposed to prove that to you, Detective Maguire?"

He looked up and down the street then back to her. "I've been a detective for a long time, Amber," he said, walking back up the stairs to stand nose-to-nose with her, obviously getting pissed. "You want me to believe your ex-husband, a man you allegedly despise, shows up here unexpectedly two days before he's brutally murdered and yet you know nothing about what he's been up to? Then on top of that, you think I should accept that he didn't give you the Blue Diamond to hide until the heat was off him and he could sell it?"

She searched his eyes for any sign of hope that he was on her side. "Yes, because it's the truth. I wouldn't have taken a damn thing from him," she said as her voice hitched, tears threatening to shed any second.

"Give me a break, lady. You want my help, then fess up to everything you know. And I mean everything or you're on your own. You've got my card."

He left her standing in her doorway, watching his back, as he entered a dark sedan and sped off.

Her heart sank as she stepped back inside her apartment and locked the door. She walked aimlessly through her rooms. If the detective spoke the truth, what the hell did Derek do to her this time? What kind of sinister crime did he involve her and his daughter in? The Mob was looking for her? *Oh great!* She didn't want to get on the bad side of any more thugs now that the main one in her life was dead. Why couldn't she just live in peace for once?

The detective had to be blowing smoke up her ass in hopes of scaring her. She took a few deep breaths to steady her shaking body. Now wasn't the time to give in to her emotions. Yeah, she was scared but dealing with police interrogations wasn't new to her.

In her head, she reviewed her conversation with Detective Maguire. Derek never did anything unless it benefited him. He could've wanted to hide stolen property with her without her knowledge. But she never let him past the doorway. The detective mentioned a prince looking for her. Surely, he wouldn't believe she held anything stolen by Derek.

And hit men? Yeah right. She wasn't about to be frightened by the detective's lies and believe all those people would chase after her for no reason, especially since she didn't have any diamond.

But Derek was killed for a reason. It was very possible the killer would look at her for whatever it was. Damn, she didn't need this to worry about.

She cursed Derek for stopping by the other day. Thank

God she didn't let him in the house or he very well may have hidden his stolen crap without her knowing it. Amber froze.

Jenna's doll. Derek had given his daughter a present when he never had before.

Oh God. The doll could have the Blue Diamond. And Jenna had the doll. And there were possible hit men for Christ's sake.

Within minutes, Amber ran from her apartment in the tight-knit South Boston neighborhood to pick up her daughter at her play date. The warm July air carried the smell of her landlady's roses and the sharp scent of salty water from Boston Harbor only blocks away as she ran down her front stairs. The neighborhood offered Amber the chance to blend in. Just blend. But how well could she blend now with the world, and its thugs, looking for her. She had to get to Jenna.

With shaking hands, Amber managed to get the key in her car's ignition after a few attempts. She rolled down the windows, needing the breeze more than the cool comfort the air conditioner offered. In the small front seat of her car, the world closed in on her once again—thanks to her ex-husband. But these dangers were the worst she had ever faced. Derek was murdered. And the police suspected her! Oh God! What the hell else could happen?

With her seatbelt fastened, Amber drove as calmly as possible to pick up her daughter. She needed to hold the child in her arms before she'd believe the girl was safe. Moments later, Amber had the chance to do just that when she arrived at Jenna's friend's house.

With trembling arms, Amber wrapped her daughter in a huge hug before whisking her into the car.

"Mommy, are you okay? You look like you just saw a monster."

Amber turned the radio on, the music cutting the air. "Sorry, sweetie. Mommy was just rushing to see you and it's hot out. Can I take a look at your doll?"

"Sure, Mommy. She's a really good doll. Me and Kelly played with her all afternoon."

"That sounds like you had a great time," Amber said calmly, searching the doll for any hidden contraband. When she found nothing out of the ordinary with the doll, she breathed a sigh of relief and handed it back to her daughter.

She hadn't found the Blue Diamond but that didn't mean the bad guys wouldn't still suspect her. How would she defend herself against unknown goons? How was she supposed to proclaim or prove her innocence when she didn't know who to tell it to?

Before driving home, Amber called her father, a retired lawyer. It looked as if he'd have to come out of retirement to fix this mess.

Damn voicemail. "Dad, it's Amber. Need you to call me as soon as you get this message. Seems Derek has given me more legal problems. It's the worst this time. Love you, Daddy."

"Is my daddy in trouble?" Jenna asked, clutching her doll.

How could Amber tell a seven-year-old that her father was dead? A father she barely saw or remembered. "I just need Papa to help me with something. That's all." Until she reached him for help, she was all alone.

Jenna smiled wide, her missing front tooth obvious. "I can't wait to show Papa my new doll. I named her Sarah."

"That's a nice name, honey," Amber tried to remain composed and concentrate on the conversation with her daughter, but scary visions of evil men chasing her, kept invading her mind. Looking in the rearview mirror continuously wasn't safe but keeping her eyes straight ahead without watching her back wouldn't protect them either. And what would she do if someone were following her? Call Mr. Big Shot Detective who thought she was a criminal?

"Mommy, can we go by Papa's house now? I really want to show him and Grandma my new doll." Jenna's voice was pleading.

"They're not home right now but maybe in a little bit. Or maybe they'll just come visit us," Amber suggested even knowing her parents hated coming over to her small apartment in a neighborhood they deemed unfit for their daughter and granddaughter. But it's what Amber could afford. The neighborhood wasn't too bad, mainly break-ins or muggings, but at least not gunshots like in other areas.

Amber parked in her small driveway and finally breathed a sigh of relief that at least she had Jenna with her and they were safe. No one had followed them home or tried to run her off the road and shoot her like in the movies.

At least Amber thought they were safe until she entered her apartment, locked her door and turned to face four men dressed in black, pointing very large guns at her and her daughter. Instinctively, she pushed Jenna behind her and prayed she'd wake up from this nightmare.

CHAPTER 4

Cody Maguire considered himself to be one damn good detective. He had learned early in his training at the police academy how to trust his gut instinct. But his gut pointed him in the wrong direction this time—it just had to be.

How could he actually consider that Amber Norris *wasn't* a part of her ex-husband's schemes? Obviously, she was not well off and could probably use some decent cash that Derek could have shared with her after selling the stolen diamond. Christ, she had even admitted Derek had been there to see her not even two days before he was found dead of multiple gunshots to the head.

And now Amber Norris was on hit lists for two very powerful men, a Mob boss and a Saudi prince. Time was of the essence. The assassins worked fast. What if she had told the truth and truly despised her ex-husband and wasn't involved in his treacherous schemes? She certainly didn't live an extraordinary lifestyle. That was clearly evident in the simple furnishings in her apartment, in her no-brand-name clothes, although he thought she'd look great in a paper bag. Even if she was an innocent lady, she still had a major price on her lovely head with every bounty hunter in the world looking for her. By this time tomorrow, this could all be over with and Amber and her daughter dead and the Blue Diamond in the hands of the Black Market to fetch the highest price.

"Goddammit, Maguire. Have you lost your mind?" Commissioner Polski yelled through the receiver.

"Sir, all I'm saying is that Amber Norris is a vital key to this case and should be afforded some protection. The price on her head is unbelievably large," Cody argued. "Every damn bounty hunter will stalk her."

"Then maybe she should confess before she gets herself killed," Commissioner Polski said, his voice thundering. "There's no money in the budget."

"We have to find the money. If not for Amber, then to protect her daughter. The child is innocent." Cody was determined to argue this through. He knew when he was right.

"Unless you show me proof, Maguire, that the woman isn't caught up in this mess, then there's no way in fucking hell I'm wasting valuable police money to protect a conspirator. No police protection. Do I make myself clear, Detective?" The last question emphasized each word.

Cody gave up the argument. He really had no right to press the issue of protection for Amber when he didn't have a lick of evidence to prove she was innocently mixed up in this mess. All he had was his gut. Even though it had never failed him before, maybe, just maybe, he could be wrong now.

Is Amber playing me for a fool with her innocent act?

"Yes, sir. I understand. No protection orders," Cody said defeated. Maybe his professional judgment was clouded with the child involved. But he still wasn't convinced Amber was guilty.

"And if you're that concerned about the child, then call Child Protective Services to remove her from a harmful home. Don't make me listen to any more of this bullshit." The commissioner hung up abruptly.

Cody slammed the handset down and rubbed his head. Politics and budgets. He hated both.

Cody sat back in his chair, staring at the pile of folders on his desk. Amber Norris. The tall, slender woman was a natural beauty, wearing no make-up and still looking young and fresh. As long as Cody lived, he'd never understand how creeps and lowlifes like Derek Norris got the pretty girls like Amber. Didn't these girls have parents to steer them clear of such vile rift-raft? Rodents would make better bed partners than someone like Derek.

Where the hell did Derek stash the Blue Diamond?

"The coroner faxed his preliminary findings of a visual inspection of Derek's body," Detective Daniel Riley said, passing the papers to Cody before taking a seat at his desk across from Cody. "Either they finally tortured the location of the Blue Diamond out of him, or they got so pissed they blew his head off before they realized they killed the one person who could help them."

Cody cringed. "Unless they believe Amber can help them." He wouldn't put it past the slime bag Derek to lie and say his ex-wife had the diamond just to save his own skin. But from his beaten and bloodied body in the coroner's file photos, if that was his plan then it sadly backfired.

Fine, the department wouldn't offer Amber official police protection, but what Cody did on his own time was his business. When his shift ended, he planned to stake out Amber's apartment and give his gut the respect it deserved.

"Why wouldn't a wimpy thug like Derek Norris give up the info to end the obvious hell he'd been put through by his captives?" Riley asked.

After studying the pictures of the battered body, Cody would almost say Derek really didn't know where the Blue Diamond was and, therefore, couldn't stop his torture. There's no way he could have held out under such horrific torment.

"Could someone have stolen the Blue Diamond from Derek?" Cody wondered, glancing up. "Wouldn't that be an ironic death for a pathetic thief like Norris, getting fucked over like he'd done to everyone he'd ever met."

"The poor bastard even endured an extensive cavity search by his captors," Riley said laughing.

"If he was stupid enough to stick the diamond up his ass hoping it'd be a safe place to hide it, then he deserved to have his rectum torn open with God knows what," Cody said, positive they didn't find the diamond since the hit was still out for Amber. There was no way in hell he wanted Amber to endure any cavity searches, or worse, so he needed to figure out this puzzle and fast. The hit men wouldn't care Amber was a female. Hell, that would only make her more vulnerable to their sadistic means of extracting information from victims.

"It's pretty shocking that someone like Derek could even get close enough to the Blue Diamond to steal it. There was more security assigned to that gem than to the prince."

"Yeah, well, my sources indicate the Mob trained Derek in jail, teaching him Special Op techniques and such."

"Sources aren't always reliable."

Cody knitted his brows. "True. But mine are. They know not to screw me over with false info. I'm up front with them and they share what they know. Haven't had a problem yet."

"So the guy gets some second-hand training from ex-military men and all of the sudden he can take on the world? Nah, I don't buy that," Riley said, waving his hand in dismissal.

"Of course, Derek couldn't have pulled that stunt off by himself. Remember, he wasn't alone." Cody tossed a file onto Riley's adjoining desk. "That's the dead man they found in the New York hotel room, stabbed to death, after the attack on the hospital. He was connected to the Boston Mob. And Norris' prints were all over the room."

Riley studied the picture. "I know this guy. Carlos Pereira. Real mean guy. Don't think he had a sympathetic bone in his body." He tossed the file back to Cody.

Cody had never wanted to solve a case as bad as this one. And never had one been as hard to figure out, always hitting a wall as soon as he got a lead. He continued, "Carlos' military file showed he was a specialist in evacuating hostages. The guy never lost a man on his team and was highly decorated. It's plausible to think he could've trained Derek well enough to gain him entrance to the hospital even with tight security. And, of course, all of the news channels have reported the timing of the theft occurred during pre-dawn prayer. Even with such a valuable rock to protect, it was customary for the prince to allow up to four guys, at once, to go and pray on another floor where the hospital accommodated their religious practices."

"So the poor bastard let his guard down. He'd been at the hospital for three weeks and hospital security reported not even one problem," Riley said, leaning back in his squeaky chair.

Cody sighed. "Don't care. If those other four soldiers had remained with the Blue Diamond, then the thieves wouldn't have had a chance." And Amber wouldn't be in harm's way.

Riley shrugged. "They are deeply religious people, Maguire. Praying would amount to the same importance of performing their jobs. And each prayer session only takes about ten minutes to complete."

"Well, at least praying saved their lives. They weren't in the room to be shot." Cody shook his head. "I'll agree the thieves had a narrow space of time to pull it off, but the fact remains that the thieves took a chance and succeeded."

"How brilliant to strike when the men were baring their souls for prayer," Riley said, staring up at the ceiling.

"Well, that and the prince was three floors down getting an MRI. Hospital security arranged the test to be performed in the early morning hours when the least amount of people were in the building." Cody laughed at the luck these thieves had. "The Blue Diamond couldn't accompany the prince since nothing is allowed in the MRI area due to the magnet. This heist was a well thought out plan with a huge dose of sheer luck."

Riley glanced across at Cody. "Yeah. The prince probably took the rest of his security detail with him, leaving the diamond more vulnerable."

"Exactly. Not the brightest move but the diamond was on a secure, badge-access only floor. And no prior threats had been established while the prince had been in town."

They were silent for a moment.

"Why'd Carlos turn into a criminal if he was such a big shot military man?" Riley countered.

"He was always a criminal. Just got his job done first and served his country well. Then he'd rob the unsuspecting slobs who crossed his path. Even after such honorable service, he received a dishonorable discharge from the service for a classified conduct matter. Could have been anything from selling military secrets to murder," Cody explained after having memorized every detail on the case. "My guess would be murder."

"That's not what he was in jail for when Derek met him. He was in there for aggravated assault."

"Yeah, like I said, he wasn't a nice man. May have had one hell of a career serving his country, but he wasn't honorable." Cody finished glancing through the coroner's report as he wrapped up the conversation.

"Criminals generally aren't nice, Maguire. Want coffee?"

"No, thanks." Cody dropped the papers on his desk when Riley left. He could use a jolt of caffeine since it looked like a long night ahead but he didn't need the jitters that came with drinking coffee so late in the day. Settling for a lame piece of sugarless gum, he sighed and rested his head on his chair staring at the dingy, white peeling ceiling.

This was the kind of case that could make or break his police career. It didn't matter if he had aspirations to move on to the F.B.I. If he screwed up this case and didn't get the Blue Diamond before it could be sold on the Black Market, then he might as well kiss his dreams goodbye. The Bureau sure wouldn't want a detective who couldn't work under pressure and solve the heist of the century.

It also wouldn't help Amber Norris live any longer if he couldn't piece together the puzzle of the missing heirloom. With every passing minute, crucial time was lost and Amber and her daughter's lives remained in jeopardy.

It wouldn't help Cody to be distracted by the intriguing, pretty Amber. Images of her shiny, light brown hair styled to feather her small face with wispy strands and her golden eyes wide and defensive would stick with him. Damn, he needed to get laid if he was attracted to a suspect.

He laughed knowing there was no way she had killed her ex-husband. But she sure could be holding the key to the rest of the mystery. If only she would be honest about what she knew. She had to know something. It didn't make any sense that her ex-husband would just drop in, out of the blue, for a visit if he wasn't in the habit of doing so.

Cody stretched, unable to stop thinking of Amber. He admired her. From what he had read about her life with Derek, it hadn't been very good. Domestic violence. Run-ins with the law. Foreclosure. She had endured it all and survived to provide a decent home for her daughter. Her criminal record since her divorce was spotless, not even bouncing a check.

"Looks like someone's deep in thought again," Riley commented, walking back to his desk with a cup of coffee.

Cody shrugged, wishing he had grabbed a coffee too when he caught a whiff of it. "I've just never stooped to lying. I hated to lead Amber to believe she was a suspect in Derek's murder."

Riley sipped his coffee before responding. "Hey, whatever works at this point, buddy. It may be the only way to get to any knowledge she may have. Besides, the judge wouldn't give you a search warrant based only on Derek's visit and the theory that he stashed the Blue Diamond with her."

Cody dragged a hand over his face. "I know but there's political consequences on this one because the Saudis won't be very willing to cooperate with the U.S. in the future on vital security measures if Prince Al-Hussein doesn't recover the Blue Diamond. With Derek dead and useless to the investigation, it just increased the odds of a diplomatic nightmare evolving over a chunk of stone worth millions. And since there's no way Amber killed Derek, I've got to discover how she's connected to this case," Cody said, logging off his computer and standing.

Cody needed to figure that out soon, with or without

Amber's cooperation, since Derek's death was a professional hit. There was his gut telling him Amber was totally ignorant about the situation. And now she'd pay the ultimate price with her life—just for marrying the wrong man.

"Heading back out?" Riley hollered as Cody walked to the door.

"Yeah, at this point every second counts. I'll be in touch. Get me on my phone if the lab results return or you hear of any new developments."

"Gonna go keep that pretty lady safe?"

Cody only smirked. He wished. *Stupid budget.*

"Damn, you get all the perks of this job, I swear," the other man complained, throwing out his empty cup.

"Not this time. Got to bring her to identify the body as his next of kin. Coroner couldn't locate any of his family so she's got to do it."

"Sucks to be her. Better bring her a barf bag once she sees him. But you still get the perks of dealing with such a pretty lady. All I ever get are the strung out drug addicts," Riley complained, shaking his head and picking up the ringing phone on his desk.

Yeah, some perks. Cody walked out of his precinct and into the bright afternoon sun.

The commissioner never said anything about not staking out Amber's apartment to determine her criminal activities, if any, related to this case. While on duty, Cody would just watch over Amber with the excuse of tracking the Blue Diamond. Technically, he wasn't providing her protection but was continuing his investigation.

His thoughts consumed him as he walked to his car. After all, if she did have the diamond, she may now decide to dispose of it since the heat was on from the police as well as every thug in the vicinity. Cody's job was to retrieve the stolen gem and solve this deepening mystery, keeping Boston out of the international spotlight.

Yes, it was his job. *For now*.

It didn't help matters that Cody and the Boston Police Department would probably lose jurisdiction once the Feds stepped in and took over the investigation, which could happen at any time.

CHAPTER 5

Jenna clutched her doll as hard as Amber clutched Jenna. Amber's cheek still stung from the slap one of the men had planted across it an hour ago when she refused to leave with them. It had been five years since she had had to endure that kind of abuse. While she knew she could get through it, she regretted Jenna witnessing the violence. If Amber had been alone, then she would've fought to the death, but she had to use her head to get her and Jenna safely away from these kidnappers.

After being thrown into the back of a van that smelled of mildew and stale tobacco, Amber and Jenna were tossed around as the driver whipped through Boston's high traffic streets to merge onto the Interstate.

"Where are we going?" Amber demanded, catching a glimpse out the windshield before a big man pushed her onto the floor. She had seen enough to know they were headed north.

"Shut up, lady. Unless you're going to tell us where to find the Blue Diamond, don't open your mouth. The boss ain't too happy right now," the burly man, who smelled of garlic and cigarettes, said between coughs.

"Who's your boss and where is he?" she asked nicely but with a bite. If these morons were doing someone else's work, then why not go to the top guy?

"Mr. DiGento will be meeting up with us shortly. You may have heard of him. Goes by Bones on the street." The fat man heaved a sinister laugh. "Got a reputation for breaking them."

Chuckles came from the other three men, an ominous feeling filling her belly. Jenna sat quietly in her arms, the little girl so brave.

Amber had hardly paid attention to what happened in a big city like Boston. She had enough to worry about making ends meet and keeping from becoming homeless. But she remembered the name Bones. Worse, she remembered her ex-husband calling his boss Bones when he had gotten busted on the bank robbery years earlier. Christ, did Derek work for the Mob back then?

At least now, Amber knew it was the Mob who had kidnapped her and Jenna. Oh God, why was this happening? She couldn't panic, it wouldn't help them any. Amber had to save Jenna on her own. Sighing, Amber concentrated her dwindling energy on thinking of a way to get her and Jenna freedom.

"Mommy, I have to go to the bathroom," Jenna whispered, her little hand tugging on Amber's. Even with the barely audible tone, the fat man still heard her.

"Too bad, kid," he said. "Hold it. And shut up."

How dare the bully talk to a little girl like that? "Please. Let me take her to the bathroom. We'll be quick, I promise. She's only a child and has behaved," Amber pleaded.

"I gotta take a piss too," the driver announced. "There's a gas station up ahead. We'll stop there."

The fat guy shoved a black gun into Amber's face, the cold barrel resting between her eyes. Her heart stopped. Her eyes widened to stare at the pock-marked, wrinkled face only inches from her. How she wanted to give him the same treatment he gave her.

"Mommy!" Jenna screeched and clung hard to Amber, who squeezed the girl's hand hoping the reassurance would be enough to keep her from becoming hysterical.

"Try something, bitch, and I'll splatter your brains and then hers. Hear me?" The man snarled, his noxious breath almost causing her to puke.

"Yes," Amber said calmer than she was, keeping her eyes on his until he returned the gun to his waist. If she didn't do something soon, she and Jenna were as good as dead. It would be only a matter of time before they arrived at their destination and God knows what more trouble. She wasn't about to let them hurt her baby, not without one hell of a fight. *The bastards!*

Being concealed in the van gave her no edge over her competition. In here, they'd kill them easily if she attempted any resistance.

From where she sat, Amber could once again see out the windshield.

The van stopped abruptly after the driver swung into the parking lot situated off the highway. The men in the front seats opened the doors and climbed out.

The fat man next to her pulled Amber by the hair, snapping her neck back. She cried out. He spoke through clenched teeth. "You have three minutes. Piss and get the fuck back out here. Understood?"

"W-we will," Amber agreed, her entire body shaking so

much she could barely walk. How was she ever going to escape these brutes? She couldn't think of what would happen to her if she got caught trying to run.

As if he read her mind, the fat man spoke again, "Don't even think of trying anything. I'll be waiting right here for you and you better hurry it up. Bones doesn't like to be kept waiting. He wanted you brought to him alive. Don't mean he won't kill you on the spot, lady."

Holding Jenna's hand firmly while the girl still clutched the doll, Amber stepped out of the van. She quickly scooped Jenna into her arms and walked to the side of the cement building and entered the bathroom on the side of the gas station.

She prayed someone would think there was something wrong and call the police. But that was more wishful thinking on her part. The only other person she could see was a gas station attendant who wasn't very likely to offer help considering he looked to be a hundred-years-old.

Once inside the bathroom, Amber placed Jenna on her feet and quickly locked the door, even though the flimsy bolt wouldn't keep the men out if they meant to come in. The smell inside the tiny space consisted of a disgusting mixture of cigarettes and urine.

Amber had to think quickly. They had two and a half minutes to escape. She looked around the small room. A toilet and a pedestal sink were the only things in the room.

The small window above the toilet was their only hope since one of the mobsters stayed outside the door. Amber had doubts she'd even fit through it, but as long as Jenna did, that's all that mattered. If she could get her daughter freed, Amber would face whatever punishment from her captors that they dished out. At least her baby would be safe and away from those jerks.

Leaning down, she whispered to her daughter. "Jenna, Mommy needs you to listen very carefully. We need to get away from these bad men, honey, or they will hurt us. I need you to wait to pee so we can escape." Jenna nodded.

Amber stepped onto the dirty toilet seat and pushed at the window. Cobwebs and dead bugs littered the windowsill but she didn't have any time to be skeeved over it. Desperation and fear consumed her when the window wouldn't budge. Was it nailed shut? Did the damn thing even open? *Oh no.* Her shoe slipped off the seat proving to be the magic touch as her stumble knocked her body weight into the rotten wooden frame finally opening it.

She hesitated only a few seconds to listen for the thugs in case they heard the window open. When they didn't rush into the bathroom, she was sure they hadn't.

She lifted Jenna and her doll onto the toilet. "Jenna, you see those woods?" she whispered, her heart pounding. "You run into them. Mommy will follow soon, but if I don't, you still run until you see someone. Then tell them to call the police. You have to be very, very quiet. Now go."

Amber attempted to take the doll from Jenna, but the girl shook her head in silent protest.

"I'll pass her to you once you're outside," Amber reasoned, her heart ready to beat out of her chest.

One minute, thirty seconds.

Amber lifted Jenna after placing the doll on top of the toilet. Jenna fit easily through the small hole, placing her feet first. Amber held her by the hands and slowly, but quickly, lowered her until she dropped silently to the dirt ground. Amber passed her the doll. Like a mouse, Jenna ran into the woods.

With a knot forming in her throat, Amber bit back her tears. She was forced to send her baby into a dangerous forest abutting a highway in the middle of nowhere. Damned if she'd ever left her daughter alone for a second longer than necessary, so she cursed the thugs and Derek silently. She heaved herself through the window, twisting and turning to fit her hips through the small opening. She was slender but this was too damn small.

Thirty seconds.

Hanging upside down out the window was not a position to get caught in. Peeking through the hair that covered her eyes, she looked toward the woods and saw Jenna waiting for her. The child was scared stiff, pale and hugging her doll. With a strength she never realized she possessed, Amber hauled herself through the window, rolling onto the ground in a somersault, allowing her upper body to take the brunt of the fall. She bit down on an oath when a piece of jagged wood scraped the side of her thigh.

No time to worry about small injuries now. Not with a gun just around the corner. Amber bolted to Jenna, never looking back. She ran as fast and as silently as she could, getting to her daughter's side and quickly assessing their next move. She wasn't made for this kind of crap. She should be home making dinner for her daughter and listening to the details of her play date.

"Get on my back, honey. Hold tight. I'll give you a piggy-back ride," she whispered through nervous breaths. She leaned down to allow the little girl to scramble on.

With Jenna clinging to her and the doll, Amber ran as fast as she could through the thick woods knowing the highway abutted it on the west, who knew what was on the east. The gas station had been the only business in the immediate area. They had driven for about forty minutes and with traffic, she figured they had managed to get up near the New Hampshire border. They were definitely in an isolated stretch of highway.

Still, they had escaped. She'd never stop running, not until they were safe and away from the Mob creeps for good.

Jenna clung tightly as Amber ran while paying attention to her direction. Getting lost in the woods wasn't on her agenda. Getting them to safety was.

Minutes later, off in the distance, the shouts of angry men wafted over the warm summer air.

Shit! They hadn't gotten far enough away if she could hear the men. Three minutes hadn't been enough time to escape *and* put distance between them. Obviously, their captors had discovered the pair missing and weren't happy about it. Thoughts of what would happen to them should they be recaptured increased the adrenaline flowing through Amber's veins. Feeling the power of a hundred women, she roared on, allowing herself to grunt at the sheer exhaustion facing her.

Amber's legs burned, using muscles she hadn't in years. Running track in school couldn't have prepared her for this jaunt through the woods. Jenna's small body bobbed on her back, the awkward position straining her neck as she leapt through sharp bushes and broken branches. The overgrowth slowed her down when all she wanted was to just run, run as fast as humanly possible. Jenna had a death grip around her throat, the choking sensation hampered what little air Amber could suck in. Her lungs wanted to explode from lack of oxygen. With every ounce of adrenaline riveting through her body, she refused to stop until she got them help.

Until she could call Detective Maguire.

Would he help them? Her father wouldn't be able to. Not at his age. Detective Maguire was their only hope. She wasn't stupid enough to believe any other cop would help her. Hell, they probably all thought she was in cahoots with her ex. But Detective Maguire, well, something in his eyes indicated he would at least protect them even if he didn't quite believe she was innocent of any wrongdoing.

It felt as if they had been running for hours and miles. When Amber stumbled and almost fell, she finally gave in to her body's demands for rest. Quickly, she hid behind a tree, lowering Jenna to the ground and taking in deep drags of air. She lay against the tree and fought a wave of nausea, knowing she didn't even have the energy to vomit. Never in her life had she been thirstier than at this moment.

Using the back of her hand to wipe the dirt and sweat from her face caused her to cry out from the pain of using muscles still twitching from her unexpected race. Jenna may be a little girl but she was far from light. Hauling her through the forest had Amber's back aching in too many places to count. She rubbed the side of her stinging thigh. A red circle covered her jeans. The cut throbbed and ached but was minimal compared to the rest of her body.

She reached for Jenna who had sat only a few inches away and held her close to her side.

"You...were a...brave girl, Jenna," Amber said through short breaths.

"I'm so scared, Mommy." Jenna's voice cracked with tears.

Never in her life had Amber wanted to kill a man with her bare hands and that said a lot since she lived with the likes of Derek for so long. But, these men made her daughter cry and she wanted to choke the life out of them for hurting her little girl. She said a silent prayer willing God to punish them before she could, because she wouldn't be held responsible for what she did.

"We've got to...just sit real quiet for a bit. Okay. Let Mommy catch...her breath."

"Okay," Jenna whispered and buried her little face into Amber's bosom. She wrapped her arms tightly around her daughter and looked at the treetops above them. Sitting the way they were, they were still too visible for her liking.

Two minutes, she pledged. Two minutes and she'd gather the strength to hide them so they would be out of sight until she could figure out what to do next.

What in the hell am I going to do?

Escaping appeared to be the easy part as Amber looked around the dense forest with its tall trees and overgrown bushes. Finding her way out of here may prove difficult since she had lost her sense of direction while running, more concerned with not falling than with keeping in line with the abutting highway. Were there wild animals they would have to contend with if she couldn't get them out of here?

"I still have to pee," Jenna admitted, whispering.

Amber sat up and looked around. "Okay. But you have to do it right here. We can't move around."

"That's okay."

Jenna listened to Amber's whispered instructions and was sitting back on her mother's lap in no time.

"We're going to hide better, sweetie. Come on," Amber whispered and moved them deeper into the bushes.

Before sitting back on the ground, Amber slipped her fingers into the back pocket of her jeans. She found Detective Maguire's business card, grateful she had stuck it in there and not in her purse.

Now to find a pay phone.

Do pay phones even exist anymore? God, please.

CHAPTER 6

The balmy summer day had climbed into the mid-eighties with high humidity. Cody's short-sleeved polo shirt stuck to his back when he got out of his car after finding an illegal parking spot on Amber's Street. South Boston's neighborhoods were so over-crowded with cars that even the police had a hard time finding a place to stop and not block the flow of traffic on the narrow streets.

Cody put on his sunglasses and walked the short distance to Amber's apartment in the gray three-story building on the corner. Once she made the official ID of Derek's body, the autopsy could begin. At least while Cody accompanied Amber to the coroner's office, she would be safe with him. He would have to be sure to drill into her head the need for her to cooperate with his investigation. Although she had ample time since Derek's visit to hide the diamond elsewhere, it would be rather stupid to keep it here where everyone, cops and thugs, would expect.

Cody climbed the stairs to the three-decker house and removed his sunglasses, preparing to confront the hostile Amber Norris for the second time that day. Entering the screened porch, he noticed toys piled neatly in the corner—bubbles, balls, and chalk looking like they got a lot of use.

A sign above the Norris doorbell indicated it was broken so Cody knocked and waited. All the shades were drawn, unlike earlier. Hell, he couldn't blame her for wanting to hide. Damn woman had better get her head checked if she decided to continue blowing smoke up his ass.

After a minute without an answer, Cody banged louder. "Amber Norris, Detective Maguire. I need to speak with you please."

No answer. Did she think she could hide inside the house and avoid him? He'd bust down the damn door.

He pounded his fist harder. "Amber Norris, open up. Now. Your car's in the driveway so I know you're home." He needed her to open the damn door, uneasiness filling him as each moment passed. She didn't seem the type to be openly defiant to a police officer.

Turning the doorknob confirmed it was locked. The frilly curtain covering the small window on her door prevented him from peering inside.

He walked back down the steps and circled the house. The back yard was empty and the rear door to Amber's apartment also locked. Cody walked back to the front, his temper becoming as hot as the temperatures outside. So Amber wanted to play games, did she? How would she feel if he brought throngs of Boston Police here to raid her apartment?

Back in front of the building, Cody once again walked up the stairs and gave Amber one last opportunity to answer the door. He pounded hard without saying a word.

What the hell? He'd just left her a few hours earlier. She did say her daughter was at a play date, but she should've been back from picking her up.

That uneasy feeling deep in his gut was growing. He banged harder and hollered, "Amber."

"What's going on out there?" an elderly woman demanded from the second floor window.

Cody stepped off of the stairs, holding a hand over his eyes against the sun's glare, and flashed his badge. "Sorry to bother you, ma'am. Detective Maguire, Boston Police. I need to speak with Amber Norris."

"About what?" she demanded, the sound of a loud television blaring in the background.

Cody normally would've laughed at the old woman's brashness if he weren't so preoccupied on why the hell Amber wasn't answering her door. "Do you know where she is?"

"No. I'm her landlady, not her keeper."

Cody rolled his eyes. "Can you let me in her apartment, please?"

"I don't think I should do that without her permission, especially since you won't tell me why."

He really didn't need this shit right now. Weren't little old ladies supposed to be nice or at least cordial? Wasn't that a law or something? He took a deep breath ready to fight fire with fire. "It'll keep me from having to break down the door."

That got her attention, her eyes widening.

"Don't you dare. Let me get the key." Her plump body disappeared back inside the window. Within five minutes, she joined Cody on the porch.

"It's my property, you know," she snarled at Cody as she walked to the other door. "I have a right to know what the hell is going on."

"Then I suggest you ask your tenant, ma'am, when you

see her." Cody spoke politely even though he wanted to tell the lady to mind her own business.

"Is this about that rotten ex-husband of hers?" the lady asked while she fidgeted with a ring of keys searching for the one to Amber's apartment.

"Do you have something you want to tell me about him?" Cody figured this woman was the type who minded everyone's business but her own. She'd be a great cesspool of information. But, of course, unless it was something she had heard or had seen first-hand, he'd have to dismiss it as gossip. While gossip could sometimes be useful in tying up loose ends in an investigation and answering unknown questions, it was rarely useful in the beginning of a case, and never admissible in court unless he could validate the information.

"Well, I've never met the man. But he did show up here the other night in a bad mood or something."

"Bad mood?"

"He looked shady...very creepy. What that pretty girl ever saw in the likes of him, I'll never know." She shook her head and tried another key in the hole. "I'm sorry. I can never remember which key is which here. Aggravates the shit out of me."

Cody smirked. The lady was a spitfire. "Anything else you remember about him?"

She glanced at him before looking back at her keys. "Do you mean today or the other day?"

"Today?" Cody asked, his senses on high alert.

"Son of a bitch must've been here again. Heard some noise down here about an hour ago but it didn't last long so I didn't call down to see what was going on. My favorite soap opera was on so I remember when it was. She must've sent his ass packing again, though, because I didn't hear any more. Finally," she said opening the door. "Here you go, Detective."

Cody didn't like this one bit. Derek was dead. He couldn't have been here. Maybe Amber fought with another lover. Time to find out.

"Thank you, ma'am. I'll take it from here. I'll need you to wait out here," he instructed, walking past the woman into the hot apartment. Amber probably couldn't afford air conditioning since he didn't spot any of the machines in her windows. And it didn't help that each window was closed allowing no ventilation, humid or not.

When Cody walked a few feet inside, he immediately froze, drew his gun, and proceeded to walk through the ransacked living room. The once immaculate area now stood in disarray with broken picture frames scattered on the carpet, along with remnants from the trinkets that decorated the room earlier.

With his gun held steadily in front of him, Cody quickly radioed for backup. "Detective Maguire at 115 Pendington Street requesting backup for B & E and possible Code 4." His use of the code for homicide sent shivers up his spine.

Before proceeding further into the apartment, his eyes scanned for any sign of Amber or her daughter. Thoughts of what he may find shook him to the core. He willed himself to rely on his training and not picture Amber or her daughter murdered.

He breathed a sigh of relief when he found no blood or other obvious signs of trauma, but that didn't mean Amber and her daughter weren't in danger. At least there were no dead bodies here. Cody sure didn't want to recover a seven-year-old's body.

The rest of the apartment was in the same damaged condition. Someone was damn angry when they came through here, obviously searching for something. Cody didn't have to be a rocket scientist to figure out what that was.

The Blue Diamond.

"Fuck!" Cody yelled as his backup arrived with lights flashing and siren's wailing.

"Responding units to 115 Pendington Street, stand down, premises clear," Cody spoke into his radio, re-holstering his weapon.

Two police officers walked in with Detective Riley, who addressed Cody with a grim expression. "Any bodies?"

"No."

"Maybe she staged this, Maguire...you know, to make it look like a hit so she could get away with the Blue Diamond," Riley said, hands on his hips and surveying the room.

Cody was ashamed that for a split second he, too, had thought the same thing. Never had he had such an internal struggle about whether a person was innocent or not. "Then why'd she leave her purse?" he asked, looking through the contents. "Cell phone, wallet, credit cards, ID, keys, everything's here."

Riley shrugged. "Maybe she didn't need them anymore. What's to say she didn't leave it behind to stage her own disappearance?"

It was a possibility. "But why?"

"Why not? Everyone in the world is focusing on her right now for the Blue Diamond's whereabouts. Hell, someone like her would have access to another identity. You and I both know she could easily change her appearance and identity and that of the kid's too. This could all be part of her plan."

"Maybe," Cody admitted. "But what if she didn't stage this?" He didn't need an answer to the rhetorical question.

"Then this ain't good," Riley said. "Looks like the bad guys got to her a lot sooner than we expected. Shows the power of money."

"No shit," Cody agreed, running a hand through his hair contemplating of his next move. "I arrived to ask her to come identify the body. Landlady had to let me in after there was no answer. But nothing looked out of place outside."

"Windows are closed on such a humid day," Riley observed. "With no air conditioners."

Cody stood, arms crossed. "Yeah. I noticed that right away. Just thought she wanted to lay low—figure out what she was gonna do, you know?"

Riley walked further into the room before turning to face Cody again. "Looks like she may have had some help with that."

Something in the room didn't make sense. Amber had very few material possessions and all were now destroyed. She didn't fit the profile of a woman well versed in criminal activities. Even if in the past she had lived with a known convict, it didn't make her guilty by association. Cody had to at least afford her some consideration in that area. She had worked steadily and struggled to pay her bills from what he discovered about her during his initial investigation. A woman like that didn't live a secret criminal life and struggle for the basic things in life.

There was nothing out of the ordinary for Amber Norris. No matter how much Cody dug looking for signs of wrong-doing, he found nothing to indicate she was anything more than a single mother raising her daughter the best she could while burying her past.

"Maguire, look over here," Riley said, grimly.

Cody turned and swore under his breath as Riley squatted near a small red spot. "I need to put out an APB on Amber and the girl."

"I'll do that, Maguire. You're more familiar with this place since you were already here. Look around for anything out of the ordinary. I'll be outside on the computer, if you need anything," Detective Riley said before walking out the front door.

What Cody needed was a crystal ball to locate Amber before it was too late. If his first thoughts were right and professional hit men or the Mob took her, Cody wouldn't be left a crumb to follow her trail. Her fate would be whatever the bastards decided for her. Without being a hardened criminal, she wouldn't last long in their hands.

His skin crawled with horrific thoughts of what she may be going through while he stood helpless in her damn kitchen. Visions of Derek's battered body played in his mind, knowing Amber would face the same treatment as well as rape or gang rape. The players in this game would be cruel enough to torture her little girl to get her to talk.

But did she have anything they wanted to hear? It's hard to talk about something you know nothing about. More and more, Cody was inclined to believe she didn't have a clue about the jewel. But until he had proof she was completely innocent, he would have to walk the fine line of protecting her as an innocent civilian and scrutinizing her as a clever criminal.

If he thought of the worst scenario then he'd be too distracted and that would lead to mistakes. He brushed any thoughts from his mind that were useless to his case.

Steady streams of Boston police officers arrived to work the scene, delegated to interviewing neighbors and scouring the neighborhood streets for any further evidence. Some police officers left to view the videotapes from surveillance cameras outside convenience stores and gas stations within a one-mile radius. Other detectives photographed the scene while Cody kept foot traffic in the apartment to a minimum. No sense disturbing possible evidence with some clod's big, clumsy feet.

After an hour and a half, the commotion cleared out of the apartment and the remaining police officers left Cody alone. Dammit! This is exactly why Cody argued for police protection for Amber and her daughter. Now it appeared they were too late to be of any help.

Cody shut the door leaving behind only yellow crime scene tape. He affixed a DO NOT ENTER sign to the front door.

"Detective Maguire, are we going to be safe here tonight?" the landlady asked from her doorway on the porch. The poor woman was pale and nervous.

"Yes, ma'am. I have no reason to believe otherwise. But I have arranged for added police patrols in this area to put you and your neighbors at ease." And to keep watch if the bastards who may have taken Amber and her daughter return to finish their search.

The landlady shook her head. "This is awful. Just awful. Where were the police when Amber needed them? You should have been here to protect her."

Cody took the verbal assault in stride. How could he argue with the woman when she was right?

"I assure you...we're doing all we can to find them. I appreciate your assistance. If there's anything you need, just call the police and someone will help you."

"Ha! Like they helped poor Amber. Yeah right." The woman entered her door and slammed it, leaving Cody on the porch alone. When he turned and again saw the child's toys neatly piled in the corner, he cringed, praying the little girl could play with them again some day.

It was six in the evening and, since he planned on looking for Amber until he found her, he had to eat. He dialed his favorite pizza shop while walking back to his car. He pulled out of his parking spot to go pick up his food. When his cell phone rang, he fought the urge to disregard it, not wanting any bad news.

"Maguire," he answered harshly not recognizing the phone number.

"Please accept a collect call from Amber Norris," an automated voice said. "Press one to be connected to the caller and authorize the charges. Otherwise, hang up to reject the call."

He swung over to the side of the road, pressed one, and waited, listening to a series of clicks. His heart was in his throat. Amber was alive.

"Hello?" the frightened female voice whispered on the other end. Never had he been so glad to hear a woman's voice.

"Amber, where the hell are you?"

"Oh, thank God. I need your help, Detective Maguire." Her voice cracked with a sob.

"I'm going to help you. Where are you?"

"I don't know for sure. We're at a payphone outside of a little store somewhere off Route 93 North."

Cody swallowed. "We? Does that mean your daughter is with you?"

"Y-yes. We were kidnapped, but managed to get away. Oh, God. They're looking for us still. They chased us into the woods."

Thank God, both of them were together. "Okay. Calm

down so I can help you. You'll tell me everything when I come get you. Can you tell me where you are?"

"The store says Russell's Variety. It's white. There's a donut shop across the street, but I can't read the name. It looks like a small highway or roadway or something."

That wasn't very helpful. "Christ. I need you to hold on a minute while I look this up. Don't hang up, Amber. Don't."

"I won't. Hurry." The desperation in her voice unnerved him.

He used his police issued laptop to research the store, his fingers not typing nearly as fast as he wished they would.

He lifted the phone to his ear again. "I'm not getting anything. Do you see a street sign or anything? A town name?"

"No. Nothing. Hold on a minute," she said, then he heard muffled voices.

Aw hell, did the kidnappers catch up with her? His hand slapped the steering wheel. "Amber," he yelled into the phone. "Amber."

"I'm here. Dracut. The lady I just asked said we're in Dracut, but she didn't know the name of the street." Her voice was a little hoarse and not as perky as earlier.

"Okay. Hold on again," he said, resting the cell on his dashboard while typing. Another search on the computer provided him the details he needed. He breathed a huge sigh of relief when the address appeared on the screen.

Picking up the cell phone again, Cody kept his voice calm. No sense in adding to her worries. If she became hysterical, she'd be of no help to her or her daughter. A clear mind was always needed to survive these kinds of situations.

"Amber, listen to me. You're about an hour from me, but

I'm sure I'll hit traffic. I promise I'll be there as soon as I can."

"Okay. Please hurry. We're scared," she whispered the last words and he could only guess she didn't want her daughter to know how frightened she was.

He drove toward the highway as he spoke. "Don't stay in the phone booth, Amber. Get outside. Is there a place for you to hide that's out of sight?"

"Yes. There's woods."

Cody merged onto the highway, heading north. "Okay then. Hide in the woods. I'll be there in about an hour. I'll flick the headlights when I pull in so you know it's me, but stay hidden until you see me get out of the car. Now hide!"

"We will. Hurry," she said before disconnecting.

His heart broke hearing the fear in her voice. He could tell she was trying to hide it, no doubt for her daughter's sake. But Cody had been a cop long enough to sense a woman's fears and he'd bet any amount of money that Amber Norris was one heartbeat away from hysteria.

Cody should've turned on his blue lights to cut through the evening traffic on the heavily traveled Interstate but that would only call attention to him if he was being followed from her apartment. Without knowing who the players were yet, and not up for playing any games, he'd remain incognito as much as possible.

He dialed his cell phone. "Captain Ferron. Maguire here."

"Maguire, just who the hell do you think you are going above my head to the commissioner?"

Cody cringed. "Please, Captain, chew my ass out another time. I've got bigger problems right now."

"What is it?"

"I'm headed north to a location where Amber Norris said she is."

"You've heard from her?" Captain Ferron asked, surprised most likely because the people after Amber were professional killers and not likely to lose their victim. Especially a female victim with a child in tow.

Cody maneuvered around a slower vehicle. "Yes, sir. It appears they were kidnapped by unknown perps but have escaped. With your permission, I'd like to keep Amber's whereabouts between you and me. We both know with the Mob involved there's bound to be a mole in the department who's on the Mob's bankroll."

There were a few seconds of silence on the other end. "And how are you going to do that, Maguire? Keep her location secret...especially with the press finally getting wind of this story and Derek Norris's connection to the Blue Diamond?" Captain Ferron demanded. The older man's bark was always worse than his bite. Still, he had thirty years experience as a policeman earning Cody's respect.

"So the press has gotten hold of the story?"

"Gotten hold? Are you kidding me?" Captain Ferron yelled louder. "It's plastered all over the evening news."

"Aw, hell. That's just great," Cody grumbled, knowing that with the press involved the men chasing Amber would be more desperate to catch her.

"There are reporters camped outside her apartment so much that I've had to call in additional officers, on overtime, just to keep the street open for access by emergency vehicles."

"What? I just left and no media was there."

"Lucky you. They all showed up for Breaking News for the six o'clock broadcast. The city can't afford the overtime. So tell me how in the hell we can get this case resolved,

Maguire. Don't answer that because I'll tell you. You're going to get that lady and find out where the hell she has the Blue Diamond stashed."

Cody swerved through traffic. "Sir, with all due respect, I'm beginning to think she really doesn't know."

"You think?" he said, his tone clipped. "Find out. Period."

"Yes, sir."

"Now what's your plan going to be when you get to her?" Captain Ferron's voice calmed a fraction, a signal that his initial temper was de-escalating.

Cody hadn't given much thought to what to do with the woman and child once he picked them up. All he had been concerned with, up to now, was just getting to them before the kidnappers did. "I'll hide them in a motel tonight over the border in New Hampshire, sir, until you and I can talk again tomorrow."

"Fine."

"Maybe now that there's been an attempt on their lives, the commissioner will grant police protection. We have to do something for them, because without protection, we both know Amber and the girl will be killed within hours. They won't have a chance." Amber's soft face floated into his memory forcing Cody to see her as the pretty woman she was rather than just a suspect-turned-victim.

"And you think you working alone can give them that chance, Maguire? I don't need a dead police detective. You really should have a partner on this." Captain Ferron argued, his words strong and sure.

"Captain, I am more than qualified to offer them protection. You know that. I've done it before by myself and have a perfect track record. Plus, it'll help keep overtime to a minimum. If I didn't think myself capable then I would never risk their lives or mine."

The captain cursed. "Yeah, but I'm sensing you're a little too personally involved in this case, Maguire. You didn't have to return to her apartment this afternoon. You could've sent a uniform to bring her to ID the damn body. Why go yourself unless you're letting yourself get attached to the case, like the child involved?"

"Well, the child is the only truly innocent one we know of at this point, isn't she? And I don't have time for a lecture. I'm just doing my damn job," Cody battled back. So what if he had a soft spot for a pretty woman in distress who had more of a backbone than she thought she had. And it went without saying that her kid was simply adorable. The pictures of her were the only things adorning the walls in Amber's simple apartment. Well, at least before intruders destroyed them.

Captain Ferron's voice interrupted his thoughts. "Fine, Maguire. You're officially assigned to Amber and Jenna Norris's police protection. And only because this is a sensitive case and you're the lead detective. Bringing them back here to Boston isn't an option until I can gather more information on what the hell she's mixed up in. I've got every available officer and detective helping with the investigation. Can't believe the Feds haven't swooped in to take it over."

"Yeah, you and I both," Cody agreed. "Makes me wonder why they haven't. They may be sitting back because they're sitting on a bigger duck."

"Without a doubt, Maguire, there's got to be a serious reason holding them back. So take advantage of this."

"Yes, sir."

"Don't talk to anyone else about this—no one but me— and don't bring Amber back to the city until I say so. Don't need the Mob trying to make a hit under a police station's roof."

"Thank you, Captain." Relief flooded Cody. He didn't want to trust anyone else, not when he wanted to be the one to save Amber and Jenna. He owed her something after accusing her of treacherous crimes.

"If I didn't believe you could handle it, I wouldn't give it any consideration. Get in touch when you can. I'll keep this part of the case between us for now," Captain Ferron said and disconnected.

Cody glanced at the clock and estimated the time that remained before he could reach Amber. He didn't want to take a minute longer than necessary. Accelerating, he sped off to rescue the woman who was now a victim more than a suspect.

CHAPTER 7

"Get my plane ready," Prince Jamal Al-Hussein demanded, rising from his massive fifteen-foot mahogany desk. The blazing Saudi sun shone brightly through the ceiling-to-floor windows in the prince's office but the air remained pleasantly cool thanks to the air conditioning and marble walls. "I'm going back to Boston." His voice shook with the fury from deep inside his gut. How dare some little fool think he could steal from the future king of Saudi Arabia and get away with it?

As far as Prince Al-Hussein was concerned, the dirty scumbag Derek Norris hadn't suffered enough for the shame he had brought down on the Saudi Royal family. If the prince's soldiers had captured Derek then he would never have been shot, ending his misery before confessing the whereabouts of the Blue Diamond.

Oh, no. Every bone, every nerve, every cell of Derek's body would have felt excruciating, never-ending pain. And so would be the fate of every family member of Derek Norris. There were effective ways to get desired information out of unwilling detainees.

"Yes, Prince Al-Hussein, at once," Lieutenant Ahmad obeyed, bowing his head slightly before hurrying out of the door.

"Sir, may I ask what is in Boston that requires your personal attention?" General Khalid asked, entering the large office. "The doctor insists you still need bed rest to properly and fully recover."

"The Blue Diamond." The prince said simply, the urge to scream so close.

"It has been found, yes?"

"Not quite," Prince Al-Hussein said, remembering to speak softly to keep his nerves calm. Not an easy feat when faced with losing a precious heirloom to an American thug. "But the thief has been found slaughtered like the pig that he is."

"How did you discover who stole it?"

"A friend in the F.B.I. was kind enough to share that bit of information with me but not soon enough. Someone got to the thief before we could."

"And the Blue Diamond?"

"Hasn't been found yet," the prince said, gritting his teeth. "The F.B.I. was investigating Derek Norris as the possible other thief, along with their connections to the Mob. It appears he knifed his partner to death in New York after they both stole my diamond. When the F.B.I. discovered the dead man, they made the connection to Norris after they viewed videotape of them together at a local New York gas station. Then when the body was discovered, the hotel manager and her fellow employees gave testimony to the agents that placed this Derek Norris guy with the dead mobster."

"Then the Boston Mob has your diamond, no?" General Khalid asked.

"Maybe. But the F.B.I. believes the Norris guy may have double-crossed the Mob and kept the diamond for himself. And now he was found murdered."

"So it was stolen by an organized crime family just as we had suspected." General Khalid paced the office.

"Yes. I'm also told that while the Mob boss, Mr. DiGento, is actively pursuing leads on the missing diamond, the wimp is in hiding, fearing retribution from me."

"As he should," the general said, his eyes darkening with his temper. "Would you like a team to look for him and drag him out of hiding for you?"

"That's a matter for another time. Right now, we only concentrate on retrieving the Blue Diamond."

"Yes, sir, as you wish."

"A man consumed by vengeance is an enemy to himself, failing to focus where needed. The Blue Diamond is our only focus, not the perpetrator of the crime. Understood?" the prince stated.

"Of course, Your Highness. As you wish." The general bowed to show respect and acceptance of his orders.

The prince pounded his fist. This didn't have to happen. "The American media had no right broadcasting that I had the Blue Diamond in my possession while I was in New York. It was a private matter and the fools gave valuable information to the damn thieves."

"Agreed. But with all due respect, Your Highness, I don't think it'd be wise for you to travel. I would consider it an honor to retrieve the Blue Diamond for you while you remain here under doctor's care."

"Your loyalty and commitment to the throne is admirable, General Khalid, but this is something I must do personally. You will, of course, accompany me. There is no other man I wish to be by my side as we launch the greatest fight of my family's history. Be ready to leave the moment the plane is ready."

"As you wish, sir," the general said. "But may I inquire? How will you find the Blue Diamond if the thief is dead and the Mob does not have it?"

Prince Al-Hussein felt his blood pressure rise as his face grew hot and his fists clenched deadly by his side. "Because I will track down Norris's whore ex-wife who has escaped with it. Before his death, he paid her a visit. It is believed by all law enforcement agencies that she has possession of my diamond but will not say where it is. She has a child, too. How can a lone woman and child face my Royal Soldiers and think she can win?"

"It would be foolish of her," the general acknowledged, the thirst for blood in his eyes, pleasing the prince. "Believe me, Prince Al-Hussein, I will personally hunt the whore down and slice her slowly until every ounce of her blood pools on the floor, after I have made her watch her child bleed."

The prince chuckled with no friendliness to the tone. "Ah, don't underestimate a conniving whore, General. Some mothers wouldn't think twice about sacrificing a child for wealth. And it just so happens the Blue Diamond would bring her immense wealth. Don't put it past her to only think of herself."

The general pondered a moment. "Well, then I'll see to it that her child watches as I make her mother bleed out slowly. This I promise you, Prince Al-Hussein. I will avenge this horrible misdeed to the Royal family and to Saudi history."

"Yes, I know you will, General Khalid. And I will watch as you do it," the prince stated, almost tasting victory and smelling the blood of the whore.

"Your Highness, the plane is ready," Lieutenant Ahmad said rushing back into the office and bowing.

Immediately, Prince Al-Hussein and General Khalid walked through the palace with a small contingent of the prince's personal soldiers providing a security detail for the future king.

"General Khalid," the prince stated as they boarded the plane. "You promised we would have the best assassins in the world to work with you on hunting down Amber Norris and I know she cannot possibly hide from the best of the best. But I want it made clear she is worth more money alive than dead."

"Absolutely, Your Highness. Will there be anything else?" the general asked as they took their seats.

From his window seat on the private jet, the prince studied the fading Saudi landscape, sandy desserts and large palaces, as they ascended into the bright blue sky under a scorching afternoon sun. He thought about the turn of events since his journey to New York in America three months earlier. A necessary trip then to save his life turned out to be the beginning of a living nightmare, the humiliation of having the Blue Diamond stolen from him like he was a common man, gnawing at his heart.

"Just bring me the woman," the prince spoke quietly, decisively. "I will personally make Amber Norris sorry for the day she ever met her ex-husband and aided him in the betrayal of my family and me. Every American will soon find out Amber Norris's fate and what happens to thieves who dare steal from me."

CHAPTER 8

"Mommy, I'm scared," Jenna whispered. She sat in thick brush with Amber in the forest abutting the little convenience store.

"I know, baby. Just a little longer and Detective Maguire will be here to pick us up." Amber hoped her voice was soothing and not still shaky.

Mosquitoes were coming out as the humid evening settled around them, darkness slowly creeping in. Despite the warm temperatures, Amber kept Jenna nestled under her arm, using the thick bushes to hide them as much as possible. She chose a spot where they would be concealed and she could still view the parking lot to watch any vehicles pulling in.

"Is he a good guy or a bad guy? I don't want to see any more bad guys," the child said matter-of-factly.

"I don't either, honey. Detective Maguire is definitely a good guy. He's a policeman from Boston who will help us. Don't worry any more. Just rest and be really quiet. Okay?"

"Okay."

Amber's eyes searched continuously for any movement around them while she listened desperately for approaching footsteps. She didn't know what she would do if she witnessed either and prayed for Detective Maguire to hurry up and get here before the goons returned. At least the pending nightfall would help hide them. Maybe the jerks would give up their search. After all, none of them was in great physical shape and running through dense woods had to be taxing on their overweight, out-of-shape bodies. God, she really hoped so.

Amber watched another car swing into the convenience store's parking lot. It wasn't unusual since the little store was situated ideally off the ramp of the highway. Every few minutes someone stopped briefly, then sped away after making a purchase. The constant activity had made it difficult for Amber and Jenna to sneak out of the forest earlier and search for a payphone. Luckily for them, there was an old-fashioned telephone booth near the side of the building. What would it look like for a woman and little girl to be seen wandering out of the woods—dirty, scratched and pale? That was the kind of attention Amber didn't need so they lucked out with only having to talk to that one woman to ask what town they were in.

Movement pulled Amber from her thoughts. A car was coming toward them. Slowly. It circled the building, headlights flickering, and drove to the edge of the parking lot where it met the bushes.

Jenna shivered. Amber held her tighter, her eyes squinting to study the tall man who had stepped from the driver's side, weapon drawn but pointed at the pavement.

Detective Maguire. *Thank God*. The breath she had been holding escaped in a loud sigh. While saying a silent prayer of gratitude, Amber hustled her daughter out of the forest, running on stiff legs, and jumping into the back seat of the detective's car without saying a word to him. Within seconds, he drove away as easily as he had driven in.

Amber watched him study the mirrors. She prayed he would make sure they weren't spotted by the goons. Her vision darted from window to window, relieved when they were the only car on the narrow road.

"She okay?" Detective Maguire asked making eye contact with Amber through the rearview mirror.

"Yes. She's fine. Thank you for coming, Detective Maguire." It took so much energy just to talk. Never had she endured a workout like today's. And never again did she want to.

He handed them a bottle of water. Amber opened it, placing it in Jenna's small hands. "Name's Cody. How'd you hurt your leg, Amber?"

How did he see that? The red spot had dried, but the scrape underneath throbbed. "We had to climb through a window."

"I'll take a look at it when we get to the motel," he said, like he was the boss.

"Motel?" She didn't want to go to any motel. Was she under arrest or something?

"Yeah. I don't think it's safe to take you two back home. Your *friends* won't stop until they find you—and this time, they won't take any chances with you getting away. So I'll hide you until my captain and I can discuss a plan tomorrow."

She blew out an aggravated breath, mostly the one she'd been holding since the escape. "First of all, they are not my friends. We were kidnapped. And I can't go to a motel. I have to work tomorrow."

Cody turned to look at her like she had three heads

before turning his eyes back to the road. "Listen, Amber, maybe you don't understand, but you can't do your job if you're dead. That's what these guys want. You dead. Sorry," he said, looking at Jenna then back to the road. "I'll keep you safe. I promise." His voice immediately turned softer. She didn't need to be thinking of how his damn voice sounded when there were killers after her and Jenna. But at least he was concerned about her daughter more than what she could say about the kidnappers.

"Am I under arrest?" she asked, worried she wouldn't like his answer.

"Should you be?" he asked without even looking at her.

Why did people answer a question with another question? "Not unless it's protocol of the Boston Police Department to arrest victims of kidnappings."

"Not at all. But most victims aren't concealing stolen items. After today's events, have you given any thought as to sharing the info you know on the Blue Diamond?"

She rolled her eyes. "Christ, here we go again about some stupid diamond. Tell me, Detective Maguire—"

"Cody."

She gritted her teeth. "*Cody*. Tell me, do you honestly think that after being kidnapped, with my daughter's life at stake, that I wouldn't gladly give up the stupid diamond you keep insisting I have."

For the first time since picking them up, Cody sighed, showing his concern and worry. Amber felt like a jerk yelling at the one man willing to risk his life to save hers and Jenna's.

"I'm sorry. I don't mean to be rude. I'm just not used to being kidnapped," she admitted, her head hung low, her eyes staring at her hands as Jenna dozed next to her in the back seat.

He laughed slightly, catching her attention. She looked up to focus on the back of his head.

When he spoke, the arrogance he had earlier disappeared. "No, I guess you wouldn't be used to something like that. Now why don't you start from the beginning and tell me exactly what happened since I left you after the search warrant. Don't leave anything out, no matter how silly or small you think the info is. You never know what is important to a case."

She swallowed another gulp of water from the near empty bottle. Glancing at Jenna, the girl was fast asleep, snuggled up against her mother's leg, clutching her doll. Poor thing would be scarred for life after today. Amber shook her head and bit back a sob that begged to escape her throat. What good would crying accomplish right now except to exhaust her more—emotionally, mentally and physically?

Amber looked toward the windshield to find Cody watching her through the rearview mirror again, his eyes looking back and forth between that and the road. Did he show her compassion just then? Wow, she almost wanted to check to see if pigs were flying since she never dreamed the detective would look at her like a human being instead of a wad of shit under his shoe. Amazing what a turn of events could do for a person's reputation.

Without a word, Amber checked Jenna's seatbelt and kissed her on the forehead. She then stood as much as the car would allow and climbed into the front passenger seat. Affixing her seatbelt, she glanced at Cody's profile. Yeah, the arrogance was still there, but not meant for her. Instead, he looked like a man in control of his own path in life, knowing exactly what he wanted or needed. He was calm, cool and collected—all totally opposite of what she felt.

She sat sideways to face him as he continued to drive north down a long two-lane highway. "Where are we headed?" she asked, staring out the windshield with the roads darkening as the sun set.

"New Hampshire. It'll be safer than Massachusetts, although not entirely."

"Not entirely? Then why head there. We could go somewhere else."

He turned and smiled at her before looking back at the road. "In case you haven't noticed, you're a wreck. Dirty and scratched up."

"Gee thanks. Not every day a girl gets a compliment like that," she teased, allowing a slight smile now that she felt more comfortable with him. He didn't seem terribly bad. Time would tell though.

"Besides, I want to get off of the road. It's not like there are a lot of cars on the road as the night wears on so we can't necessarily blend in. Now start telling me what happened. I should warn you I love details, the more you talk, the better it will be."

Now she laughed. "I don't think I've ever heard a man want a woman to talk as much as she could. You are one of a kind, Cody."

"Now that I can admit being accused of." He turned and flashed her a killer smile, her breath hitched. He should be the one arrested for having such a deadly smile. "They only made one of me and my fellow officers are pretty glad. Now start talking, Amber. It'll help pass the time on the road."

"I want to say it happened so quickly, but I would be lying," she began, nervous to put words to her thoughts.

"I don't understand."

She shrugged, the simple movement tiring. "It was all in

slow motion. All I wanted was to speed it up so we could get away. When I brought Jenna home from her play date, I walked into my house to find four guys waiting for me."

As he drove, she talked. Not leaving out a single second of what happened, she was overwhelmed listening to her recollection of the events. "And then you picked us up."

"I'm sorry you had to go through that, Amber." Cody's voice was soft and soothing, a big change from the accusatory tone earlier in the day. "For what it's worth, when I left you, I fought with my commissioner to secure you police protection."

"So you finally realized I wasn't guilty or involved with Derek?"

"Not exactly. I'm still sorting this case out. But I knew, with the scumbags involved in this mess, that you wouldn't last long without police protection." He glanced at her. "Innocent or not."

"I see. So it took me and my daughter almost getting killed to get this protection?" Her temper ignited with his admission and the police's lack of response to her needs. "Thought you were sworn to protect people."

"I'm afraid so. With budget constraints being what they are, the commissioner couldn't agree without more to go on."

She sat silent for a minute, not wanting to yell at him for something that was out of his control. When she finally spoke, her voice was firm. "So Jenna and I are basically on our own in this mess."

"Hell no. Not anymore. You've got me. I'll be by your side until this case can be worked out—whether the department likes it or not."

"You mean until I give you the Blue Diamond that I don't

have, have never seen, and until this morning, had never heard of?" The bite in her words reflected her aggravation at being unwillingly thrust into a criminal probe.

"Yeah. Or until we recover the Blue Diamond elsewhere."

She glared at him. "But, Cody, then you'd have to admit I'm not involved in my dead ex-husband's shit. Oh my God. Then you'd actually have to do some detective work and stop focusing on me as your only option. Surely, you must've been taught better in detective school or wherever you went to get that useless badge you liked flashing at me earlier."

Now it was his turn to glare at her as they stopped at a stop sign on a deserted rural road. "Look, Amber. I've been worried sick about you and that little girl back there. I happen to have seen first-hand what these men are capable of and there's no way I wanted that as your fate, even if you are guilty of something."

"And—"

"Shut up and listen. I was planning to give you protection on my own time because I don't give a shit about budgets and finances when people's lives are at stake."

"Really?"

"Yeah, really. I know that doesn't fit with the big, bad detective picture you've no doubt painted of me inside your head." His temper had bite. Interesting.

"Much like I'm not fitting with the picture you've no doubt painted in your head of a convict's conniving ex-wife holding the missing link to an international theft."

"Touché," he said with a slight grin that showed his weariness. "Can we call a goddamn truce? I'm not looking to waste time battling you. I'm on the line of believing all of what you've said about your innocence but the detective in me struggles with why your ex-husband shows up, out of nowhere, to visit you unexpectedly only two days before he's murdered."

Amber took his words in and organized her own thoughts. "Okay. Truce. You're right. I understand you're just doing your job and I probably wouldn't believe me either, not after my history with Derek. But, please believe me. He gave me nothing to hide. I've never, ever seen the diamond."

Cody drove calmly, even as his hand held the steering wheel in a death grip. "I'm trying to believe you, Amber. Really I am. I just need a little time to sort out all of today's events so I can figure out what the hell is going on. Police work isn't like on T.V. where cases are solved miraculously in an hour's time. It's long boring hours sorting through people's lives and lies."

Amber exhaled, her breath shaky. "I know. I've lived on the other side of the law. It's just as long and boring when you're trying to prove you're innocent after you've been deemed guilty because of your association with someone." If she had the strength, she would burst out crying.

"When I entered your apartment and saw it ransacked, I was beside myself with fear. Yes, police officers can have fear. I thought the worse."

"You went back to my apartment? What for?"

He looked at her, his features barely visible with the minimal light from the dashboard. "Needed you to identify Derek," he whispered.

Her stomached turned. "Oh God. Why? He has a brother."

"Couldn't get a hold of him. You, being the ex-wife, were the next best thing. Okay. We're here. This should be an ideal motel for the night," he said, entering the parking lot of the Greenbrook Motel on a street littered with small businesses that were mostly closed.

Cody parked in the small lot in front of the one-story wooden motel and kept the ignition running.

He leaned back to look at Jenna who was waking up. "Ladies, stay in the car until I get back out. I'll get us a room. It'll be better if no one sees you so they can't tip off anyone who probes about your whereabouts."

"My God, do you think they'll look for us out here in the middle of nowhere?" Amber asked.

"You can bet your next paycheck on it. There's civilization all around us and that means nosy people. Stay put. The car's running in case..." Cody looked back at them as he opened the car and stepped out. "Well, you know...just in case, I can't help you."

"But you promised to keep us safe," Jenna finally spoke after pure silence since she'd gotten into the car.

Cody leaned back in the car and stared at Amber then at the little girl. "You're absolutely right, sweetheart. I don't break promises. I promise you'll be safe. I'll be right out, okay?"

"Yes," Amber whispered.

"Just in case we have company show up, don't hesitate to take off, okay?" he directed to Amber who nodded.

Cody quickly walked into the motel office. Bugs converged on the lone light fixture above the front door. Amber watched as giant moths fluttered about in the quiet night air. *Hurry up, Cody.* She hated sitting in a car, alone with her daughter, in a place she didn't even know.

"Mommy, I'm still scared," Jenna whispered.

Amber motioned for her to climb in the front seat. "It's okay to be scared, honey. But we're going to be all right. Cody is going to help us."

"I like Cody. He's really nice. And he smells good."

Amber laughed at her little girl's observant behavior. "He does, huh?" *A lot better than what Derek smelled like the other night.*

It was hard to believe after wishing him dead for so long that it had finally happened. Maybe once this mystery was solved, Amber could actually give Jenna a good life without fear. That would be so nice.

Amber studied the surrounding darkness but found nothing unusual. She reminded herself that Cody was just inside and he had a gun. He would defend them, if necessary.

Cody emerged from the office and Amber let out a sigh of relief.

"Jenna, are you going to drive?" he asked, sitting back in the car.

Jenna giggled. "No. I don't have a license like Mommy does."

"And why's that?" he asked while driving into a parking spot.

Jenna giggled louder. "Because I'm too little, silly."

Amber laughed. It was music to her ears to hear the little girl's laughter again.

Cody hustled them out of the car and walked them inside the rented room that had one queen bed, an armchair, and a black and white television. Cody checked the windows, locking them and drawing the curtains. He turned on the small air conditioner. The room was hot and humid, but at least there were no damn bugs or mosquitoes. Amber shivered at the memory of having to endure the bugs in the forest for so many hours.

"You and Jenna share the bed. I'll take in the chair," Cody said double-checking the locks on the door.

"I don't think I could sleep," Amber confessed, yawning in spite of herself.

"Mommy, I'm hungry," Jenna said, yawning as well, her nap in the car obviously not enough sleep after what she'd been through.

Amber had no money. Her purse was at the house. How could she feed her daughter?

"There's a pizza place across the street," Cody said simply.

"But I don't have any money on me," Amber said softly, totally embarrassed by her predicament. Granted she didn't have a lot of money usually, but she always had been able to feed Jenna.

Cody looked at her, his eyes soft and friendly. "Consider dinner to be on the Boston Police tonight," he said and leaned down to Jenna pretending to be a confidant. "Does your mommy let you drink tonic?"

Jenna shook her head.

Cody smiled, the simple act warming his hard features instantly. "I'll tell you what, if you be a good girl and listen to Mommy while I'm gone, then I'll sneak some tonic back and cookies too. How's that sound?"

Of course, Amber could hear every word but when Jenna leaned forward to whisper in his ear, Amber bit down on a laugh. The pair made an adorable sight trying to pull a fast one over on her.

Considering the hell Jenna had been through today and that Cody had saved them, Amber would just let them get away with their sneaky plan. Just this once though.

"That sounds good. But I don't want to make Mommy mad. She says tonic rots teeth and I don't have my toothbrush with me."

Cody's eyes caught Amber's, a warm feeling filled her belly as those bright blues studied her. "I'm sure Mommy will agree that tonight's special."

Amber hugged Jenna. "Yes, of course. It's fine, honey. Your teeth will survive a few glasses of tonic. Now go into the bathroom and wash up as best you can, okay?"

Jenna and her doll bounced across the bedroom into the bathroom, the sound of running water soon filled the air.

"Thank you, Cody. For making her feel safe."

"And her mom? Do I make her feel safe, too?" His tone was too sexy for her own good, the thrill racing from her belly to her womb too noticeable to ignore. She didn't need this right now. It didn't matter how handsome he was, or how toned his body was, or the smell of his woodsy cologne or aftershave. What mattered was keeping Jenna safe.

"I'm not looking for a lover right now," Amber blurted out when he studied her too long.

His grin was so mischievous, like she'd just challenged him to the greatest contest of his life. "Good thing I'm not either." He moved to the door and turned back to her. "Because I'm damn good at getting what I want." This time his smile was promising.

"Don't answer the door to anyone. And stay away from the windows. I'll be keeping an eye on you from across the street. You'll be fine. I promise. You might want to check both of you for ticks after sitting in the woods so long. I'll be happy to assist you when I return, Amber...if there are any spots you can't reach."

With a wink and a twinkle in his eyes, he left Amber to stare at the closed door. Just how in the hell was she supposed to sleep in the same room with that confidant man when what she really wanted to do was crawl into his wide arms and let him rock her to sleep? Okay, so maybe not to sleep.

It looked like she had a sleepless night ahead. It had nothing to do with armed kidnappers wanting to kill her but everything to do with one very sexy cop.

CHAPTER 9

Cody felt like a caged animal waiting in the small pizza shop for his order. He kept the motel in his constant sight, only turning away to check the progress of the food.

Across the road Amber and Jenna awaited his arrival, no doubt nervous with being left alone again, but he couldn't risk them outside even at night. Not when the Mob thugs who kidnapped them wouldn't be too far away, determined to collect their lost victims. It still amazed him how Amber managed to get away from professional hit men. Cody didn't even know if she realized how unheard of it was for someone to escape the Mob's hold, especially with a child in tow.

Pacing didn't help calm his nerves. Every muscle in his body tightened on high alert just in case he needed to react to any danger immediately. His thoughts were not only consumed with keeping Amber and Jenna safe but with figuring out at what point he had lost control of this investigation. How did he let the Mob get a step ahead of him and capture Amber? What was he missing in this case?

He had to get control back and solve the case before anyone else got hurt. Now his determination was addictive.

First thing he needed to do was determine, once and for all, if Amber was in any way involved with stashing the Blue Diamond. The only way to do that was to choose to trust her declared innocence. Never once had she wavered in her insistence of being not guilty so maybe it was time to go with his gut. Then he could move on to figuring out where Derek had hid the diamond. That would prove harder with no damn leads.

"Sir, here you go," the pizza clerk said handing Cody his food.

With long strides, his leg ate up the ground back to the motel. And back to the investigation of his career.

"PIZZA HAS NEVER TASTED SO GOOD." Amber sighed as she chewed her second piece. Jenna stuffed chicken fingers into her mouth almost as quickly as she could pick them up.

"Slow down, Jenna, honey. You're going to choke," Amber explained, passing her a napkin.

"But I'm so hungry and these are so good," Jenna said in her typical dramatic fashion. It was amazing how well she was doing after being kidnapped, chased, and stashed away in a less than desirable motel for the night.

"Yes, everything tastes great. Thank you, again, Cody, for dinner. Seems we all worked up an appetite tonight." Amber hoped small talk would ease the tension in the room. Cody seemed distracted, deep in thought. Maybe he was planning her arrest. That wasn't even funny, but she had lost faith in convincing him she was a victim and nothing more.

"Yeah, Mommy never eats more than one slice of pizza,"

Jenna confessed before chugging tonic, burping and giggling. "Excuse me."

Cody smiled wide. "It's my pleasure. I don't get to dine with two pretty women very often so this is a treat for me."

Oh, he's a charmer. Amber would bet any amount of money that, when Cody wasn't detecting things, he was out playing the field. He was desirable enough to have any woman he wanted.

When a flare of jealousy hit Amber, she winced. *What's gotten into me—acting like this?* She wasn't some kind of hopeless romantic. Her experiences with her ex-husband had pretty much ruined her for life in the romance department. Trusting another man with her heart would be foolish and just lead to more heartache.

"Mommy, I'm so full. Can I watch T.V.?"

"Only for a few minutes before bed, but first wash your hands. And rinse your mouth out since you can't brush your teeth."

Jenna did as told and plopped on the bed with her doll to watch cartoons.

"Jenna," Cody said, standing and taking Amber by the hand. "I need to check out your mom's cut. We'll be right here in the bathroom."

"We will not," Amber said, trying unsuccessfully to pull her hand out of his grip.

"Don't be a baby," he teased walking into the bathroom and flicking on the light.

"Don't call me names."

"Pull down your pants." Those words rolling off his tongue instantly awakened something deep inside her. She squashed the urge to squeeze her knees together to deal with the ache forming between her legs. She wasn't used to having such a reaction to a man.

"I will not. What the hell are you up to, Cody?" she demanded, her voice hitching on his name.

He kept his tone even. "Not what you may be thinking. Just tug down the jeans enough for me to see the side of your thigh. Panties can stay on." His mischievous eyes caught hers. "That is, if you wear panties."

She playfully slapped his arm and whispered, "Of course I do, and you'll never see them." She had to fight not to smile with his teasing.

"I don't believe in the word never."

"Oh, for God's sake. If I do this, then will you let me get some sleep?"

"Of course."

She unbuttoned her jeans to slide them down just enough for him to see her upper thigh, but she ignored the fact that he would also have a glimpse of her ass cheek since her bikini panties didn't cover much.

"Hurry up." Her face burned. "Ouch."

"Sorry. Just wiping it with some water."

"Does this mean I'm no longer suspected of killing my ex-husband?" She needed conversation to keep from concentrating on his fingers touching her skin inches below her panties.

"You were never a suspect in his death. Sorry about that." His eyes glanced up sheepishly.

"What?" The swine! "But you said I was the *only* suspect. You made me think you'd arrest me at any second. Do you know how scared I was? How worried I was for my daughter?"

His body stiffened. "It was for your own good. I didn't believe you would share any info unless you thought you'd be accused of something you didn't do."

"You're a jerk. You used my daughter against me,

knowing I am all she has and couldn't risk being arrested. That can't be acceptable police protocol." His intentions may have been good, but the worry she went through had sucked.

"I've learned to do what is necessary to protect the innocent and I knew you were innocent in killing him, my dear."

"Oh really? And how did you know that? You even had eyewitnesses that I threatened to kill him."

Cody continued cleaning the cut before pressing a rolled wad of toilet paper to the area to dry it. "Derek's murder was a professional hit. Not something his ex-wife could've done no matter how much you hated him. I also knew you didn't have the financial resources to pay for such a hit. Scrape looks good." He patted her leg and stood.

She immediately pulled her pants back up and buttoned them, relieved the peep show was over, but concerned why it had affected her so much, awakening feelings deep inside her for a man's touch. Feelings she didn't think she could feel.

"I'd say thank you, but I think you actually enjoyed that," she accused to mask her embarrassment.

He smiled, the effort easing the tension she had briefly witnessed etched on his face. "Would be lying if I said I didn't enjoy seeing some of your skin. Hit the bed. We'll get up early."

He swatted her bottom as she left the bathroom. "Hey."

"Enjoyed doing that too," he said smiling.

Damn man was too sexy for both their sakes.

Cody's stiff neck cursed him after spending the night sleeping upright in the armchair while Amber and Jenna slept a few feet away in the bed. Based on how much Amber tossed and turned all night, the bed couldn't have been that much more comfortable.

Rubbing sleep from his eyes, Cody stood, stretched and hit the bathroom. When he came out, Amber was sitting on the side of the bed.

"Manage to get any sleep, Amber?"

Her answer was a yawn, as she rose and walked past him into the bathroom. "I should warn you I'm not a morning person. And I'm not nice until my second cup of coffee."

He laughed when she disappeared behind the bathroom door. After a few minutes, she appeared looking like she'd washed her face and finger brushed her hair. They had all slept in their clothes and kept their shoes on just in case a fast get away was needed during the night. Cody was damn grateful one wasn't.

Amber gently woke Jenna with a few shakes and held her hand to walk her to the bathroom with whispered instructions to clean up.

"How about we get some breakfast and coffee?" Cody asked once Jenna came back out to the room.

"I want waffles and whipped cream," Jenna said.

"Then that's what we'll have," Cody said, unable to resist the little girl's happy disposition.

"You know you don't have to give her everything she wants," Amber said as they walked to the front door.

"I don't mind. I like waffles," Cody said, opening the front door, having only seconds to throw Amber and Jenna down as a hail of bullets whizzed over their heads. "Fuck! Get up!" he screamed, returning fire with his weapon. He could clearly see the men shooting at them from across the parking lot, using a van as a shield.

"Those the kidnappers?" he demanded of Amber

without looking at her but keeping his eyes on the men as he reloaded his weapon and fired again.

"Yes," she screamed, not hiding her fear. Amber and Jenna staggered to their feet.

"This way," Cody yelled, shooting at the van as he dragged Amber and Jenna to the side of the building.

Cody replaced his weapon in its holster knowing he was outgunned. Lifting the little girl, he cradled her to his side as he grabbed Amber's arm and ran around back and into the woods.

"Jenna!" Amber screamed.

"I've got her. Just keep running. Don't stop!" Cody demanded as bullets sliced the bark off the trees around them.

"Oh, Christ, not again," Amber cried out.

Their only hope to escape was if the fat bastards gave up running after them. That didn't seem likely, so Cody needed to find a car and quick. There was no way he could have gotten them into his car, not with the barrage of bullets raining down on them. And hiding out in the woods to circle back when things calmed down wasn't a good plan. Someone would be left behind to watch his car just in case he tried to do that.

"Come on, Amber. I said run." He hoped his yelling would keep her from going into shock with this latest episode. He needed her alert and able.

"I'm running as fast as I can." The bite in her words was what he needed to hear to feel confident she was holding it together.

Cody kept a strong grip on Amber's arm, pulling her alongside him as he carried Jenna. They jumped over fallen logs and through thick bushes that scratched their exposed arms. Amber's agility impressed him. There were no complaints from her as she ran as fast as him, of course her daughter's weight hampered him somewhat. But he hadn't run miles in the woods the day before like Amber did and her muscles must surely be tight this morning. She didn't show any sign of that as she plunged ahead with an admirable dignity.

The air was cooler in the shade of the forest but, still, after running at high speed for over five minutes, sweat trickled down Cody's chest and back, and over his face and neck. He hated feeling clammy, but it was better than not feeling anything at all. Cody was grateful that the bullets had stopped.

He dared to stop running, using the wide trunk of a maple to hide them while he scanned the edge of trees behind them. Gasping for breath and sweaty, both Amber and him doubled over, keeping Jenna between them as they sucked air into their deprived lungs.

"Are the bad guys gone?" Jenna asked, clutching her doll. How she managed not to drop that thing was beyond him.

"I think so, but we can't be too sure. Got to keep walking. Come on," he ordered, scooping Jenna into his arms. "We're going to do a reverse piggy back, sweetheart. Need you to sit in front of me while I hold on to you."

"In case the bad guys shoot at us again?"

He smiled. For a little thing, she was not hysterical like he had expected. "Yes. You're very smart."

"I can carry her," Amber said through deep breaths.

One look at her and Cody didn't doubt she was strong enough to carry her child to safety. Hell, she had already done so once, the determination set deeply in her golden eyes. She was walking proof that it wasn't wise to mess with a woman's child. Amber looked mad enough to shred a man to pieces with her bare hands. Did she even realize how strong a woman she was? And he didn't mean with physical strength either, although it was obvious she had that too.

"I've got her," Cody said simply. "You can trust me to keep her safe, Amber."

"I don't know who to trust anymore." Amber's wounded voice only hinted at her anxiety over the situation when she should be hysterical or worse.

"I had plenty of time to hurt you last night if that was my intention," he snapped, the frustration of their plight growing in him too.

She glanced at him then lowered her eyes to the ground. "I'm sorry, Cody. I know you're trying to help us. But why don't you have a partner or something? Why are you alone? Shouldn't you have help? I mean you alone couldn't fend them off with bullets just now. It's damn lucky we had somewhere to run."

So he fucked up and didn't pay attention to his surroundings when they left the motel room. Jenna was just such a delight to talk with that she threw him off his game. That can't happen again. Didn't matter what paternal instincts he'd discovered he had during the night while watching the little girl snore gently.

He picked up the pace now that they had caught their breaths. "I trust no one either. Just my captain. He's the only one who knows you're with me. We aren't foolish enough not to realize the Mob's money reaches into the rank and file of the police department. Greed is a powerful weapon. I want to operate as confidentially as possible. The fewer people involved means less chances of information about you getting to the wrong people. Make sense?"

"Yeah. But you're a bit late since the wrong people knew exactly how to find me." He welcomed sarcasm over hysteria any day.

They walked for the next twenty minutes in silence until they came to the edge of a clearing. The woods had ended leaving them on a dirt road.

"Look over there," Cody said, pointing to an old pickup truck. "That's our ride, ladies."

"You silly guy, you don't have keys for it." Jenna laughed, her little arms wrapped tightly around his sweaty neck, her doll in between them. At least the doll looked the part of a hiker with the small backpack attached to her shoulders.

He smiled and kept watch behind them so they had no more surprise visitors. "No, but I can hot wire it. Want me to teach you?"

"Yes," she said excitedly, bouncing in his grip. Her minor weight felt like a truckload after the run through the woods. The muscles in his arms protested her movement, but he didn't say a word. He much rather have her squirming around than motionless from a bullet.

"Cody!" Amber admonished. "Now why in the world does she need to know something like that?"

He shrugged. "Why not?"

"Don't you think it a bit ironic that a cop teaches a little girl how to steal something?" Amber challenged as they walked across the road to their ride.

"Now I never said anything about stealing something. I simply said I'd teach her how to hot wire, you know, in case someday she lost her keys or something."

"Yeah, right," Amber said, effectively dismissing him.

Cody was eternally grateful to find the truck unlocked. He set Jenna down on the bench seat in the front of the truck and Amber climbed in next to her, rolling down the window before shutting the door.

Jenna watched intensely as Cody crouched under the steering wheel, peeled back the plastic around the column and worked with the exposed wires until the engine roared to life.

"You did it," Jenna exclaimed, clapping her hands. Amber sat with her arm around the child's shoulders.

Cody sat behind the steering wheel and studied the gauges. "We have half a tank of gas. That'll be enough to at least get us out of here." He looked around to see if there was a sign to indicate exactly where here was. "You two duck down so that if those bad guys come back you won't be a target. Plus, they'll be looking for three of us. If they see only me, it may throw them off track."

"Hopefully," Amber quipped and crawled onto the floor-board with her daughter.

"Yeah. Hopefully," Cody agreed, knowing he was running low on bullets and luck.

The old truck didn't have a lot of speed to it as it bumped along the rural road. Finally, a sign gave Cody the direction he needed.

"I'm staying off the highway even though it's the fastest route. The back roads will offer a bit more seclusion. The men looking for us will expect us to use the highway to get as much distance as possible."

"That sounds like a good idea," Amber said. She looked adorable hiding out on the floor of the truck, her temper etched on her face but her eyes betraying her fright.

"Not such a good idea to be on one road where the bad guys can spot us like moving targets. It may be a faster route but definitely not the safest. Believe me, they are extremely desperate right now to catch you. It's their lives in jeopardy for screwing up and losing you in the first place."

"Mommy, it'll be okay. Cody promised to keep us safe and so far he has. Right?"

Cody glanced down at the little girl and what he

witnessed melted his heart. Jenna's tiny hand caressed Amber's scratched arm. Then Amber's eyes caught his, the shiny tears on the verge of spilling over. It tore at his heart fiercely, so much so he forced his eyes back to the road and left mother and child to comfort each other while he kept an eye on all mirrors for any sign of danger.

They drove for an hour in silence, deeper into the heart of New Hampshire. "I think it's safe for you two to sit back up here. There's been no sign of anyone."

"Thank God." Amber didn't waste a second scrambling up onto the bench seat and hauling a napping Jenna up beside her. "Just when I didn't think my body could hurt any more than it already did." Finding the seatbelt stuck behind the seat, she pulled it free and fastened it around her daughter.

"Yeah, sorry about that. I know it wasn't the most comfortable position but I had to err on the side of caution."

"I know," Amber said, and stretched like a cat, long and hard. He expected her to purr at any second when he saw the pleasure on her face. "Suppose it wouldn't be safe to stop and stretch yet."

"Do you have to pee?"

"Not really," she answered without looking at him, the soft pink color dotting her cheeks delightful.

"Then we can't risk stopping yet."

"Cody, where are we headed?" Amber asked quietly, Jenna restless but still napping beside her.

"My grandfather's fishing cabin," he answered, glancing at her, enjoying the way her light brown hair feathered her cheeks as the warm wind wafted through the open windows. "It's about another hour away. Believe me when I say no one will find us there."

"Sorry if I don't share your belief. You said it yourself...

these men will stop at nothing to get me. And so far, their track record isn't too bad. We barely escaped."

"Granddad's cabin is so secluded and deep in the woods that unless they're following us, and I mean on our bumper, they won't find us. The dirt trail leading to the cabin doesn't even resemble a road. If you don't know to take it, you won't find the cabin."

Amber sat silently for a few minutes, staring out the window, her gorgeous face filled with worry. When she finally looked at him and spoke, her voice sounded defeated. "How are we going to eat? If the cabin is that secluded, it's not like we can order pizza."

Now this was where Cody could ease her worries. He had a plan. "We'll fish. There's an outdoor fire pit for cooking. It's what people used before the invention of barbeques. Grandpa keeps the cabin well stocked with non-perishables...I promise we won't starve, Amber."

She smiled, the first he'd seen from her since yesterday. "You've been making a lot of promises, Detective. I hope you live up to them. Especially the one about keeping us safe."

"On that, my dear, you have my word."

"I'm hungry," Jenna said, waking up from her nap, stretching like her mother had. *Too cute.*

"Hungry? That's right," Cody said. "We never did get our waffles. We'll see what we can do about that, Peanut. Promise," he said, looking at a smiling Amber and winking.

Her smile was delightful. He'd love to see it more often and when they weren't part of a manhunt.

Cody dug out his wallet from his back pocket, steering the truck with one hand. "Jenna, look inside here and take out all of the cash. You count it and let me know what we have."

Jenna followed instructions perfectly. "Seventy-four dollars. Wow, you're rich. I've never seen so much money."

Cody laughed and glanced at Amber, her cheeks reddened. Why would she be embarrassed about not having money? She was a single mom raising her daughter without any handouts from government agencies. His investigation on her proved that.

"Well, now I need you to be in charge of it. Hold onto it tight. That's our waffle money. And gas money, which we're going to need soon." Cody kept a constant watch in the mirrors, not wanting another surprise visit. "Speaking of gas...there's a gas station up ahead. We'll stop, use the bathrooms and see what we can get to eat."

"Look, Mommy, I have an important job now."

"Yes you do," she agreed, kissing the top of her daughter's head.

"I only want to use cash," Cody said to Amber. "If my suspicions are correct, then the players involved will have access to trace my credit cards and cell phone—easily leading them right to us."

"Oh, brother, not again," Jenna quipped, slinging her head back on the seat in an overly dramatic fashion.

Cody laughed. He would much rather have the little girl making light of the situation than consumed with worry.

CHAPTER 10

N ow that Jenna had some food, she quietly ate. Amber was glad to have a decent cup of coffee, her appetite non-existent.

"So, Amber. Why don't you tell me everything that happened when Derek showed up at your house the other night so I can try to piece together this puzzle?" Cody said, his profile as relaxed as she'd seen him so far, odd considering they were still chased by monsters.

"There's not much," Amber said. "Jenna opened the door to find him standing there. He looked awful—filthy, smelly, thin, sickly."

"He brought me a doll," Jenna included.

"Yeah, that was just his way of sweet talking his way into my house. He was looking for a place to crash—as usual, it was all about him. He excelled at using people to his benefit."

"Most criminals do. Did he say anything about being in trouble?"

Amber sighed, hating having to talk about this in front

of Jenna but knowing time was of the essence so Cody could figure this out and save their lives. "Derek was always in trouble. If he had said he wasn't, then I would've been shocked."

"He didn't ask you to hold onto anything for him? A box? Package?"

Amber shook her head. "He just wanted to bully me into letting him stay at my house. That's when I threw him out."

"Was he carrying a bag or a box? A backpack or gym bag?" Cody asked, his questions going in circles.

Amber sighed at the meaningless information she had to offer. "Nope. Just a coat. He sounded like he was homeless. I'm sorry, Cody, but don't you think I've dissected that night over and over in my head? It would make this a heck of a lot easier if he had just mentioned the diamond or referred to a windfall or something, but he didn't." Amber rubbed her finger on the side of her coffee cup, looking up to gaze into his eyes. "I have to tell you, though, if he expected a windfall, he would definitely brag about it. He was great at bragging."

"I'm afraid Derek may have smartened up in the years since your divorce, my dear. He stole the diamond and went into hiding for months before being found. And only after visiting you."

She gasped. "Do you think those men have been watching me all along?"

"It's possible. Since Derek didn't have many relatives, it's logical to think he'd come by his daughter's home if he were in trouble."

Oh my God. Each new detail only worried her more.

"Cody, how did you discover Derek stole the Blue Diamond? I mean, he wasn't caught so how can you be sure he ever had it?"

Cody looked at Jenna sitting between them on the truck's bench seat, belted in tight and gobbling her food, then turned his attention back to the road. "I didn't. The Feds did. The F.B.I. has been investigating this case since the heist in New York. There was a body discovered, and I'm choosing my words nicely for little ears."

Amber glanced at her daughter then to Cody. "Thank you. I appreciate that since she doesn't know of, well, Derek's fate."

"What's fate, Mommy?" Jenna asked, her innocent voice so delicate.

"Something we'll talk about later. Let Mommy and Cody have their adult conversation. Okay, honey?"

"Okay. But when I'm an adult, I'm gonna have adult conversations too."

Amber smiled at her daughter's slight back talk. She was definitely growing up. "So what happened in New York?"

Cody kept his driving steady as he spoke. "The man found expired had help getting there, if you catch my drift. His partner was Derek. Probably the one who helped him get to the expired stage. Hospital cameras caught them entering and exiting the hospital on the day of the heist. Then that was the last anyone saw of Derek. It's believed they were both connected to the Boston Mob, who orchestrated the theft of the Blue Diamond using Derek and his partner."

Amber laughed, her brain not fully comprehending everything she had just heard. "That can't all be true. Derek was a petty thief, a loser criminal. He would never have the skills to steal such a valuable item. No way."

"Of course not. That's what his partner was for. Derek trained in jail during his last stint for the armed robbery charge. Mr. DiGento, the man you said you were being taken to, had been planning the theft of the Blue Diamond for many years. Derek was teamed with a partner who had a decorated military background and specialties in black-op affairs, the perfect match for the prince's security team. Obviously, since they got the diamond."

Amber was more than stunned. "Wow. I just can't see Derek making that kind of effort."

"It was for millions of dollars, enough for him to disappear forever and live a king's life in some non-extradition country," Cody said, taking a tight turn on a long curvy road.

"He sure didn't look like a king the other night on my doorstep."

"I'm sure he didn't after laying low for so long. The Feds think he was having a hard time selling the diamond on the Black Market since he hadn't a clue how to do so. That was DiGento's area of expertise."

"Yeah, now that sounds more like Derek—the not having a clue part."

Cody laughed.

"Can I ask you something, Detective Maguire?" Amber asked, watching him closely.

When he turned and grinned, it was enough to spin her head. "Back to calling me by my official name? Oh oh. Looks like I've done something wrong. Okay. Spill it."

"Do you believe me, yet...that I have nothing to do with the Blue Diamond? Do you believe I'm totally innocent?" She had to ask the question even if she braced for an answer she didn't want from the stubborn man.

When he spoke, he sounded sincere. "Yes, Amber. I know you're completely innocent in this whole mess and I'm sorry you and your daughter are caught up in such a dangerous situation."

"My my. A declaration of belief *and* an apology," she teased, relieved he was now completely on her side. "To what do I owe the sudden change of heart?"

He glanced at her and winked. "Your eyes."

Now that she could honestly say she hadn't expected to hear. "My eyes? What's that supposed to mean?"

He shrugged, those broad shoulders hidden under his dirty shirt. "Your eyes have only ever showed honesty. I've been waiting for you to slip up and show your guilt. Every criminal eventually exposes it, usually in the eyes first and the way they avoid eye contact, not looking at you, trying to conceal their faults."

"And my eyes didn't do that?" Amber asked, the relief in her voice obvious.

"Hell, no. You glared at me. You kept eye contact, never flinching when declaring your innocence over and over. You never blinked when I accused you of something you didn't do. Instead of guilt, your eyes held temper, anger and fright, none of which you'd have if you were guilty."

"So the eyes have it," she teased. "Thank you for finally believing in me. I know your job ain't easy but I'm glad you're good at it."

"Thank you," Cody said while turning onto another rural road. "Now since I didn't have a chance earlier to ask you, due to being shot at, why don't you tell me how you got that bruise on your cheek?"

Her hand rubbed her face where he indicated, the purplish mark growing visible overnight. "Oh, I forgot about that since the bullets had my attention." She laughed slightly for Jenna's sake to take the edge off the story. "Yesterday, when the kidnappers went to pick up Jenna, I lunged at them. I know it was a stupid move, me being outnumbered and all, so save any cop lecture, okay? But I just lost it. I didn't want them touching her." Remembering the awful day, she drew Jenna closer to her, keeping an arm around her daughter.

"You'll get no cop lecture here. I understand maternal instincts. Hell, that's what's saved your asses...excuse me, Jenna...I mean behinds, until I could get to you." Cody spoke with a genuine admiration. Wow, how had she ever pegged him as an asshole, snooty cop? Then again, the circumstances under which they had met yesterday weren't conducive to a civil thought.

"The bad guy hit Mommy in the face so I kicked him," Jenna added matter-of-factly.

"She did," Amber said, proudly and kissed the top of Jenna's head. "But they still managed to throw us in the van. They threatened to shoot Jenna if I made a sound while we walked out of my apartment."

"Of course. They needed your cooperation."

She stared at him. "Do you think I should've screamed for help?"

He quickly looked at her like she had three heads before turning his attention back to the bumpy road. "Hell, no. If you'd done that, we wouldn't be talking right now. They'd have kept that promise. The Mob's never been afraid of a public spectacle. But it's easier to kidnap a compliant woman than a fighting one, so of course they used your daughter against you. Typical. Use the threat to a loved one to get someone to cooperate."

Amber shook her head and watched the trees pass by in a blur. "Amazing no one saw us, but even if they did, people are so used to minding their own business now-a-days I'm sure no one would've helped or even bothered to call the police."

"Sad but true," Cody agreed. "Except your landlady, but she was busy watching her soaps."

"Yes. She loves those," Amber said. "When the kidnappers mentioned that Mr. DiGento went by the name of Bones, I remembered the guy Derek had said he met in prison. He called him Bones and eventually went to work for him. I was too young and naïve to realize he was working for the Mob doing things like stealing and collecting gambling debts. Found all that out at Derek's bank robbery trial."

"Yeah, Bones is definitely the Mob boss. But you said he wasn't there yesterday, right?"

"No he wasn't in the van, but that was who the men told us they were taking us to meet."

"Then we ran into the woods," Jenna added. "Mommy gave me a piggyback ride and ran forever and ever like that. She's strong."

"That she is, sweetheart. That she is," Cody said, sending Amber another look of admiration that caused a shiver to run the length of her spine. How could he heat her body with only a look or a smile?

"We ran until I found the store. Then I remembered your business card in my back pocket," Amber said, trying to keep her mind on her plight and not on how interesting Cody Maguire was.

"Ah, so you hadn't had a chance to throw it out yet, huh?" The half smile he flashed her was wicked.

She laughed. "Well, at least you're perceptive. And yes, the thought had crossed my mind but then I got kidnapped and forgot all about it."

His laughter filled the inside of the truck, but his eyes remained serious. "Those jerks are definitely the Boston Mob and Bones their boss. I haven't had any run-ins with him, although I do have some unsolved homicides with his name linked to them. So far, I've been unable to prove squat against him. Bones' pathetic followers won't stop looking for you because he won't let them. Plus, they know people will look the other way when they confront you, even if it's in public."

That made her shiver even with the hot temps. "Great. Then what do I do?"

"The added problem is the Saudi's Royal Soldiers, who are probably watching you as well. Everyone believes you have the Blue Diamond thanks to Derek's little visit the other night. The Royal Soldiers will probably let the Mob do the dirty work since they're local guys and would be much more familiar with the area. Then they will swoop in to recover the Blue Diamond. Believe me when I tell you they won't hesitate to kill anyone who gets in their way. That includes you, her, the police, or the Mob."

"Oh, God." The shiver turned into a tremble. If only this nightmare would end.

"Amber, do you have any idea how valuable the Blue Diamond is?" Something in his voice, the concern, unnerved her.

"No idea. Before yesterday, I didn't use the words 'blue' and 'diamond' in the same sentence." She hated talking about this in front of Jenna. Seven-year-olds shouldn't have to worry about mobsters and foreign soldiers chasing them.

"Fifty million dollars," Cody confirmed quietly, an eerie feeling settling around them in the cramped truck.

"You've got to be kidding me." Her heart stopped. "Fifty million? And they think I have something that valuable? Oh my God. No wonder they won't stop looking for me." A headache quickly settled between her eyes. Massaging her temples didn't do a damn thing.

"Unfortunately, since the jewel wasn't discovered on Derek and he never gave up its location, the Mob and the Saudis will logically think you have it. Remember, they don't know or care about your troubled past with Derek."

"Daddy gave me this pretty doll," Jenna interrupted, but Amber and Cody just smiled to acknowledge her before looking back to each other.

Her heart started to beat again, hard, strong and wild. "Do you have any good news to share, Cody?" Amber asked, the weight on her shoulders ready to collapse her.

"Yes, I actually do. We're here. The cabin is right over there," Cody announced as they drove off a dirt road into a clearing in front of a small log cabin. He parked in the middle of some trees.

"Wish I could offer you a hotel room, ladies, but we'll be safe here. That's the important part."

"That's an understatement," Amber said, climbing out of the truck, her sore muscles revolting against the sudden movement. What she really wanted was a long, hot bath. *Wishful thinking.*

"Yay, we're here!" Jenna exclaimed, scooting out of the truck after Amber, excited like they had arrived for a vacation instead of seeking a hideout. Who could blame the girl's excitement? They hardly ever made it out of the city for special trips. And this was shaping up to be the most memorable.

"Don't run off, Jenna. Remember, we're here to hide out, to stay safe," Amber ordered, cautiously looking around, praying no one jumped out at them, or worse, shot at them. She never wanted to hear a gunshot ever again.

"Yes, Mommy."

Once out of the truck, they stretched. When Cody stood beside Amber, his arm brushed against hers, an impulse to lay her lips against his overwhelmed her. The only thing stopping her insane need to touch this man was Jenna's presence. Amber didn't understand where these feelings came from or why they felt so natural. Maybe it was because she hadn't spent so much time alone with a man in a very long time. Even when she was married, Derek was around long enough to only eat and sleep, before disappearing again.

"I've seen that look on a woman before. Should I be scared?" he teased, flashing a smile that should be outlawed for its intoxicating effect on her.

"What look is that, Cody?"

He leaned closer, his warm breath tickled her ear. "The look of a woman who knows what she wants but not sure how to get it."

So he was good at reading people, was he? Of course, he was a detective after all.

"Oh, I know how to get it. Just not quite sure if I want it bad enough yet."

Did he just growl? She laughed. It had been so long since she flirted. It was good to know she hadn't lost the touch. She may be a bit rusty in the flirtation department, but she discovered it was easily coming back to her. The playful teasing and light banter between her and Cody was just what she needed to calm her frayed nerves and relax now that they had left danger hundreds of miles behind them.

When his hand latched onto hers, heat shot up her arm leaving a trail of fiery goose bumps. Now that reaction she hadn't expected.

"Then we're a lot alike, darling. Come on, I'll show you the inside."

"How are we alike?" she asked as they walked with Jenna around to the rear of the cabin.

"When I want something bad enough, I know exactly how to get it."

The promise in his eyes did something that hadn't happened in years. It aroused her. Soft aches pulsed between her legs, reminding her of her femininity. When her cheeks grow hot with a blush, she swore it would cover her entire body if she continued thinking this way.

"I'll keep that in mind," she said, hoping he didn't hear the slight tremble in her voice and think of her as pathetic.

The smile he offered only fanned the heat creeping over her body. When her panties dampened, she was in trouble. Her body had never reacted this way to a man. Just how was she supposed to conceal it or ignore it? It was all too new to her. She didn't know how to handle herself with such a virile man. Suddenly, she was very aware of every inch of her body and the unbelievable need to feel Cody's hands on her.

"Careful walking around here, ladies," Cody said, interrupting her thoughts.

"Yeah, we know. The bad guys are still chasing us, aren't they, Cody?" Jenna asked, but her soft voice didn't hold fear. Instead, she sounded disgusted. Amber bit her lip. Her daughter had a bigger backbone than she did.

Cody stopped walking and knelt down to be eye-level with Jenna. "Yes, sweetie, the bad guys will be chasing us until I can solve this mystery. But for now, I know they're nowhere near here. You don't worry about them, okay? I made a promise to keep you safe and I plan to keep that promise."

"Okay, Cody," Jenna offered with a smile. "Can you teach me to shoot your gun?"

Amber almost choked. "No!"

Cody laughed. "Sorry, I'd get in trouble with work, and your mom, if I did that. But what I wanted you ladies to be careful of is poison ivy."

"What's that?" Jenna asked, hanging on every word Cody spoke.

Cody pointed to some plants with shiny leaves behind them in the woods. "That there is poison ivy, and if you brush against it, then it's gonna give you the itchies like you wouldn't believe. You'll scratch and scratch."

"Yuk, then I'm not going in the woods," Jenna said and crinkled her nose.

"Good idea. We don't want any itchies," Amber agreed, emphasizing the last word as Cody stood again.

"So I made up a word. As long as it gets the point across, right?" He laughed quietly.

He looked adorable standing there in the middle of a wilderness trying to explain to a seven-year-old the hazards of some of its plants.

"Right."

The quick lesson in how to avoid unwanted scratching did nothing to deter Amber's brain from thinking of Cody and her body's reaction to him. She chalked it all up to lack of sex. Working two jobs and raising a seven-year-old by herself hardly gave her time to shower let alone.

Oh, God. Her cheeks heated. What would Cody think if he could read her mind? Would he be intrigued? Flattered? Aroused? Unless she had really misread the signals from his conversation or his actions, there was no doubt he was interested in her. But timing was everything and now wasn't the time to dwell on such things. She had to figure out what they would do next about being moving targets for the mobsters.

Despite the unfortunate circumstances that brought them here to the fishing cabin, Amber was pleasantly pleased at the fresh air and serene surroundings. She couldn't afford to take vacations so this would be the next best thing to getting away. She bet it would be a relaxing spot if she weren't constantly glancing over her shoulder for the bad guys, expecting the jerks to find them any minute. The jumpiness reminded her of how she lived during her marriage, always wondering when Derek's fists would fly. A wave of nausea hit her like it always did at the horrible memories. But she wouldn't have to deal with Derek any more, a slight comfort in this crazy situation.

Cody, Amber and Jenna walked over hard dirt covered with decaying pine needles and small twigs.

"Grandpa had this patch cleared out where he built the cabin," Cody said. "It makes for easier walking rather than slumping through overgrown bush since he doesn't really get up here often enough to keep it mowed."

"Yeah, I've had my fill of that," Amber countered.

The only grass lay in the surrounding woods. The large pine trees circling the log cabin provided a decent amount of shade around the perimeter, with just enough of a clearing to accommodate the structure and nothing more. It almost appeared like someone dropped the cabin in the middle of the trees. Amber looked above and noticed some large maple and oak trees that swayed in the mild afternoon breezes, not a cloud in sight.

Wasn't this the life?

"There's no electricity and the bathroom is the great outdoors," Cody announced, as if going without toilet facilities was acceptable. Maybe to men it was. "Sorry, ladies. This place was never intended for a woman to stay here so the modern amenities are nil."

Amber and Jenna were wide eyed as they stared at each other. Did Amber just hear him right? No electricity? Well, that she could live without. But no bathroom? What the hell?

"You're joking, right? Please tell us you're joking." His smirk said it all. He wasn't joking. "We have to, well, go to the bathroom out here?" she asked looking around only seeing woods.

"Yes, but the good news is we do at least have toilet paper."

So much for living the perfect life while here. "That's not comforting," Amber retorted. "What about the poison ivy you just warned us about? How can we possibly crouch with the risk of getting a rash?"

"Grandpa is always thinking. He made a special clearing around back but that doesn't mean all the plants are gone. You just have to be careful and look for those leaves I pointed out."

Jenna giggled. "How do we wash our hands?"

He leaned down, hands on his knees. "There's an outdoor well. I'll show you how to pump it and you can use that as a sink. Works great because it splashes your feet, too."

"Cooool." Jenna's exaggerated reply warmed Amber's heart, filling her with relief that her daughter adapted well to their current situation.

"Why don't we just go to another motel?" Amber asked, the thought of squatting butt naked in a forest with bugs and animals all around her creeped her out.

Cody stood and faced her, the serious cop guy back. "No way. We'd be sitting ducks like this morning."

She crossed her arms, not caring if she looked like she was acting stubborn. "Oh, and we're not here?"

"At least here I have the upper hand on any attackers."

"How?"

"I know the lay of this land. The bad guys won't. At least here we'd have a decent chance to escape. Plus, we don't want to use a credit card that can be traced for a motel."

"We'll be fine here says you," Amber complained. "You get to go to the bathroom standing up."

Cody laughed heartily, annoying her more. "Not always."

She only rolled her eyes.

"Come on. Let me show you around. It's really not a bad place once you get past the lack of a toilet."

They walked around back, following Cody as he pointed out the land. "There's a dock down there and a boat. Have you ever fished, Jenna?"

She shook her head.

"Then I'll teach you. We'll have fish for dinner. You can help me clean the fish, too, if you want."

Amber gagged as Jenna jumped up and down. "Count me out. I can't stand the sight of blood," Amber admitted.

"That's why I try not to get into scrapes," Jenna said to Cody who laughed.

He continued with the tour. "The shed has the fishing supplies. Here's the well. You move the handle up and down like this and water comes out." He demonstrated to Jenna's squeals of delight until water splashed onto the concrete slab. "Here's where we'll cook our dinner," he said, pointing to a large stone circle with a blackened metal grate lying across it. Big, fat, long logs were strategically placed around it. "These are close enough to sit and cook with a long branch but far enough not to get burned," he pointed out once he followed where Amber stared.

"It doesn't look very clean," Amber mentioned, studying the soot.

"Nah. That's just black from use. Perfectly fine. I won't poison you." There he went flashing that addicting smile again. "That tire hanging from the tree is a swing you can play with, Jenna, but only after I check it to make sure no bees or hornets have made a nest in it, okay?"

"Sure. I wouldn't want to get stung. My friend got stung by a bee and she cried," Jenna said before turning to Amber. "Mommy, this place is so cool."

"Yes, it is. If you think peeing in the woods is cool." Looking up, tall trees hovered above them, birds flew back and forth between treetops. As majestic as Mother Nature was, it certainly would take her some time to get used to living like this.

Cody laughed, taking Amber's hand as if he'd done it a hundred times. "Come on, it's not so bad. I'll show you inside."

Amber swallowed hard. Why was he holding her hand? She could walk just fine on her own. She dared to look at him, but he was too busy pointing out a rabbit to Jenna.

"Mommy, if I catch a rabbit, can I keep it as a pet?" Jenna asked excitedly.

"I don't think it'd be fair to take the bunny from its family, do you?" Cody said, intervening quickly before Amber could think of a decent excuse to keep her daughter from asking a hundred times for the rabbit.

"Oh, well, I never thought of that," Jenna said, abandoning the idea.

"You're good. That was too easy," Amber whispered, her hand still in Cody's.

He turned his head and looked at her, smiling and winking. "I've got a few tricks up my sleeve. All my brothers have kids so I've learned a thing or two."

"How about you? Any kids?"

"Not yet. Someday if I'm lucky. Just haven't met the right woman I guess," he said, letting go of her hand as they neared the entrance.

When they walked through the unlocked front door of the small log cabin, Amber was shocked. For a cop, he didn't practice safety. "You don't lock your door?" Amber was hit by a sudden jolt of worry. The goons who had kidnapped her had gotten into her locked apartment. Here they could just walk right in. Jeesh, some kind of security he offered them. Amber admonished herself for over-reacting and not being grateful to Cody for risking his life to save them. Guilt forced her to offer a smile.

Cody only shrugged, no worries like hers. "Why should we? It's not like there's any close neighbors here to catch anyone if they broke in. Grandpa figures if he has something someone needs to break in and steal, then they must need it more than him and can have it."

"Interesting philosophy," Amber said. "Sorry, but your grandpa would be robbed blind in the city for his graciousness."

He snorted. "Agreed. Now, ladies, we wash our dishes down in the lake since there's no running water in here and it's easier than using the well. We store our plates and pots in this cupboard. Not much that we go without up here even though by the look of concern on your face, Amber, you must be thinking we're going to be roughing it big time."

She sighed. "I wasn't trying to be ungrateful or rude. It's just that...well, I'm used to going without a lot of things but not this much. But I trust that you know what you're doing. Jenna and I will make the best of it."

"Sure will. Mommy this is so cool. Wait until I tell Papa about this place. He'll want to come too."

"Papa?" Cody asked.

"My dad. They're very close, him and Jenna."

He stared at her. "I know it's a big adjustment, but I'm afraid since our options were limited, it was the best I could come up with on such short notice."

"It's okay. Really, Cody. I'm just glad we're safe." She looked at him, caught those blue eyes and held the contact. "We *are* safe here, right?"

"Promise." He raised his palm. "Now there's an old-fashioned, cast-iron claw foot tub in the bathroom that gives a decent hot bath. Interested?"

Her eyes widened. If he were joking, she'd contemplate committing assault and battery on a cop. "But if there's no running water, then how do you fill it?" she asked, loving the idea of sinking into a deep tub and allowing the hot water to work on her tired muscles and countless scrapes. She felt like a pincushion.

"Grandpa built a contraption for the fire pit, warms the water you get from the well and you haul it inside. I'll set a bath for Jenna, then for you if you'd like."

Amber practically drooled at the offer. "I'd love it. I'm so filthy from sweating and running. But how do you drain the tub?"

After bringing them into the bathroom to show off the massive tub, Cody pointed to a plug underneath. "Grandpa installed this so we can drain it and throw the water out the window. Again, this place was built without the comfort of a woman in mind. It was built solely for us men to fish and enjoy the great outdoors."

"And to hide women in distress," Amber teased.

"Well, I admit that was never in the plans, but I'm not

complaining. Never expected a woman's presence up here to be so pleasant."

Suddenly, the room felt a lot smaller. "Yeah, we'll see if you say that the first time I need to use the woods as a bathroom."

His laugh was contagious as Jenna first joined him then Amber. God, she needed that bath.

CHAPTER 11

"That's it, Jenna. You got the hang of it now." Cody encouraged the girl while he kept a careful eye on the surrounding woods. There was no way any one would find them here. They hadn't been followed; he had made sure of it by taking the longest route here. The never-ending stretch of deserted rural roads would've given away anyone in pursuit. And no one, not even his captain, knew this place existed. Only Grandpa and Cody's four brothers knew how to get here.

"I got one!" Jenna screamed, sitting on the edge of the dock with him, her little legs kicking wildly. Sure enough, she had a fish, the desperate fight under the water evident in the splashes breaking the surface.

"Good girl. Reel it in like this." He placed his large hand gently over her tiny ones, and twirled the reel until the line shortened and the fish emerged, wiggling in its dire struggle.

She did exactly as he had taught her, a quick learner, and had her first bass in the bucket. "Just need two more," she exclaimed, baiting her hook before tossing the line back into the lake like a pro. Pride surged through him. "This sure is fun. Wish Mommy would learn, but she's too girlie for these things."

"Is that so?" Of course, he had guessed the exact same thing about the pretty mommy.

"Yeah, she doesn't like dirt or bugs or...well, icky things in general." Jenna continued to kick her legs leisurely while keeping her eyes on the water.

Cody laughed and just listened to the little girl carry on. He managed to learn more about Amber in the past hour than he had the whole trip or through his prior research. Little Jenna was more mature for her young age than most adults he hung around with. She talked about school, her grandparents, her new doll, her old dolls, the dolls she wished she could have but understood that money was tight for her mom. Cody just shook his head as he listened intently, not wanting to miss one detail about the intriguing woman who trusted him to protect her and her daughter.

"So when Mommy works I get to go to Grammy and Papa's house. They don't like where me and Mommy live. They say it's too dangerous. But really it's not. Unless you park in the wrong place then you get a ticket. The men who get tickets get really mad. So I think that's why Grammy and Papa think it's dangerous."

Cody chuckled. *If it were only just that I'd probably be out of a job.*

"Cody, I've got another fish. Help."

"Nah. You know how to do it now. You're an old pro. Reel 'er in like I showed you."

Jenna didn't complain but did as told. "I did it," she exclaimed while Cody removed the fish from the hook and re-baited.

"You're a very fine fisherman, Jenna." He couldn't help

smiling at this infectious child. "Catch us one more and we'll start dinner."

"Okay. I've never had fish like this before. I hope I like it."

"Have you ever had fish sticks?"

"Yes, Mommy makes them for me sometimes. They're really good."

"Well, these will be really good, too."

"Thank you, Cody, for making my mom smile," Jenna said, the change of subject sudden.

"Oh, come now. I bet your mom smiles every time she looks at your pretty face."

Jenna giggled. "Yeah. But not like you get her to do. She laughs with you. That she never does. Mommy works really hard. I try to help her but I'm still too little. She's the best mom ever."

"I bet she is." His heart swelled with an unfamiliar feeling of excitement.

"Hey, I caught the last one we need." She reeled it in quickly. "There's three fishes, Cody. Now let's clean them," Jenna said standing and running down the dock to the shed. Cody held the bucket and the fishing rod, walking quickly to keep up with her so she didn't get too far ahead. While he had complete confidence in the solitude of the cabin, he still needed to remain on guard. Not a good idea to get to complacent in the serenity of the country.

After hanging the rod in the shed, Cody led the way to the fire pit, but first stopped at the well to fill the bucket with water. He had begun the fire before they began fishing to give it a good chance to take since he was starving and wanted to waste no time.

"First, we check the fire, Jenna. Need it roaring so we can bake them." He added firewood under the grate and the flames grew new life. "Now we take a sharp knife, got to be very careful, and slice like this down the belly, remove the yucky stuff, then scrape the skin off it like this. And you're done. Rinse in the water and you're ready to cook. Here, toss that onto the grill. Be careful."

His little helper was a good student. Soon the smell of baked fish wafted through the smoky air. Using a long branch that he had chiseled one end into a point with his hunting knife, Cody inserted it into the open belly of each fish and flipped it to cook the other side.

"Few more minutes, Jenna," Cody said, watching as Amber walked toward them, her slender hips swaying seductively as she moved with short strides.

Fighting his attraction to her grew harder by the second. Never had he mixed business with pleasure. Just made for easier living. But there was something about Amber that aroused him immensely. Maybe it was the way she handled herself in tense situations. She didn't fall apart like most women would do. Instead, she kept a clear head, assessed the situation, and then dealt with it. He liked that characteristic.

His job kept him away from home for long, mostly unpredictable times. It'd be nice having a woman who he didn't have to worry about being alone while he worked. He shook his head.

Where in the hell did that thought come from? One minute he's on the run for his life with two victims and the next he's having thoughts of coming home to Amber and what it'd be like. One look at her as she stopped at the pit and he knew it was because Amber was the type of woman who could make a man really happy with her smile, her heart, her mind. The exact combination he had always searched for in a woman but had never found. Until now.

"Something smells fantastic out here," Amber said, stooping by Jenna who sat perched on a log beside the fire. "I can't wait to eat."

"Were you able to rest any to get rid of your headache?" Cody asked from his seat on the other log beside Jenna's.

"A little. I'm okay. I couldn't sleep with Jenna out of my sight. No offense."

"None taken," Cody quipped. "But remember, I'm the one with the gun."

"Yeah, the gun that's almost out of bullets."

He grinned. *Smart-ass woman.* He liked that quality in her too. She was never afraid to speak her mind and say things bluntly. "Well, I hadn't planned on a multi-state trek and shootouts with mobsters. They have SWAT teams for that crap. When you called me, I had just ordered my dinner because I wasn't planning to stop looking for you guys until I found you."

Smiling seemed to be easier for her to do lately. The simple gesture helped to warm her soft features. "My bad. I should've given a laundry list of what to bring and put bullets at the top of the list."

"Would've helped. But let's not worry about bullets and bad guys right now. Your daughter has caught and cooked dinner."

"Wow. You did all that, honey?" Amber asked before kissing the top of Jenna's head and standing.

"I did. But Cody helped a lot."

Cody forced himself to tear his eyes away from Amber and how she looked with the fading sun bouncing off of her whispy brown hair and turned back to the girl. "Gonna need a plate for the fish. Jenna, will you run inside and get one from the cabinet on the side of the sink?" Cody hardly finished talking and the girl was off and running.

Amber laughed, the soft sound tightening Cody's gut painfully. *Why do I want the one woman I really shouldn't have?* She was involved in the biggest case of his career.

"You're very good with her, Cody. It's hard to believe you don't have any of your own," she said, sitting next to him by the fire.

"Not yet, but lots of nieces and nephews who I love to spoil. She's a great kid, Amber. You've done well by her." *How in the hell am I supposed to keep my mind on work if she looks so damn good?*

Her smile was more sad than happy. "I haven't told her about her father yet. Don't know if she'd understand or be hurt because she hardly knew him."

"I figured as much. That's why I was careful to screen what I said in front of her on the ride here."

"She's had a rough time over the past day and a half. Too much for a seven-year-old to have to go through just because she had a loser for a father."

"I don't want to tell you how to do your parenting but you really should speak to her soon considering what's going on now. She's bound to find out somehow. It's all over the news and she overhears our conversations. At some point, she's bound to hear it."

She sighed, long and hard. "I'll tell her after dinner."

"Don't underestimate her. She's smart and attentive. Kids are resilient. She'll be good. How about you, Amber? How are you doing?" His throat suddenly felt dry and he couldn't keep his hands still. They had to touch her.

She shrugged, her delicate features showing her stress even when she tried to put on a happy face. But part of his job and expertise was to read people, figure out what they were hiding, what they didn't want him to know. Amber was clearly hiding her feelings, something she excelled at, but

Cody just happened to excel a bit more at his training. If she needed a shoulder, he would give her his.

"How did Derek die?" Her direct question stunned him. *Does she still love the loser? Is that the sadness I read in her eyes?*

Sharing the horrific details wouldn't be wise. Dead is dead. No need to explain the torture he suffered before the bullets ended his misery. Given that she hated the sight of blood, explaining how much Derek shed wouldn't serve any purpose other than to make her sick. "Shot. He was shot in the head."

"He deserved a lot worse for all the shit he's done in his life," she said with no heat.

And Derek got plenty worse, but Cody kept that to himself. "You'll get no argument from me, darling."

Her eyes widened at his use of the endearment. Christ, hadn't anyone ever given this beautiful, kind-hearted woman the compliments she deserved?

Nervousness settled into her with her hands kneading her jeans. If he had the price on his head that she did, he'd be unable to sit still too.

When she spoke, her voice was soft, the sound giving him vivid images of awakening in her arms. "I want to thank you, Cody. For everything. If it weren't for you, we'd probably be dead by now. I didn't have anyone else to turn to that could get us out of that jam."

When her eyes teared up, it broke his heart. He wanted to reach for her. Touch her. Hold her. Wipe away the pain embedded deep in those beautiful golden eyes.

"Just doing my job."

She shook her head, her brown hair whipping around her shoulders. "No way. You've gone above and beyond the call of duty. Most cops wouldn't have done what you have."

"Now I don't know about that. The cops I work with are pretty top notch."

"I'm sure they are. But they weren't the ones to save my daughter and me. All I'm saying is thank you. I can never repay you for your kindness and compassion."

Oh, he could think of a number of ways, like for her to stop tormenting him with an inviting smile, or those eyes that reminded him of soft sunbeams, or the laugh that always managed to tie his stomach into knots. He banished any sexual thoughts from his mind, not wanting to even think about something he couldn't have right now.

Jenna ran back with the plate, a welcome intrusion as Amber inched over for Jenna to take her seat on the log again. Keeping a distance from Amber was imperative for Cody to keep his wits about him.

Jenna held the plate while Cody used the chiseled branch to lift the baked fish from the grill.

"You got that, Jenna, or do you need me to carry it?" Amber asked, standing up.

"Nope. I got it. Come on, guys." Jenna hollered and walked quickly to the cabin.

One glance at Amber and Cody was doomed. She stood there wiping her hands over her bottom to brush away the dirt from the log.

Doesn't she realize how sexy and exciting she is? With a slight smile for him, she turned and followed her daughter, giving Cody a view of her very fine ass in those tight jeans, the vision making his mouth water until he forgot his damn name. How could hips swaying back and forth during a simple walk be so arousing? He finally had to admit Amber Norris had somehow gotten under his skin and into his heart without even a kiss. Now didn't that just make no damn sense.

Shaking his head, Cody willed himself to remain a gentleman and not ravish the beautiful Amber at first chance. He wanted to take his time with her—if he could convince her to give him a chance.

Inside the cabin, the three of them sat at the rustic butcher-block table eating barbequed bass compliments of Jenna's fishing skills. Cody couldn't remember having a more enjoyable meal, not even at any of the five-star restaurants Boston proudly offered.

After licking his fingers, he wanted to keep the mood light with conversation and see if he could discover new information to help the case. "Jenna, I must say you've outdone yourself, girl. Grandpa doesn't know what he's missing and I sure ain't going to tell him and make him jealous."

Jenna giggled. "Oh, Cody, you are funny. I'm already full, Mommy." She had eaten half her fish.

"Mommy, too, honey," Amber confessed, polishing off the last of her dinner.

"Cody, Mommy always says we shouldn't waste food so do you want to have the rest of mine? I promise I don't have any cooties."

Now there was a word that quickly transported him back to his grade school days. He smiled, totally enjoying the company of mother and daughter. "Well, since you promised you don't have cooties then I will definitely take you up on your offer to share," he said and scooped the remainder of her fish onto his plate. "And I happen to agree with your mom that food should never be wasted. Grandpa always used to say don't eat with your eyes, eat with your belly. When I was a kid, I'd put so much food on my plate that I could never finish it."

"I do that with ice cream and then get a brain freeze cuz

I eat too fast," Jenna admitted with a giggle into her hand. "Mommy, can I play with my doll?"

"Yes, for a little bit."

Jenna sat across the room with her doll and played quietly.

"Dinner hit the spot. I've never seen Jenna so excited."

Cody tried his best not to look at Amber since just the sight of her revved his heartbeat and caused him to think naughty thoughts of just what he'd like to do with her in the privacy of his bedroom. Dimly lit candles so he could watch the flames dance over her smooth skin played a big role.

"She should be. She did a fantastic job making it," he said.

When he took the last bite of the bass, Cody stood to collect the dishes.

"Uh-uh," Amber said, standing and taking the plates from him. "You two cooked dinner, the least I can do is clean up. You said wash them in the lake, right?"

The cozy scene should've been awkward for two people who hardly knew each other but it felt so natural to work on domestic chores with Amber. Her eyes mesmerized him, the softness finally showing her relaxation. "Your parents named you for your eyes, didn't they?" he asked, totally captivated by her and finding it harder and harder to hide. He should've made the connection before, the unique name for a woman whose golden eyes highlighted the soft, delicate angles of her face.

She only smiled before walking outside. If only she realized the power of her smile to make him want to beg for a chance to kiss those lovely lips.

"Jenna, how about I heat some water for your bath?" Cody asked, hoping the manual labor would help him wear off some sexual frustration.

"Can I help?" she asked excitedly, running toward him carrying that silly doll.

"Sure. I can always use an extra pair of muscles." Before he turned away, he tweaked her nose.

Her giggle sang against the log walls of the cabin. "I want lots of bubbles."

"Afraid we have no bubbles, sweetheart," he admitted, knowing she was right on his heels without even having to look. Her pigtails bounced in the shadows on the ground.

"Oh, well, that's okay. We'll bring some next time," she said, her voice adorable.

Next time? Oh, boy, he should've thought the girl would like it here, but he didn't expect her to become attached. But then again, what the hell did he know about kids? He was an uncle, not a father. He hadn't learned all there was about kids yet.

"The boys in school said they make bubbles in the tub by farting." Jenna burst into a doubled-over belly laugh.

"Jenna!" Amber scolded as she walked back with the clean plates. "Young ladies don't talk like that."

"Sorry."

Cody jumped to his feet as soon as he heard the rustling in the woods at the edge of the clearing. "Get behind me. Now."

Amber dropped the plates and grabbed Jenna and ran behind Cody, who leveled his gun at the woods. From where he stood, he couldn't determine the source of the noise but the bushes were definitely moving.

Fuck! How the hell did someone find us?

"Amber. Jenna. Lie on the ground and stay there. I'll be right back." He kept his voice low but his eyes never strayed from the forest.

Cody crept silently toward the rustling, knowing he

was a walking target. There was no place for him to take cover in the middle of the clearing so he continued on, using his eyes and ears to figure out who he was up against. Holding his gun in front of him as steady as he could, he sought the bastards who dared follow them here.

Why aren't they shooting? They had a clear shot and could pick him off before he'd get a round off. Then they'd have Amber and Jenna. Anger surged through his veins, his heart thudding hard against his chest, creating an echo in his ears. Whoever it was hiding in the bushes, they'd get Amber and Jenna over his dead body.

He increased his pace, taking larger steps as he got within a few feet of the bushes. There was no doubt someone was there when the branches crackled more.

"You son of a bitch! Come out here and fight like a man," Cody said between clenched teeth.

Without warning, a large deer popped his head out from under the foliage where he had been feasting on berries. Cody lifted his gun without getting a shot off. The deer, startled and massive, leapt to the side and ran into the woods. Cody scanned the area, dragging in deep gulps of air. They were safe.

He re-holstered his weapon and walked back to where Amber and Jenna lay on the ground by the fire pit. Amber had covered Jenna with her body. Cody would've expected nothing less.

"It's okay, ladies," Cody announced. "Was just a deer."

Amber looked up, her face pale, her golden eyes wet and wide. "Only a deer?"

He offered her his hand. When he helped her stand, she trembled. He rubbed her back hoping to soothe her and take away her fears.

"Wow. A real deer?" Jenna exclaimed, standing up quickly. "I wanna see."

Cody smiled even though he didn't feel happy. He didn't like how Amber suffered so much heartache and fear. "Sorry, sweetie. He was just snacking on some berries, but he got scared and ran. They don't like being near people." Cody looked down at Amber. "You okay?"

She shook her head and stepped out of his reach. "Yes. I'm going to go put the plates away and see if I can clean up any inside." She picked up all the plates on the ground.

He knew there wasn't anything to clean up, but also sensed why Amber was scurrying away like a rabbit. Looking like she'd burst into tears at any moment, the poor thing probably wanted the privacy of the cabin to regain her composure.

"Jenna, let's get that bath water started for you." He picked up two large buckets. "We'll fill these with water from the well and heat it on the fire."

"Mommy's scared, Cody." Her little voice was filled with concern.

"I know she is. I'll make sure she gets a nice bath after yours. Deal?"

"Deal."

Jenna proved to be a decent helper. She kept watch over the fire and stirred the buckets for even heating, as Cody lugged water from the well to the fire pit to the tub. The afternoon was settling lazily around them, and by the look of Jenna's heavy eyes, Cody expected her to be asleep within the hour.

When Amber called her inside for her bath, Cody's paternal instincts slammed into him like a freight train. He had never wondered about having a family of his own because the job was his life. But now watching mother and daughter perform the domestic ritual of bath time tugged at Cody's heart. Suddenly, his once exciting single life was dull.

Yeah, he couldn't deny it any longer. He was falling for the sexy mother and her darling daughter. Cody retrieved another bucket of water and sat by the fire waiting for Amber to call him to drain the tub. There was no doubt Amber would deny she was exhausted, but being a dedicated mother, she never complained. Just wanted her daughter taken care of. So admirable.

"Cody, can you show me how to drain the water?" Amber yelled from the front door.

Of course, she'd want to do it on her own. He should've expected her not to ask for help when she was so used to not getting any.

Cody strode inside to the bathroom, a man on a mission. "Rule number one, Amber. While I'm around, there's no need for you to do everything on your own." He opened the window to dump the first bucket of water. When he turned around, she was staring at him with cool eyes, arms crossed, and foot tapping. Good. At least he had her damn attention.

"Rules now? Okay. What's rule number two?" He loved the fire in her voice. Sexy as all hell.

"Haven't a friggin' clue," he said continuing with his chore.

Her laughter filled the cramped room. "Can I at least help with getting my bath ready?"

"Sure. Strip." Maybe he would decide that was rule number two. A smile creased his lips. This could be fun.

Her face was priceless. Wide golden eyes, pink cheeks, mouth opened in an O. "You'd love that, wouldn't you?"

"Hell, yes. In case no one's told you lately, Amber, you're one hot lady with a body to make a man fall to his knees begging for mercy."

She stared at him for a long moment then looked him up and down slowly. "You're still standing." Oh, he loved her spunk when she dared to show it.

Now that the tub was emptied, he was ready to fill it. If he continued to think of her naked then he'd be joining her for that bath. "Barely, babe. Just barely I'm standing." He brushed past her but stopped when their bodies were inches apart. "I'll have that bath ready for you in a few minutes. You should start getting ready."

"Mmmm. I will. And I won't take long in the bath so you can get one too."

He needed a friggin' cold shower but pride made him keep that info to himself. "Don't worry about me, babe. I'll bathe. You just enjoy yours. I think you've earned it."

As he fully expected, and to his utter disappointment, Cody didn't catch glimpse of a naked Amber. Instead, his imagination was left to create the scene of her stripping down and stepping into the tub, the water covering her slender body as she sank into its warm depths.

Aw hell. He needed a cold shower or he'd suffer all night. Since a shower wasn't possible, he opted for the next best thing now that Jenna had fallen asleep and he was assured privacy. He grabbed a towel and headed to the lake. The fresh water would be cool enough to calm his raging hormones. Maybe not. But he hoped.

CHAPTER 12

Amber was in heaven. The water may have lacked bubbles and fragrance, but submerging her sore body into the fire-warmed water was the best medicine. Every muscle relaxed as she just laid there, her head resting on the edge of the tub, a small towel folded as a pillow, eyes closed, ears listening for Jenna who had fallen fast asleep in the next room after her bath.

Cody had left Amber an oil lamp that glowed across the room. No electricity meant they needed to use lanterns once the sun settled. No big deal really since the flame gave off a decent light. Leaving behind modern technology intrigued her. It made life simpler, no television or computer meant they would be forced to enjoy each other's company to pass the evening. It meant she could relax, something she wasn't accustomed to doing as a single mom with a never-ending to-do list.

Life had taken a turn for the worse but that didn't mean she couldn't make something good come from something bad. She would treat this short excursion into the wilderness—and there was no doubt they were roughing it—like a much needed mini-vacation. There were no phone calls to interrupt her bath, no terrible stories on the ten o'clock news, although she did wonder if she and Jenna were still a breaking news story.

Yes, if she was smart and took full advantage of this unexpected vacation from her hectic life, then she just may come out of this horrible living nightmare as a better, well-rested woman.

Cody. He floated into Amber's thoughts more easily with each passing hour. What was she going to do about him? Keeping her eyes closed, she sank into the water and rinsed her hair as best she could, coming up for air a few times before she felt satisfied that her hair was as clean as she would get it without shampoo and conditioner.

After rubbing the water from her eyes, Amber lay back and thought again of Cody. She envisioned the handsome man, his dark hair and blue eyes looking better with a day's growth of beard shadowing his face.

Amber couldn't deny the attraction. Hell, they could set off smoke alarms with their sparks. She wanted him like she had never wanted any other man. Probably because of his acceptance of Jenna. He was a natural with her and would make a great father some day. He proved that some men were cut out to be great dads and others, like Derek, were just sperm donors, too consumed with themselves to give a shit about the child they helped create.

Amber refused to dwell on bad memories, especially when visions of hunky Cody kept forcing their way back into her mind. Even with exhaustion consuming her, she was vividly aware of the desires pulsing through her body, needs she hadn't a clue as to how to address, and ignoring them was proving to be an impossible feat. Never had she been so pre-occupied with a yearning to experience intimacy. But then again, never had a man like Cody Maguire been interested in her.

Lying in the water, she dragged in slow, deep breaths to calm her racing heart. Each thought of Cody had her excitement growing wildly out of control. What would he look like naked? Would his kisses cause her to shriek in delight as he nibbled along her neck? Was he imagining what she looked like?

The lap of the water against her skin was like the soft stroke of his hand over her hot flesh. Her body heated at the idea of his touch. She sank deeper into the warmth and just let her aches dissolve.

When the water finally cooled after about twenty minutes of pure heavenly bliss, she reluctantly dragged her water-logged body out of the deep tub. Wrapping herself in the scratchy towel Cody left her, she wished for clean clothes. But at least her body was clean now.

Drying off, Amber couldn't help remembering how Cody had teased her before her bath. He admitted thinking she was a hot woman. Her cheeks grew hot with the blush that was surely covering them. Her? A hot woman? Why not? She took care of herself. Lord knew she got plenty of exercise running around after a seven-year-old and working two jobs. But still, she'd never thought of herself in this way.

Quickly, she toweled off, her thoughts once again imagining his hands floating over her body instead of the stiff fabric. What would he feel like naked? His hard body against hers. His warmth adding to hers. Her belly did somersaults just wondering about intimacy with Cody.

After reluctantly dressing in her dirty clothes, Amber walked to the bedroom she would share with Jenna during their stay here. Her little girl was still asleep and clutching her doll. If there was anything ever good to say about Derek, it would only be that the doll he had given his daughter had given her comfort during this harrowing ordeal. Amber was grateful her daughter at least had that much after all that she'd been through thanks to her deadbeat father.

Amber walked to the curtain-less window and couldn't believe her eyes.

"Oh. My. God," she whispered, her hand clutching her throat.

She lost the ability to breathe as she spied Cody standing hip deep in the lake, his ass barely covered. Water sluiced off his muscular body as he cupped water with his hands and let it run over his body. Amber had to squint to make out details since the final rays of the sun setting in the distance made it difficult to see. The fading sun's golden glow only highlighted every muscle of Cody's hard, sexy body. The sight of such a rugged man had her thinking again of her own needs, needs long dormant but blossoming rapidly tonight.

How could she be preoccupied with such naughty thoughts and desires when she was a wanted woman with a huge price on her head for some diamond she knew nothing about? She had been chased by mad men and all she could think about was Cody, the one man able and willing to help her and Jenna. Amber sighed. Why did life always have to be so damn difficult? For once she'd like a break.

When Cody suddenly turned and looked in Amber's direction, his smile grew wide when their eyes met. He could see her from the lake? Damn lantern!

Slowly, he walked out of the water like an ancient God. Even though she knew she should give him his privacy, she couldn't take her eyes off his nakedness. Squinting to see in the diminishing light, she kept her eyes glued to him. His tall, lean body rippled with hard muscles. His hand wiped through his short black hair, droplets flying off him. Immediately, and with no control, her eyes descended to his long erection. His lack of modesty only turned her on more. A man comfortable with his body was very desirable. Visions of him lying on top of her danced in her head, that long, hard body crushing hers deeply into the mattress while he was buried deep inside her, thrusting over and over as she cried out his name.

When he picked up the towel and slowly hugged his hips with it, disappointment filled her. The show was over, his erection hidden under the cloth. Her cheeks flamed hotter with her embarrassment for getting caught. She sighed and rubbed her temples to fend off the headache that hadn't completely healed earlier. She walked to the mirror over the single bureau and busied herself with drying her hair, shaking it in the towel before using her fingers as a comb.

Another stolen glance outside showed Cody was no longer near the lake. When she heard movement in the cabin, she knew he must've returned from his bath. She wondered what had taken him so long and then she caught sight of fading white smoke hovering under the trees outside. Must've put out the fire in the pit.

Jenna's soft snoring was the only sound in the room. Amber paced the floor knowing she had to face Cody at some point. She checked on Jenna one more time before shutting the bedroom door and walking into the parlor.

Cody was dressed in the same clothes again, at least they had that much in common.

"So what's the plan now, Cody?" she asked, sitting on the lumpy couch, tucking her bare feet under her. If only her cheeks would cool down then she wouldn't feel so much on display.

Cody walked toward her holding two ceramic mugs. "The plan is for you to relax now," he said simply, handing her one of the mugs. "It's a hot toddy. Grandpa's special. I warmed up some brandy on the fire while I bathed. Thought we could enjoy a nightcap before heading to bed." He laughed when her eyes widened. "Don't worry...I meant in separate beds. Unless you decide different. Cheers." He lifted his cup to tap hers before sipping.

Unless she decided different? She could only stare, torn between her needs and the complexity of their situation.

A lantern sat on the small table in front of them, blanketing the room with enough cozy light to be comfortable. Looking out the window, the night sky was pitch-black, only the half moon and stars sparkled.

The caramel colored liquid was sweet as she sipped, her belly warmed with the drink. "I should thank you, Cody, for all you've done for me and Jenna. You've gone above and beyond your duty when you got stuck with us."

"I never said I got stuck with you, Amber."

She watched him, his bright eyes alert and edgy. He was a man of many moods. That only added to his appeal. "I'm scared, Cody. If anything happens to Jenna, I'll never forgive myself."

His hand covered hers while his knee brushed against hers, the minimal space on the couch taken up by his large body. "I promise you we're safe here and I don't make promises lightly."

"So you've said." Her hand tingled where his fingers danced over her skin.

"My granddad always told me the two things a man absolutely has in this world are his word and his last name."

"Your grandfather sounds very wise."

"Taught me everything I know about the outdoors. Now tell me about you, Amber."

She laughed. God, he was so different than any man she had ever known. "There's not much to tell. I work and raise my daughter. Until we were kidnapped, I led a very boring, dull life. All I ever wanted was to make Jenna happy."

"Then you should be very proud of yourself because she's a well-adjusted, happy little girl who happens to idolize her mom. Why don't you tell me what life with Derek was like?" He sipped his drink while keeping his eyes on hers. There were no accusations this time, just friendly concern.

"I don't want to think of the past." Humiliation always consumed her when she thought of how stupid she had been where Derek was concerned.

"Well, sorry, honey, but the past is now the present. It'll help me to know everything I can about the jerk so I can figure out where he stashed the Blue Diamond. If we can find it, we can save you and your daughter's life and I happen to have a high interest in doing that. Remember, they want you both and won't hesitate to use your daughter as leverage against you. I'm not trying to scare you. Just being honest, honey."

Amber sighed, the events of the past day weighing heavily on her shoulders. "I already said I was young and dumb when I met Derek. He was my first boyfriend. His wild ways excited me because I had strict parents with lots of rules. We started dating, I got pregnant, and we got married. Soon after, things went downhill fast." She took a deep, steadying breath before she could continue. "He loved to gamble, ran up huge debts and stole to pay them off. He also had an appetite for coke and pot. I swear I didn't know what he was doing until it was too late. I had a baby, and every time I threatened to leave him, he threatened to take my baby. I had no family to depend on because they disowned me when I married him."

She had to take a deep breath to calm herself when the emotions bottled up inside of her threatened to spill over into weepy tears. She had held it together this long, no reason to break down now.

"Amber, take your time. There's no rush. I know it isn't fun for you to relive a past you want to leave behind."

Looking up at him, she found understanding eyes staring back at her and was no longer humiliated over her past. At least not with Cody. She continued slowly trying to sort out the memories long ago buried. "I've only recently gotten back into my parents' good graces. They know they abandoned me as much as I disappointed them, but that's all in the past. But during the first years of my marriage, I was all alone with no connection to my family. I had no money. And I was scared of Derek. He started beating me when I would stand up to him and ask questions about his mysterious ways." She wanted to cringe remembering the awful sounds of Derek's fists hitting her face, the nauseous taste of blood filling her mouth, the throbbing pain of the bruises left behind.

Cody cursed under his breath. "He didn't deserve you, Amber. Any man who hits women is a fucking coward."

Shrugging, she sank back onto the couch, allowing her body to relax. "Unfortunately, I figured that out too late. As bad a husband as Derek was, he was a worse father. He complained when Jenna would cry, whined about spending money on diapers and formula. One night when he refused to give me money to buy her some medicine for a high fever, I went to the store and stole it. With Jenna in my arms, I shoved the bottle in her snowsuit. I shoplifted. He was turning me into a criminal too. But I swear I had no other choice."

His hand covered hers, held it, stroked it. "I'm not here to judge you, Amber, but it sure seems to me that you were just trying to survive. That's pretty damn admirable. You are stronger than you realize."

"I wish I felt that way." She sighed. "That's why it was so strange for him to visit his daughter." Huffing out a disgusted breath, she spoke again, "How dare he bring her the doll as a present when he never bought her anything before? Always complained about having to spend money on her."

Amber ran a hand through her wet hair hoping she wasn't rambling. "Knowing him, he probably found the doll in the trash as he walked to my house, thinking he could sweet talk me by being nice to Jenna. Then he wanted to stay the night. When he tried to use his old scare tactics on me and bully me into letting him stay, that's when I threatened to kill him."

She swallowed hard, still not able to accept he was truly dead. "Don't get me wrong, I was scared to death and totally expected him to beat me again. His eyes were black, like he had no soul. And I'm not foolish enough to believe I could match his rage." Daring to glance up, she caught his gaze and read the understanding deep within those calm eyes.

"I don't know about that. You got away from four armed mobsters. I think that motherly instinct in you would get you through pretty much anything. Not that I'm encouraging you to challenge mobsters again." He cracked a wide grin. "I'm just saying I know why you did it and even I'm not brave enough to come between a mama and her baby."

Her eyes roamed the room with its dancing shadows

from the oil lamp's flame. "I'm not sorry to say I'm glad someone beat me to it and killed the asshole. I was never going to be free of him while he was alive. And now, even from the grave, he continues to haunt my life."

"We've got to figure out where he stashed the Blue Diamond. I need you to think of anywhere he could've possibly put it. Like maybe hid it at a family member's house. Or stashed it at a friend's place." Cody said, the detective in him surfacing with the line of questioning. How cute the change from citizen to cop.

"Derek's parents are dead. He had a brother but he was also in and out of jail. I wouldn't even know what city or state the guy lived in. I only met him twice, and that was so briefly, I could only describe him as a taller, scrawnier Derek." In her lap, she twisted her fingers unable to stop fidgeting. "As for friends of Derek's, well...I never met them either. I wasn't privy to his social life or his work life, if you can call what he did work. I do know Derek always said he never called another person a friend. They were only acquaintances because they'd all just as soon stab him in the back and then sit down and eat dinner without a blink of an eye."

"Surprised he told you that much."

She grunted even if it was unladylike. "Oh, he spoke plenty, or rather slurred plenty, when he got drunk. There were times he'd come home in a rage because someone fucked him over—as he put it. Then after too many black eyes, I learned to just sit and listen to him ranting and raving until he exhausted himself and passed out on the couch."

"I don't think I've ever hated a man like I do your ex-husband."

"That makes two of us. But to answer your question, I know of no one Derek would ever trust the diamond to. No one at all. And I'd be at the bottom of that list. He knew I would turn it into the authorities right away. I never wanted anything to do with his crimes but somehow I still got dragged into them just because I was his wife."

"Guilt by association. I understand how you'd feel being innocent and all. But you've got to realize that usually the wife is involved in some way, even if it's just helping to cover up a crime or lying about his alibi. So the cops have to look at every possible angle and that starts with those closest to the suspect. Did Derek ever have a safe deposit box?"

"No never. We never had anything worth safeguarding. Our money went up Derek's nose."

Cody sighed. "This sucks because it leaves us absolutely no leads, not even a hint that could suggest you're not the only person he could've stashed the diamond with. That's why I was so adamant you had the Blue Diamond. My investigators and I believe Derek sold you out before he was murdered."

"Why would he do that...knowing I had nothing?"

Cody shrugged. "I don't know. Probably to get the heat off of him, but we figured that when he gave you up, then they killed him, no longer needing his pathetic ass for a connection to the diamond."

"Then they came after me." Her heart pounded.

"Yes."

"But you said it was stolen months ago. Why did the Mob wait this long to see if I had it?"

"Probably because Derek was in hiding...up until a week ago. Whatever happened with Derek is the key to finding the Blue Diamond. That's why it's important to remember if he said anything about where he had been."

"Nope. He said nothing. He just argued with me about staying at my house."

Cody was silent for a long minute. "Well, not much more our frazzled brains can think of tonight so let's discuss it more tomorrow. Maybe something will jog one of our memories."

"I agree." She stood and placed her empty mug on the counter, looking out the window at the dark sky speckled with stars. He followed her, standing beside her.

"Tell me, Amber. Did you enjoy your peep show earlier? I must say I wouldn't have expected you to be a voyeur." The teasing sound of his voice soothed her embarrassment and was just what she needed to transition from their serious conversation.

Still, her mouth opened and no words came out.

He laughed hard. "Relax, honey. Just wanted to let you know I was flattered to catch such a lovely lady checking me out."

"I wasn't checking you out," she said a little too defensively. He cocked a dark eyebrow and she smiled. "Well, okay, maybe I *was* checking you out a little. But so what? I'm not used to seeing naked men bathing in a lake."

His fingers massaged her neck, the sensation tingling all the way down her spine as he spoke into her ear. "There's an open invitation for you to watch me any time, sweetheart."

His words warmed her better than any hot toddy ever could.

"That's really nice to see," his voice whispered, his arm brushing against hers.

She had to crane her neck to look at him. "What is?"

"You smiling. You have a beautiful smile and are an amazing woman."

"Cody." Her heart pounded. The look in his eyes, like he could eat her up, thrilled her.

"Tell me not to kiss you, Amber," he whispered against

her lips when he turned her slowly into his arms, her fingers resting on his chest.

She couldn't find her voice, and even if she did, she wouldn't say a word. When his lips touched hers slightly, her body stiffened. She was so out of practice sexually there was no way she could ever please a virile man like Cody.

Then his tongue swept over her closed lips, enticing them to open, and she was lost to his spell. Anchoring her hands on his shoulders, she leaned her head to accept his kiss. Slowly, her lips opened to allow him entry. He tasted of smooth brandy, smelled of the fresh air, and sounded like a lion, his growl swallowed by their kiss.

His hands didn't grope her when they could have. There was nothing she would deny him in the heat of this kiss. Her mind failed to register a thought, except for the wonderful sensations of his tongue sweeping across hers over and over. While his strength was evident in the way he held her tightly against his body, he was gentle and caring. Taking her pleasure into consideration, his hands strummed up and down her back, barely skimming the top of her ass.

God, she wanted Cody more than she wanted to breathe. *What in the hell is happening to me?*

Without warning, she broke the kiss, but not the connection. "I...I should get to bed. It's been a long day," she said against his lips.

When she leaned back, the wild look in Cody's eyes could never be mistaken for anything except desire and lust. Her head spun like she had just jumped off an amusement ride. Breaking away from his embrace was easy to do since he didn't hold her in place but slowly let his hands drop from her body. Walking away from the best kiss of her life proved to be almost impossible as her traitorous body begged her to return to Cody's room with him.

"Amber," he called to her as she crossed the floor to her door. Turning, she faced him, willing herself to be strong in the face of such delicious temptation.

"If you give me a chance, I promise I'm not like that scumbag."

"No. You could never be like him, Cody. Good night."

Once behind her closed bedroom door, Amber got a hold of herself when she glanced at Jenna sleeping soundly still clutching her doll. It wouldn't do them any good if she were to begin thinking about anything other than their safety. Maybe some day there would be a chance to do that, just not now. Crawling into bed beside Jenna, Amber draped her arm securely over her daughter and closed her eyes.

Sleep failed her. With her free hand, her fingers traced her lips where Cody's were moments earlier. The tingling sensation stayed with her into the night. Until exhaustion won and she gave in to sleep.

CHAPTER 13

W
hen Cody awoke the next day he didn't feel any more rested than when he had finally fallen asleep after midnight. Tossing and turning all night had nothing to do with the summer heat or the bad guys that lurked somewhere out there. Instead it had everything to do with a hot, sexy woman sleeping in the next room. So close. Yet so far.

Climbing out of bed, he stepped quietly from his room and removed the thick branch he had rigged as a beam against the door. It wouldn't keep the thugs out but at least it would foil their sneak attack, if they had decided to pay a visit during the night, and give him a fighting chance. He stepped outside into the cool, early morning air, the sun already beaming bright. He surveyed the surrounding woods for any sign of visitors, and seeing none, walked into the woods to go to the bathroom.

Returning to the clearing, he washed his hands at the well and sat at the pit and started a fire with the matches Grandpa kept well -stocked. He needed coffee bad, hoping it would help to clear his mind. He was still very much aware of Amber's presence within the log walls of the small cabin. The woman wanted him as much as he did her, yet she fought it. She had to believe he was nothing like her loser ex-husband. But Cody couldn't blame her for being cautious. After what she had been through in her marriage, it was probably really hard to trust again.

After the flames kicked up, Cody walked to the well to fill a metal kettle with water and placed it on the fire before going to the supply shed for the coffee grounds. He chose corned beef hash, packaged oatmeal and canned peaches for breakfast. Once the coffee was done and he had enjoyed the first strong cup, he began cooking.

Little feet soon approached. "Morning, Cody, can I help cook?" Jenna asked still clutching her doll.

"Sure. Ever use a can opener."

"Yes."

"Here's some peaches. I need you to open these, okay?"

She did as told and soon they had breakfast prepared. The corned beef hash was warmed in a skillet and the oatmeal was topped with the peaches.

"Wow, you two sure know how to cook," Amber announced, walking toward them from the woods where she must've first went to relieve herself. "I smelled it all the way inside." She continued on to the well and washed her hands before joining them.

"Have a seat," Cody said, patting the log where he sat. At least she seemed to be getting used to the outdoor bathroom idea. "We were just going to call you." He was pissed at himself for being so forward with her last night when he knew better. Hell, he'd seen plenty of scared women in his career to know that they didn't trust. She needed his protection, not his sexual advances. He planned to apologize as soon as he could. Figuring out how to hold his growing feelings in check was another story.

Cody dished up breakfast and they ate quietly by the fire.

"This is the best coffee I've ever tasted," Amber said, practically purring.

He laughed. "Is that so? I'll be sure to mention that to Grandpa since he always complains I make it too strong."

Amber smiled and held her mug out to him. "Mmmm. Just how coffee should be. Refill please."

"My pleasure, ma'am." Cody topped off both their cups and finished eating.

"I'll clean the dishes," Jenna announced, collecting the plates before her and her doll headed down to the lake.

For a moment, Cody and Amber sat silently and watched the little girl trot away to the water's edge just feet from where they sat enjoying the last of their coffee.

Jenna ran back up to collect their cups and disappeared again.

"She's a great little helper," Cody said, standing with Amber, hoping to break the silence and start a conversation so he could apologize.

Amber didn't respond, just kept her eyes on her daughter.

Aw hell. "Amber, listen, about last night—"

Before he understood what she was about to do, she leaned up and kissed him. A simple kiss, her closed lips against his. It was enough though to wake up his cock, the erection instant and painful as it strained against his jeans. Her little tongue briefly traced the outline of his mouth before darting inside to tease him with the sweetest tongue wrestling he'd ever known. To say shock filled him would be an understatement. All he could do when she stepped back and looked up at him with dancing eyes was watch her. Idolize her. Crave her.

"Yup," she said. "I didn't dream. You do kiss good."

"Is that so?" His hand squeezed her waist, but before he could extend the kiss, Jenna ran back with the clean plates and disappeared into the cabin to put them away. "Does that mean you're not mad at me for kissing you last night?"

"I believe I kissed you back so it would be unfair to place all blame on you. No?"

Cody liked her style. A lot. "True. But here comes Jenna. We'll pick this conversation up later, okay? How about we go for a hike in the woods? About a mile up, there's a payphone on the side of the road. Hopefully, it still works. I need to check in with my captain, but I'd rather not drive since we're more likely to be spotted that way."

"Sounds good to me," Amber agreed and Jenna jumped around voicing her approval.

After gathering some supplies for the hike, Cody donned the backpack and trekked into the woods with Amber and Jenna. The hike wasn't a bad one. The temps climbed into the low eighties but the high trees blocked most of the sun's rays so they didn't get sunburned and provided a breeze as they walked.

Cody gave Jenna and her doll a piggyback ride every so often so the girl didn't tire. But she never complained. Neither did Amber who still must be exhausted from all the running she had done the past two days.

They took their time, stopping to enjoy sights along the way, but reached the payphone in about an hour. Relief flooded Cody when he lifted the handset and heard the dial tone. He would've used his cell if absolutely necessary, but this was a much safer way. Yet, he'd still be cautious and be sure not to stay on very long.

"Captain Ferron. Maguire. I've got Amber and her daughter with me. We're safe," Cody reported, watching the surrounding area for any sign of the hit men. He couldn't shake the feeling of being watched, but whether it was an over-active imagination or a sixth-sense kicking in, he didn't know. But he kept his eyes and ears open just in case.

"Listen, Maguire. There's an awful big bounty on Amber's head. Five million to be exact. And word is that the kid needs to be disposed of, too. No witnesses. That's how it's to go down." The captain sounded nervous, concerned, very unusual for a man who spent a career dealing with criminals of every element.

Fuck! Cody expected the amount to be high, but that was outrageous and unheard of. "Any lead on the Blue Diamond?"

"Everything points to Amber having the block of ice. If she does, then she better hand it over and make it public or she'll be dead soon. Maguire, are you absolutely sure she's clueless on the jewel?"

Cody spoke quickly, seconds ticking by. "Yes, sir, absolutely sure. She'd never risk harm to her daughter." His chest tightened at the thought of any harm coming to Amber or Jenna. Not on his watch!

"Yeah, well, that kind of money can make a normal person do the unthinkable. Her ex-husband stole the diamond with the help of a Mob member. Then Derek killed his partner to wipe out any witnesses who could prove he had the Blue Diamond in his possession. Spurned by pure greed, Derek disappeared underground until a week before he was murdered. No one knows why he came out of hiding when he would've known his life would be in danger."

Cody looked back to where Amber and Jenna hid

amongst the trees. "I know all that, sir. And, yeah, it was an awfully stupid move for a man who had planned everything out to that point and had a successful heist. Maybe he came out of hiding to sell it. But Amber's not involved, sir."

"I trust you. Stay hidden until I can figure out the next move. I don't even want to know where you are. Just keep in touch but do it infrequently and short. Let's end this now," Captain Ferron said.

With that, the captain cut off the conversation by hanging up. Cody understood phones could be tapped and secret locations found when it was worth it. And five million would sure be worth it to a lot of bounty hunters. Hell, this one job would set the lucky hit man up for an early and desirable retirement. That kind of reward could buy a private villa in many tropical nations with all the pussy a man could buy. But the problem was, Amber didn't have the damn diamond and it would be very hard to convince any bounty hunter of that without a solid lead to its whereabouts.

Cody walked quickly back into the cover of the forest where Amber and Jenna greeted him, eager for any news they could go home. "Let's head back to the cabin. No news yet." He ushered them deeper into the forest and into the camouflage of the tall trees.

"What do we do now?" Amber asked as they crossed over a trickling creek. "We can't live in these clothes forever."

"We just sit tight and wait it out until the captain has a plan. We'll just have to make do."

"If we wash the dishes in the lake, then why don't we wash our clothes, too?" Jenna asked.

"We could. But then we'd be naked while our clothes dried," Cody teased.

Jenna burst out laughing. "That's so funny." Her laugh was contagious as Amber and Cody joined her.

"Maybe if we get back in time we can wash our clothes like Jenna said and dry them in the sun. We can use the towels and blankets to cover up until the clothes dry," Amber wondered.

Yeah, sure. Like he could possibly survive watching Amber walk around the cabin in only a towel. He sent her a weary look.

"What?" she laughed. "It was only a suggestion."

"Hardly one that I could live through the temptation, darling. Keep walking."

Jenna trudged ahead of them, her little legs keeping a good pace. Cody held Amber's hand as they walked over the rocky path.

"You know, Amber. I don't make it a habit to kiss women I'm protecting. There's something about you I just can't explain."

She kept her head down. "I don't know what it is, Cody. There's really not much I can offer a man."

A fallen log blocked the path but they simply stepped over it. "What? Of course you have a lot to offer. You're beautiful, independent, smart. I know you've had a rough go of it but you deserve so much better."

"Thank you. I know you mean that."

"Wouldn't say it if I didn't. So what does the future hold for you? Do you think you'll still stay in South Boston after everything's that's happened?"

"If I don't get this price off my head, I'll have no future," she said, grimly.

He scanned the forest, glad not to find a soul. "I assure you that every available resource of the Boston Police department is being utilized for just that purpose. I think

I've finally managed to convince my superiors of your innocence so we've got police working on this case 24/7."

"A little too late now. We can't hide forever, Cody." Her voice shook a little but he couldn't tell if it was from fear or tiredness.

He squeezed her hand. "We won't need to. I have faith we'll get through this and get your life back."

She looked ahead to where Jenna skipped. "Yeah. What's left of it. I've probably lost both my jobs for being a no-show."

"I think your situation warrants a little understanding on the part of your employers."

She shrugged. "Doesn't matter. Who wants a woman working for them that's part of a criminal case."

The sun was bright as they passed through a small clearing. He squinted when he glanced at her. "Once this is solved, I promise you I'll personally see to your good name being restored."

She looked up and smiled. "You make an awful lot of tough promises, Detective Maguire."

He matched her smile with one of his own. "Only the ones I plan to keep, sweetheart."

She was quiet for a minute before she spoke again. "You know I was thinking about what you asked about Derek's friends."

Could she have triggered a memory after their discussion? God, he hoped so. "I'm listening."

Stepping over a small muddy puddle, she didn't try to pull out of his grip. Instead, she held his hand tighter, thrilling him. "I told you Derek trusted no one, but that wasn't true. The more I think about it the more sense it makes. He trusted Bones. Practically idolized the guy, thinking his boss was a genius when it came to crime and the law."

"Well, Bones has beaten a lot of raps. Gone to prison a few times but nothing longer than about six months. His men end up getting caught doing his dirty work and then they do hard time."

Her voice grew stronger, a steady determination lacing each word. "Tell me about it. That's what happened when Derek got pinched for the armed robbery. But don't you understand what I mean? Derek stole the Blue Diamond for Bones, right? What if it was all a ploy for Derek to pretend to steal the diamond *from* Bones and go into hiding? Then everyone would think that Bones was pissed and also looking for Derek."

"But no one would be looking at Bones for the Blue Diamond. Son of a bitch!"

Excitement filled her tone. "Exactly. It's very likely that Derek gave the gem to Bones and then was double-crossed and killed by Bones."

Finally, the pieces of the puzzle he needed. "And Bones lets everyone think you have the diamond to keep the heat off of him."

She looked ready to jump up and down. "Yes. This way he can do whatever he needs to with it, pretty much right under everyone's noses."

Cody wanted to dance a friggin' jig. "Hot damn, Amber. You sure you're not an undercover detective or something because you just nailed the best lead we've had in this case since..."

"Since me." Her golden eyes watched him as they walked. They were serene, forgiving.

"Yes, since you," he agreed, continuing to scrutinize the land. "Okay. Listen. It's too risky for me to call my captain back just yet. If the phones are tapped, then we risk getting caught. We'll have to wait until tomorrow to share this with him."

"I understand," Amber said as she watched Jenna. "But that makes sense. Derek trusted no one but Bones. It would also explain why Derek resurfaced last week in the same neighborhood Bones rules. You don't go into hiding for a major crime and screwing over a Mob boss then all of the sudden pop out of nowhere."

"True. Probably was the plan all the time. And Bones would understand that while the prince is pissed at him for orchestrating the theft, the prince is more concerned with getting the Blue Diamond back. So right now even all efforts of the Royal Soldiers are for the recovery of the gem. Bones knows this and has time to sell the diamond, make his millions and disappear forever."

"I believe everyone eventually pays for their sins. Bones will get his someday. Just like Derek did."

"Have I told you how amazing you are, Amber?"

Her laughter echoed in the dense brush, like sweet music. "Maybe. But a girl never tires of hearing those kinds of words."

Had he ever felt this content with someone? He couldn't remember a time when he had. "Ahh, careful. I may take a chance and say them more often. Care to join me later for another hot toddy?" he asked, winking when she looked up at him.

"I'd like that."

He raised her hand to his lips to place a loud kiss on it. Then released it, ran ahead, scooped Jenna up onto his shoulders and made the girl laugh for the rest of the walk as they dodged low hanging branches.

When they arrived back at the cabin, Cody quickly

scanned the area before they emerged from the forest to ensure they didn't have any unwanted guests.

"Jenna, want to learn how to skip rocks?" Cody asked when Amber excused herself to go to the bathroom.

A few minutes later, Amber joined Cody and Jenna at the edge of the water, leaning down to wash her hands.

"Cody, teach Mommy how to skip rocks."

"That's okay. Mommy doesn't really need to learn that particular talent," Amber said.

"Better idea," Cody said, walking to the supply shed and returning with fishing poles. "Let's teach Mommy how to catch dinner."

"Oh, I don't think that's a good idea. I'm not very good at outdoorsy things, Cody."

"Won't know until you give it a try, right?" he asked, knowing he made complete sense. Besides, if she didn't stay busy, she'd just end up dwelling on their situation.

Jenna took control of the lesson, showing Amber how to hook a lure and cast the line. Before long, Amber had a nibble.

She jumped up from where she sat on the end of the dock. "Oh, I think I caught one. What do I do? Tell me what to do," Amber squealed, half laughing.

Cody stepped behind her, his arms circled her middle as he showed her how to reel in the fish. When the bass came out of the water, it flopped, struggling to get free, spraying them with drops of water. "Good job, Amber. That's quite a fish."

"This is hard work. I'll appreciate seafood a little more now," Amber commented while Jenna offered her a worm for bait. "Ah, no thanks. I draw the line at touching worms, honey."

"Told you she was a girlie girl," Jenna said to Cody

through giggles.

"A what?" Amber's jaw dropped. "Just because I don't want to touch insects doesn't mean anything. And where did you get the worms?"

"Cody and I dug them up while you were in the woods."

"Well, stand back. I'm going to try to cast this thing on my own," Amber announced confidently.

"Awesome," Cody shouted when she sent the hook far out in the lake. "Catch us some more big ones, darling. I think Grandpa has a stash of quick-cooking rice in the storage room. We're gonna have a feast tonight, ladies."

"Mommy, Cody says if you catch them, you clean them."

Amber looked horrified. "Now that will not happen."

Cody rubbed Amber's back. "Oh, I think your mommy could convince me to help her clean them."

When she flashed those golden eyes his way, he laughed. "Good thing I know just how to convince you, Cody."

The teasing sound of her voice shot straight to his cock. Having an erection now just wasn't suitable. Instead, he opted to change the subject until he could revisit it with Amber in private.

"No convincing necessary, but I'll take a rain check on any ideas you might have used. Since I'm a gentleman, I'll clean and cook the fish. Besides, I've got a great little helper here. Right, Jenna?"

"Right."

A branch snapped along the edge of the lake and the three of them froze.

Hand on his gun, Cody quickly scanned the perimeter but saw no one. "I'll go check it out. Probably just an animal again."

Amber held Jenna close. "Yeah. Hopefully not the two-legged kind."

Cody walked quickly to the bushes where the noise emanated from but didn't see any animals. The hair on his neck raised, an uneasy feeling like someone was watching again. There's no way someone found them without taking action. Cody was wide open for a shot. He didn't have a chance of fending off an enemy who used the woods as cover.

Suddenly, a branch fell and hit the lower branches of a maple. Cody drew his weapon and pointed up. A large hawk took flight, scattering leaves in its hasty departure. When he placed his gun back in his shoulder holster, that's when he found what had gotten the hawk's attention. A bunny darted out from the bush and zigzagged into the woods.

"Just a hawk chasing a bunny," Cody yelled as he turned and walked back to the dock where Amber and Jenna huddled.

Amber was pale. "I think we caught another fish, but I couldn't pull it in when you were in the bushes."

He would do anything to take the fear out of her voice. Instead, he grabbed the pole and reeled in the fish. With two large bass in the bucket, they were ready to start dinner.

"Jenna, think you can carry the bucket? I'll carry the poles."

"Sure."

Cody offered his hand to Amber and helped her up. When she stood beside him, he didn't release her hand. Instead, when Jenna walked toward the fire pit, Cody quickly brushed his lips against hers for the slightest kiss. Without a word, he tugged her with him as they walked behind the bouncing girl. He wanted this ordeal to end soon for Amber, but he didn't want his time with her to end. This was shaping up to be the most difficult case of his career, in more than one way.

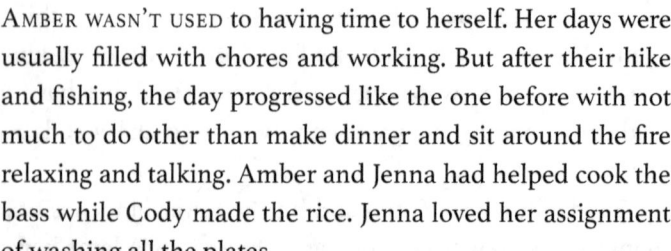

AMBER WASN'T USED to having time to herself. Her days were usually filled with chores and working. But after their hike and fishing, the day progressed like the one before with not much to do other than make dinner and sit around the fire relaxing and talking. Amber and Jenna had helped cook the bass while Cody made the rice. Jenna loved her assignment of washing all the plates.

"I think she just likes to play in the water," Amber commented from her seat by the fire.

"Nothing wrong with that. Keeps one of us from having dish duty."

"True. But you still have water duty. Can you warm some up for Jenna's bath? I think she's ready for one after another long day of exercise."

"Nah," Cody said. "I think her mom needs to bribe me with a kiss first."

Oh, he was impossible. He made her laugh with such attention and she was discovering she had a flirtatious side. "But Jenna..."

Cody just shrugged. "She's going to see me kissing her mom eventually."

"Oh, you think so, do you?" Amber teased, amazed at how sure of himself he was. She would love to have a fraction of his self-esteem. "Come on, Jenna, honey," Amber said, standing when her daughter returned from the lake. "Bath time. Cody's going to get the water ready."

Amber flashed him her sweetest smile and ignored his low growl when he stood. She laughed when he lifted her into his arms and pretended to get ready to toss her into the water.

Clinging to his neck, she yelled, "Don't you dare, Cody. I swear I'll make the bad guys look like angels."

His laugh was so loud it echoed over the lake. Jenna's giggles topped his. Amber squirmed but was stuck in the iron grasp of his arms.

"Kiss me and I'll let you down."

Her eyes narrowed and she thought of all the ways she would get even with him for this. But she relented since she felt silly in his arms with her daughter watching. She lay her lips on his briefly with the intent to linger just a second but when the connection was made it sent heat down her spine igniting her passion for this crazy, genuine man who was showing her how to laugh again.

Remembering her daughter nearby, Amber broke the kiss. "Satisfied?"

"Very," he said, placing her back on her feet. "I'll get the bath water started for Jenna."

Jenna took Amber's hand and walked into the cabin. She whispered. "Mommy, I think Cody likes you."

Amber laughed, her belly filling with butterflies. "Yeah, sweetie. Mommy likes him, too."

"That's so cool." Jenna walked ahead into the cabin. "Sarah's gonna nap while I take my bath, Mommy." She tucked the doll under the sheets on the bed.

"Sounds like a plan," Amber agreed, hiding her giddiness at being the center of Cody's attention. Even with their current circumstances of hiding out in an isolated cabin, she still felt like she had been given a second chance. Maybe her luck was finally changing for the better.

CHAPTER 14

Prince Jamal Al-Hussein paced the plush carpets of the Millstar Hotel in the center of Boston unable to focus his thoughts on anything but finding the Blue Diamond. His penthouse suite overlooked the bustling city. The heat of the summer day was kept at bay with the chill of the hotel's fantastic air-cooling system. But it did nothing to cool the prince's temper.

Somewhere out there was his priceless family heirloom. How dare those men disgrace him, and his family, and think they could live to tell about it? He would've killed Derek Norris if someone hadn't beaten him to it.

The prince's head throbbed with a headache that hadn't left him since the day of the theft. His personal pain was trivial when it came to his family's dishonor.

General Khalid entered the room and spoke. "Prince Al-Hussein, may I please have a word with you?"

The prince faced the general who was dressed in his green military fatigues. "Any update?" he demanded.

The general bowed before he spoke. "The apartment of Amber Norris hasn't been approached by anyone of significance. The Boston Police have departed their watch over the property as of midnight last night. At two this morning, three intruders entered the apartment. My men remained hidden outside as instructed and just monitored the situation." General Khalid spoke eloquently, his attention to detail welcomed.

"And what did your men discover?" the prince spoke calmly even if he really wanted to scream. It wouldn't benefit his blood pressure if he allowed his emotions to rule his brain.

"The intruders left the premises thirty minutes after entering. My soldiers detained them immediately. A search of their persons and a subsequent interrogation did not discover the Blue Diamond. I am sorry, Your Highness. My men identified the intruders as bounty hunters from South America. They were advised to turn the jewel over to us if they find it or they and their families would face a long, painful death."

Anger boiled just below the surface of the prince's skin, anger so volatile it would take no effort at all to kill a man with his bare hands. "Ah, so every piece of shit in the universe is seeking to bask in the glory of my disgrace, are they?"

The general remained silent.

"They are lucky that I allowed the snakes to live. I should slit their miserable throats and use their tainted blood to remind others what happens when I am crossed."

"I'll do as you wish, of course."

The prince expected nothing less than obedience from his staff so the general's comment didn't stun him. While he usually appreciated such dedication and rewarded it accordingly, everything in the prince's life now took backseat to finding his diamond.

The prince spoke through clenched teeth, "In time, those responsible for my shame will suffer at my hands. But for now we continue to concentrate on finding the Blue Diamond. Our number one concern remains that. Then I will personally deal with this maggot Bones and all others who assisted him."

The general continued to stand with his hands behind his back in perfect posture. "Within the hour, the telephone taps will be in place on all lines for the Boston Police department's precincts. Anyone discussing the Blue Diamond will be heard by my men. Then we can take the necessary action."

The prince didn't like the news his general had provided him so far. Breathing exercises prescribed by his physician to help relax him were useless. "There's been no sign of the Norris woman and child?"

"No, Your Highness. We are searching every second of the day. I assure you."

"Then search more!" the prince yelled, pacing again, his fist in the air. "Your men had better do more. I want that diamond found. It is inexcusable to be waiting this fucking long. Three damn months."

"Yes, sir. I can tell you we have discovered that Amber Norris and her daughter were kidnapped by Bones' men but then they managed to escape."

The prince let out a long, bitter laugh. "Fucking fools. Shows their incompetence. How does a woman, with a child, escape trained men? She will not escape my men, I promise that."

"Of course not, sir. Never." The general looked mortified at the mere thought of ever losing a prisoner.

"Another interesting development is that the lead detective working the case for the Boston Police has also disappeared."

The prince stared at him and frowned. "What do you mean? How can a detective just disappear? What are the police doing about it?"

"It appears there is no search for him currently."

The prince crossed his arms and waited a long moment before speaking again. "So now that is indeed interesting. Where do you suppose he went?"

"Not quite sure, Your Highness. But my men are investigating reports that Detective Maguire may be in hiding with the woman and child."

"What?" the prince yelled. "So then it will be easy to find her now. When the phone taps are in place, you get me the location of where they are hiding. They are bound to be in contact with someone. If the police aren't searching for a missing fellow officer, it indicates to me Detective Maguire isn't truly missing."

General Khalid bowed and spoke clearly. "Yes, sir. I was thinking the same. Given the nature of the criminal element involved in this case, if Detective Maguire disappeared without warning, his fellow officers would suspect foul play and launch a massive and public investigation. Since they don't appear to have done that, the detective must have permission to be in hiding."

"Or, maybe the detective has located the Blue Diamond as part of his investigation and has gone into hiding hoping to get a fortune for my loss."

"That, sir, is highly unlikely. I've personally researched Detective Maguire's background. He's never even had a complaint against him. From all accounts, he's a very clean cop."

"You know the value of the diamond, General Khalid.

That kind of money can make the most decent of men turn sour. Don't dismiss any theories unless you have evidence absolutely proving them wrong. We will look at Detective Maguire's sudden disappearance either as work-related to protect the woman and child, or as an indicator he has the Blue Diamond and has gone into hiding to sell it. Either way, the man is dead once I get my hands on him. And that I will do once he either calls someone helping him hide the whore or he surfaces to sell the gem."

"Yes, sir."

"I want to know all the family Amber Norris and Detective Maguire have."

"Amber has parents only. Detective Maguire has an extensive family including a grandfather he is close with and four brothers."

"Find every last blood relative," he ordered.

"I will keep you informed hourly, Your Highness. Will there be anything else?"

"Yes." The prince spoke slowly, keeping eye contact with the shorter man. "I am holding you responsible for a positive outcome of this matter, General Khalid. Do not disappoint me. Do you understand? You will not like the consequences."

The general paled. "I understand, Your Highness. I will speak with my men immediately to review where we can improve our efforts."

"I suggest you do just that." The prince returned to looking out the window when the general left the room.

Three months ago, the prince had come to the States in search of medical treatment and had placed his faith in doctors and his Blue Diamond. While the doctors had performed a great service to him and restored his health, nothing would make him feel better until the Blue Diamond was back in his possession and honor restored to him and the Al-Hussein royal family.

Until that day, he vowed to track those responsible for his shame until every last one of them took their last breath in his merciless hands...beginning with that whore Amber Norris and her child along with Detective Maguire.

CHAPTER 15

Jenna was in bed before the sun had set. She clutched her doll and snored softly. Amber had stayed with her until she had dozed off. Just watching her little girl sleep peacefully was incredible. It was obvious that because of Cody's efforts to include the girl in all camp-related activities, from catching dinner to cooking it to playing, it had ensured her daughter's mind stayed off of the bad things.

Amber smiled and kissed her daughter's forehead before leaving the room in search of Cody.

She walked through the cabin holding an oil lantern for light against the falling night. She had never quite felt so at home in a place and, yet, she did here even if it wasn't hers. There was only minimal furniture and no decorations, but she felt comfortable and relaxed—as best she could under the circumstances. The simplicity of life over the past few days at the cabin had given Amber a new outlook on life and the importance of quality time with those she loved. The fact that she and Jenna were moving targets reinforced the notion that life was precious and no one was guaranteed a tomorrow.

Stepping out into the yard, Amber rested her thoughts as she walked to join Cody by the fire. Looking forward to some rare adult company, she placed the lantern on the ground and sat next to him.

"How's Jenna?" Cody asked using a long branch to poke at the debris in the pit. The flames rekindled slightly.

"I've never seen her fall asleep so fast," Amber said, the scene too cozy at the pit not to stir romantic visions of stolen kisses under the moonlight. Her nerves wound up like butterflies in her belly.

He turned his head, the light of the campfire highlighting the angles of his handsome face. "It's the fresh air. It really does wear kids out."

"Can I help you with anything?" she asked, watching as he began to smother the fire, thin white wisps of smoke dancing up to the sky. The smoky smell, combined with the scent of the pine trees blowing in the gentle breeze, was refreshing, relaxing. She craved to be lazy and just sit about like this forever.

She inhaled sharply. Clean air. It smelled so much better than the stuffy, humid air in South Boston that was riddled with exhaust fumes.

Cody glanced her way, his bright blue eyes reflecting the dwindling flames. "As a matter of fact, I have an itch you can help me scratch."

"Okay." She stretched behind him, looking at his back. "Where?"

Before she knew what he meant to do, he lifted her and had her cradled in his lap looking up into his mischievous eyes. "All over, baby. You're driving me wild. I usually have much more finesse, but I'm afraid I lose my manners around you, especially when your very fine ass struts in front of me."

"Then I'll remember not to strut in front of you," she teased, tracing a finger over his unshaven face.

"You strut any time you want to, babe. Any time."

She laughed, sinking deeper into his strong arms.

"I know Grandpa has shaving gear hidden around here somewhere," he said, catching her hand in his and laying soft kisses to her knuckles. Her skin heated to match that coming off the fire. "I promise to shave so I don't scratch your delicate skin when I kiss you."

"I don't mind a little scratchiness. Keeps it real."

"Real?"

Her smile came easy, all she could think of was him and being the center of his attention. "Helps to remind me I'm not dreaming."

He growled and lowered his head catching her lips with his for a smooth, short kiss. Her hands rested on his shoulders, the feel of hard muscles under her fingertips proof he must work out religiously.

When he ended the kiss, he only moved away until they were nose to nose. "I want you to dream, Amber. Of me and you. Of these stars. Of this."

He broke off his words to re-capture her mouth in a devastating kiss. This time greedy lust replaced the softness. His tongue traced her lips until they parted. When she allowed him entry, his tongue stroked hers, sending a wave of need throughout her body. Every inch of her came alive and wanted to feel his mouth, wanted to feel the wet heat of his kisses gliding over her tingling flesh. His slight beard lightly scraped her jaw as he twisted and turned his head to kiss her from every angle. She didn't care about the scratchiness, the slight pain it caused lent awareness to the edginess rippling through her body.

Cody tasted of coffee from dinner, smelled of smoke and sounded like heaven when he groaned her name against her lips. How would she recover from such a kiss? Wrapping her arms around his neck, she sank into the kiss, wanting to commit every second to memory. Her mouth moved with his, wanting control, relinquishing it, taking it. All of her energy poured into the kiss, needing Cody's touch more than she needed air.

It was him who broke the connection, leaning his forehead onto hers and sucking in gulps of air. "Amber. God. You are amazing. I need you." The desperation in his voice turned her on more, the knowledge of driving this man wild with just a kiss overwhelming.

His hand found her breast and lightly squeezed. Just like that, she was a goner. Dropping her neck back, she moaned as heat settled between her legs. "Oh, God. Cody...I haven't in so long."

His lips trailed wet kisses along her neck, his words fell against her throat. "Damn that's so hot. Kiss me again," he demanded, not waiting for her response, lifting her head up. His head dipped to take her lips in a hot possession, his tongue forcing her mouth open. Never had she felt so wanted by a man, to have him lose control and act like she was the only thing that mattered. Had she possessed such power all along? Why now was she learning how to use it? To enjoy it? She must have had to wait for Cody to come along to awaken these desires deep within her, to show her how desirable a woman she really was. She loved every second spent in his arms.

Amber whimpered when Cody's lips deserted hers.

"My God, Amber."

Without another word, he stood with her and placed her on her feet. He held her hand tightly while kicking dirt onto the remaining fire. Satisfied it was extinguished, he spoke nothing. A glimpse of his stormy eyes when he picked up the lantern showed his lust, his intense stare capturing her attention. Silently, he hauled her inside with him, her jogging beside his long strides.

"Cody?" What was he up to? She wasn't so naïve to not know when a man wanted a woman in his bed, but how could they?

As she expected, they walked into his bedroom, but not before Cody fastened the wooden branch at the kitchen door.

Shutting his door, Cody leaned Amber back against it, after placing the lantern on a short bureau. His lips covered hers, her mouth responding like it had been denied the sweetest candy for too long. Eagerly, she matched his kisses, her mouth bruising under his possession but not wanting to end the delicious encounter. His hands worked magic as they manipulated her body with long massaging touches, squeezing her arms, trailing her hips, dancing over her sides. Her hands worked through his hair, grabbing it to hold his mouth against hers, losing the connection would be unacceptable.

Amber's body responded like it never had before to a man's touch, heating up in spots she had only ever read about. Places deep within a woman that would offer her the immense pleasure she had never experienced—just dreamt about or read of in her romance books. Intimate depths that before this moment were only in her imagination, never having the opportunity to explore her sexuality and desires. Never had she trusted a man like she did Cody, willing to lower her defenses and explore what could be.

Now she was like a firecracker just waiting for the right fuse to be lit before she exploded in a multitude of wondrous brilliance.

"Oh, God. Cody," she blurted out against his lips, breaking the kiss only briefly before he covered her mouth again, his kiss torturous for the sensations swirling inside her.

Wanting to touch all of him, her hands maneuvered over his arms and shoulders, the only places she could reach while pinned against the door. His body was taut, muscles flexed. God, what she wouldn't give to sink her teeth into him. When his lips traveled to the sensitive side of her neck, she bit down on a cry to prevent waking Jenna.

"Cody," she murmured. Her plea echoed her desperation.

"Don't tell me no, Amber. Please. You'll destroy me," Cody whispered, leaning his cheek against hers, his heavy breaths as much a turn on as his hard body pressing hers into the wood. "Let me make love to you, Amber. I crave your touch so much. I can't imagine not having it."

Oh. My. God. A thousand 'I Love Yous' wouldn't have stolen her heart any faster than his declaration just did. With the confidence of the desirable woman he had awakened in her, she worked on stealing his heart too.

She pushed him back to look in his eyes. "Condom. We need one. I'm not protected."

"Don't care. Having babies with you would be a blessing."

She swallowed hard. She had always wanted a sibling for Jenna. Now wasn't the time though. "Maybe someday, Cody. Tonight we use a condom."

"Thank...fucking God...I have some," he exclaimed, removing his wallet from his back pocket. The room danced in a yellow glow from the lantern, the smell of its oil lingering in the air.

"Hurry!" she demanded, clawing at him, wanting to sink her teeth into every inch of him.

He threw his wallet onto the floor once he had the condom in hand. "You're so beautiful." With an arm wrapped around her waist, he twirled her to the bed, lowering her to the mattress. His mouth skimmed her neck and ear, sending goose bumps marching down her arms and back.

Cody tossed the condom onto the nightstand beside the bed. When his hands shimmied up her sides taking her shirt with them, she swallowed hard, her throat suddenly dry. Oh, God, this was really happening.

What if he didn't like how she performed? Or maybe he didn't like her body? Or maybe...

"What is it, Amber? You look like you've seen a ghost or something," he asked after pulling her shirt over her head, keeping her in the sitting position as he sat next to her.

Her hand caressed her throat. "Nothing. I'm just...oh, I don't know. What if making love to me isn't what you expect it to be? Then what? We still have to live together for the near future."

His smile didn't mock her like most other men would do. Instead, it comforted her. His lips laid a gentle kiss to her forehead.

With his hand behind her neck, he stared into her eyes. "Amber, I'm positive making love to you is going to surpass any expectations I may have. If not then, well, we'll just have to keep at it until my expectations are met."

Her smile came automatically. How he could put her at ease without any effort at all was beyond her. "I like how you think."

"And I like how you look." He kissed her breast over her bra. "Taste." He buried his head in her hair. "Smell."

"Mmmm. Get naked for me, Cody. Otherwise, you're just a tease." Her voice didn't even sound like her own, laced now with a huskiness that flashed her excitement.

"Where do you want my kisses, Amber?" he asked, undoing her jeans and pulling them from her as she lay back on the mattress.

With her finger, she traced her body, feeling very wanton but wanting to bask in the glory of this unbelievable love-making. "Start here," she said, pointing to her belly button. "Then here." She pointed to each breasts. "Then here." She pointed to her neck.

"Then back here again," she said, stopping at her breast.

"How about I start here," he said, his finger circling her navel. "And travel down here," he whispered, his finger trailing over her abdomen to her pussy.

Heat immediately filled her face. "No. I'm not ready for that. I've never done that."

He studied her face for a moment before removing his hand. "Okay. There's plenty of other times to explore every inch of your gorgeous body. You'll get comfortable with me, baby. I'm in no rush other than to make you feel great."

He was so damn adorable looking at her like he had the patience of a saint when his cock strained noticeably against his jeans. She couldn't help but stare at the bulge with pride that it was her who had done that to him. Her belly did somersaults but she couldn't decide if it was a reaction to the nerves of facing intimacy for the first time in years or her body's sudden craving to be touched.

"Thank you for understanding but you probably should start to get naked since I'm lying here feeling a little under-dressed."

He pulled his T-shirt over his head exposing flat abs and wide shoulders. Only a tiny patch of dark hair covered his chest. When her hand brushed over the soft mat of hair, she had a new appreciation for a man's body. He was toned and obviously took care of himself, well groomed, clean...well as much as possible after being on the run.

"I wanted our first time to be special. I'm sorry, but I just can't wait to be inside you." His fingers latched in the edge of her panties, whisking them down her legs. To her bent knee, he placed wet, loud kisses. God, she would die with this kind of teasing attention.

"It is special. Please...Cody, I'm dying here. Hurry up!"

His smile was devastating when he slid up her body and hovered above her. "Now that has got to be the hottest thing anyone has ever said to me, darling. Who knew such sexy words coming from your pretty mouth would turn me on so much."

He rubbed the erection still trapped in his jeans over her pelvis. Her hips bucked as much as they could under the weight of him.

"Cody, please. It's not fair to make me wait any longer. Kiss me. Hold me." She didn't care if she had to beg, too delirious for his touch to care about anything else.

"Anything you want," he whispered into her ear before getting up and removing his jeans and sneakers.

Standing naked before her, the sight of him had her heart pounding, her breathing deepening. They were really going to make love. It was all too surreal. One minute they were running from mobsters and dodging bullets, then the next they were tangled in each other's naked embrace.

Cody's body was magnificent. Wide shoulders, narrow waist, flat abs, muscular thighs. But it was the look in his eyes that captivated her, the way he studied her like she was the only woman in the world, like he could devour her with kisses.

He pulled her back into a sitting position. His hands worked quickly behind her back removing her bra. When the cotton material fell away from her shoulders, he tossed it onto the floor, using his body to slowly push her backward. When his mouth captured her breast in its warmth, she bit down on a cry, remembering they weren't alone in the cabin.

"Oh, please, Cody. Yes. More. I want so much more."

He groaned but never took his mouth from her breast. With his lips firmly over her nipple, he sucked and licked, nipped and stroked until her nipple was hard and aching. Her head tossed back and forth on the flat pillow, the bed hardly comfortable but she didn't care. Without hesitation, he moved to her other breast and applied the same glorious manipulation of her nipple, sucking until she thought she would die from the ravenous need building throughout her body. Her pussy hummed with a new life of its own, the soft quivers running over her most intimate spot begging her to squeeze her legs shut just to bear the pressure building.

Cody's knee, strategically placed between her legs, wouldn't allow her to close hers. He kept her legs apart while his body leaned over hers, the heat between them enough to coat their skin with a fine sheen of perspiration.

"Cody. I can't wait much longer. You're driving me wild."

He laughed quietly. "Ah, now I guess we're even, darling, since you've driven me wild since the first time I saw you. But far be it for me to not want to oblige a lady."

The stiff bed sprung up when he climbed off. Amber leaned up on her elbows and watched him. "What do you mean when you first saw me? That was when you came to my house to tell me I was a murder suspect."

His smile emphasized how relaxed he was compared to that day in her apartment. "Yes it was. And all I remember thinking was there's no way in hell someone as pretty as you could've been mixed up with such a dirt bag."

She watched as he quickly sheathed his massive erection, the simple action taking longer than she wanted it to. "Pretty?"

He stared at her, his latex covered cock in his hand. "Gorgeous." He leaned over her again pushing her onto her back. "I didn't have words to describe your beauty. You were the first woman who ever interested me enough to think of more than a few dates and time between the sheets."

She laughed, circling her hands around his neck. "That's because I came with built-in action. Like bullets and mobsters." She ran her fingers through his hair, keeping his stare, those bright blue eyes darkened by the evening. "Never a dull moment with me, huh? But I need to warn you my life is usually very boring."

"Thank God," he said, before laughing.

The nerves finally hit her. She lay naked under his body. Her body begged for his touch. Her mind didn't want to think of tomorrow, just now, just being in Cody's arms, in his bed, in his thoughts. "Make love to me, Cody Maguire. Show me how much you've thought of me."

He lowered his lips to hers accepting her challenge, silencing her words. The man sure knew how to kiss. Every time it was like the first time. Amber's heart pounded and her breath escaped her. The taste of his coffee still lingered and the smoke had blanketed his hair with its own scent, keeping her mind on the rugged outdoors and thinking of that bright moon shedding its light on the night's darkness.

This was romance to Amber. Being the center of a man's attention where he wasn't rushed to get finished, wasn't concerned with only his needs, wasn't thinking of anything or anyone else but her.

Cody kissed her like he was starved for the taste of her, the thick head of his cock nestled against the entrance of her pussy. Deep kisses designed to erase all thoughts from her mind had done their job and relaxed her body, preparing it to accept his lovemaking.

Tearing his lips from hers, he spoke quietly. "Tell me now if you've changed your mind, Amber. Tell me now if you want to stop, or I won't be able to."

"Um, I don't want you to stop but I don't know if I'm, well..." She swallowed hard, swimming in the pleasure of the way he stared down at her like she was delicate and treasured. "I'm sorry. I'm out of practice."

"You have nothing to apologize for so stop. If you're not ready, I'm not doing my job here." His smile was comforting. But when his hand slipped between their bodies and his fingers probed closer to her most private spot, she squirmed, unable to stay still knowing what he was about to do. To his credit, he didn't allow her nerves to distract him. His fingers gently slid over her aching pussy lips, trailing up and down the entrance.

"Oh. Cody. Mmmm."

"Baby, you're so wet." His fingers slid over her, spreading the moisture over the entrance. She nearly catapulted from the bed when he brushed her tiny nub, sending waves of pleasure rippling through to her womb. "Nice."

The thick head of his cock replaced his fingers. With his eyes set on hers, he slowly probed into her, his thickness stretching vaginal muscles so long unused. The pain was minimal, creating the feeling of losing her virginity all over again. Except this time, it was with a man who was willing to protect her and her daughter with his own life. God, she loved Cody Maguire.

She what? She stilled under the weight of Cody as his hips continued their gentle thrusting. Did she really love him? She hardly knew him. No, that wasn't true. She knew what kind of man he was, how kind and caring, how protective and considerate. She knew he was the man she had always hoped to find but had given up on, never believing she'd find someone who could compete with the troubles of her past.

Yes. She loved Cody. But she swallowed her confession when he thrust into her, fully seating his cock deep inside of her.

"My God, Amber. You're so tight. Am I hurting you?" His arms held his weight off of her.

She wrapped her legs around his hips. "No, it feels so good. Oh...Cody. Please. Don't stop."

With smooth motions, he pumped his hips into hers, the old mattress squeaking under their combined bodies. There was no rush to finish, just long even strokes, caressing her, propelling her closer to her release. The tightening within her pussy gripped his cock, slightly restricting his thrusts, still he pumped into her. The smell of sex clung to the air, the sensual scent teasing her already heightened senses.

She had missed this, had missed everything about sex, had missed the closeness two people could share. The sounds of two bodies connecting, the closeness, the heat.

It had never been like this for her. Only in her dreams could she imagine this kind of gentle lovemaking. Suddenly, her heart pounded. What if Cody never felt this same way about her?

Her body refused to let her dwell on those thoughts any more. Cody laid wet kisses along her neck and shoulders while he thrust into her. The tingle from his stubble scratching her skin shot heated goose bumps all over her body. Her nails raked over his back, the need to keep him close to her, connected to her, overwhelming.

She clamped her mouth shut before she screamed out, her orgasm slamming into her, hard, fast, and unexpected. She had hoped to at least hold out a little longer to continue enjoying Cody's body over hers. This orgasm was so different than any she had experienced. The power of it threatened to steal the breath from her lungs. Her body couldn't possibly survive the strong waves of pleasures rolling through her body, deep inside.

"Cody!" She gritted her teeth to keep more words from flowing, not trusting herself to keep the words inside. Each spasm in her most intimate places reached into the depths of her womb, the strange sensations new and exhilarating. She never wanted this moment to end, never wanted this exquisite feeling to leave her, never wanted to move from Cody's embrace.

When he stiffened, holding his hips to hers, she rode his release with him, every tremble remarkable.

"Sweet, Amber. So sweet," Cody said, gasping, his skin wet with perspiration. "Stay with me. Let me hold you, baby." His soft kisses along her jaw were convincing, but Jenna came first.

"Jenna."

With the mention of her daughter's name, Cody immediately understood her concern and lifted himself off of her. He quickly disposed of the condom before extending his hand to help her stand in front of him. They both dressed without talking. When they finished, Cody did something she would never have guessed he'd do, especially after having sex. He hugged her. A tender, strong hug.

She melted into the embrace, her heart hoping for much more than just tonight. Her head being reasonable and knowing the odds were against anything more serious, more permanent.

"I wish I could stay, Cody. I really do," she said, her cheek resting on his chest.

He gently pushed her away from him but kept his hands on her arms, sharing long caresses, heating her body all over again. "It was irresponsible of me to even suggest you sleep in here when Jenna is in the other room. I'm sorry for my lack of judgment."

"No, Cody. It was really sweet. Heck, it's better than kicking me out of your room." She smiled and ran her fingers over the soft hair on his chest.

"I'd never kick you out of my room or my bed, darling. But I wouldn't interfere with your need to be with your daughter either. Come on. I'll walk you to your room."

"What for? It's right next door, silly."

Still, he took her hand and they slipped from his room into the darkened parlor.

"If I didn't walk you to your door, I'd miss out on this." He lowered his mouth to hers, kissed her deeply. The more he kissed her, the more she appreciated how his wicked tongue stroked hers to make her body hum everywhere.

The kiss ended, much too quickly.

Without another word, Amber quietly stepped out of Cody's embrace and into her room.

Jenna slept peacefully. Amber crawled in beside her and, for the first time in years, fell asleep without the loneliness that had usually consumed her.

CHAPTER 16

Cody drew his gun while Amber and Jenna hid in the bedroom. The unmistakable sound of a truck approaching was nerve wracking.

Fuck! He checked his weapon once again and went down a checklist in his mind. He knew he had a limited supply of bullets here in the house. The rest lay in the trunk of his car that he had left behind at the motel. There was ammo in the shed for Grandpa's hunting rifles, but the rifles weren't here. Grandpa always took them home with him. All in all, he didn't have many options.

Cody gripped his gun firmly, leaned his head back against the wall and prayed whoever drove into the clearing was a lousy shot. He felt perspiration form on his forehead as he leaned an inch forward to peer out the window. He moved at a snail's pace not wanting any sudden movement to be seen through the windows and alert the approaching intruder of his presence. No doubt whoever it was would see the pickup truck and know someone was here. Or maybe the thing looked old enough to appear abandoned and the visitor wouldn't expect someone to be here.

Aw hell! He blew out a long breath. *Who in the hell am I kidding?*

The only people who would be around these parts would be those who were chasing them. But how could they have found them here in the middle of nowhere, isolated from all humanity. He was sure no one had followed them. Hell, he would've seen someone on those long, deserted rural roads.

Whoever it was, the truck stopped. The sound of tires slipping on the pine needle covered dirt ground tracked the progress. Cody cocked his head to peek out the window and caught a glimpse of the driver.

With a sigh of relief, Cody holstered his gun, watching the old man step from the massive pick-up truck and stride toward the cabin.

Cody walked through the parlor to the kitchen door and removed the wooden branch to open it. "Amber, Jenna, come on out. It's okay. It's only Grandpa," he yelled, looking out the door as he approached.

"Only Grandpa?" the old man bellowed, shuffling his tall body into the cabin, ducking slightly as he walked through the doorway. "Well, that's some how-do-you-do for an old man who almost had a heart attack wondering where his youngest grandson had disappeared to. Boy, do you know you're all over the news?" It was good to see Grandpa hadn't changed his exaggerating ways.

Cody laughed and shook his grandfather's hand, pulling him into a quick embrace. "Good to know I'm finally a celebrity."

"Don't you get smart with me. Those news people keep hounding anybody with a connection to you. Your brothers are ready to kick some asses let me tell you. So many stories out there, I don't know what to believe."

"So you came all this way to find out for yourself, huh?" Cody cracked a grin, happy to see the old man.

"Damn right." His chin shot up with the arrogance of years in tactical training.

Amber and Jenna entered the kitchen, their steps hesitant and tightly holding onto each other while Amber's eyes flashed from Cody to Grandpa. Cody offered a smile he hoped reassured her.

Grandpa removed his baseball hat, showing off a full head of thick, white hair, and tossed it on the counter. Dressed in carpenter jeans and a short-sleeve button-up shirt, he appeared as confident as ever standing with his hands on his hips, his typical stance for when a lecture was to follow. "One reporter's got you as maybe being a victim of foul play. Another one says you may be involved in criminal activity with the Blue Diamond. Still another news station reported just this morning that you're a possible hostage of the lady's."

Cody cocked an eyebrow at that piece of news. "You don't say. Now that has got to be the most far-fetched news story I've ever heard. Amber would hardly hold me hostage." His heart yes, him physically, no. "She's much more sophisticated than that." He winked at Amber.

"Now tell me what's going on," the old man said, sitting at the table, his attempt at being tough defeated by the worried expression on his wrinkled face. "And get me something to drink. Heat's not good for me, you know."

Cody crossed his arms and leaned back against the lone counter in the kitchen. "Amber, Jenna, meet Grandpa. He constantly thinks he's having a heart attack and usually has either me, or one of my brothers, to blame it on."

"It's usually the truth. They're all hellions if you ask me. Always getting themselves in some bit of trouble and giving the rest of us a fair share of worry." His strong voice echoed authority.

Cody laughed, his grandfather's words holding a world of truth. "He also claims to be old but don't let him fool you there. Even I wouldn't mess with him."

The old man laughed with pride. "Nice to meet you, young ladies."

"Same here," Amber said, her smile lighting up her face. Wasn't she the most beautiful creature? She offered her delicate hand and it disappeared when Grandpa enclosed it in his for a strong shake.

"Cody's been teaching me to fish and skip rocks and cook," Jenna said, skipping over to stand by Grandpa's leg. Little Jenna was the splitting image of Amber, the same light brown hair and golden eyes. By the way Grandpa's pale blue eyes lit with amusement, Cody could tell Jenna had instantly stolen his heart, just like she had Cody's.

"Oh, really? He better be letting you have some fun, too."

Jenna giggled and glanced at Cody then back to Grandpa. "Yeah, he has. I've played on the tire swing and went swimming. We went for a hike in the woods. It's been fun. But we have to pee in the woods and Mommy doesn't like that."

The men erupted in laughter as Amber's face turned red. "True, it hasn't been the highlight of this trip. And that's saying a lot considering why we're even here," Amber said, taking her embarrassment in stride.

Cody watched her as she talked with Grandpa. She was always a trooper, no matter what hand she was dealt. Wasn't that one of the qualities that most attracted Cody to her? Well, that and her fine ass—actually her entire incredibly sexy body. His hands ached to touch her again. Memories of last night flashed through his mind, the amazing feeling of her naked body against his, the innocence that flowed through her, warring with the sensual woman hidden under the surface just waiting to be seduced out of hiding. No doubt their future lovemaking would only improve and drive him wilder but thinking of such encounters now would only torture him with a hard-on he couldn't put to use until Jenna, and now Grandpa, weren't around. Since that wouldn't be until much later tonight, Cody would have to keep his thoughts of Amber platonic. *Yeah, right, like that's even possible.*

Amber brushed a long strand of hair behind her ear and took her daughter's hand. "Jenna, let's go see about doing some fishing now and let the gentlemen catch up."

"Can I swim? My clothes will dry before tonight." Jenna turned to Grandpa. "That's how we've been washing our clothes since we didn't have a suitcase with us."

"You don't say," Grandpa said and tweaked her nose. "Guess then you won't want the new clothes I brought along with me just in case you didn't have a chance to pack." He smiled ear to ear. He was a goner with the little girl.

Amber's eyes widened. "You...you brought us new clothes?" she asked with hesitance, like she was afraid he was teasing her.

"Yes, dear. I enlisted the help of my one of my grandson's wives who happens to look for any reason to shop. Since you and your daughter have been all over the news, well, it was pretty easy for her to judge your size. And she knew what a woman needed for clothing. Hell, if I have a clue." He laughed hard, his tall body still toned for his age. "Bags are in the backseat of the truck. Go ahead and look. I think you'll enjoy that more than fishing, huh?"

"Oh my God. I think I love you," Amber said, leaning

down and smacking his cheek loudly with a kiss. "Thank you. I'll repay you. I promise."

He held onto her hand and pinned her with a stare. "Now I might be getting on in age but I've still got my hearing. I sure don't recall hearing myself say I wanted to be reimbursed. So I'll forget you said that, my dear." His words were soft, gentle. Grandpa never talked to him or his brothers that way.

Amber's smile slowly creased her lips. From his view on the side of her, Cody could see the glistening of her eyes and it touched his heart that her genuine goodness remained unaffected by the wretched scumbags who had been so much a part of her life. The woman, who had been through hell for the last few years, now faced death for her and her daughter through no fault of her own. Yet, she still possessed such humbleness, still thought of others, still thought of doing the right thing.

What an amazing woman. Right then, Cody promised himself to do whatever necessary to keep Amber in his life after this ordeal ended. If she wanted to leave Boston, then they would. He'd follow her wherever she wanted to go. Without her, his life would be empty. Much like it had been before their chance meeting. Wishing she was out of harm's way, he couldn't help but be thankful he had been assigned to her case. This was indeed the case of a lifetime. It would hopefully give him a life, too.

Amber ushered her daughter outside, the little girl running to the truck shrieking and hollering. Cody laughed when he looked out the small window above the bucket they used as a sink since there was no running water. He swore some of the happy shrieks came from Amber as they pulled out bags and bags of clothes.

Cody turned to his grandfather. "Thank you. I can't

believe you thought of that. They've been through hell. At least clean, fresh clothes will make them more comfortable."

"Oh, there's some in there for you, too. Can't have you smelling like crap around such a pretty lady."

Cody grinned. "True. Thanks."

"Brought other supplies too. Food. Ice. Ammo. You name it, I brought it. Packed that truck until I could barely fit in it." He laughed but his face remained serious. "Wasn't sure how long you'd have to be up here, but from the sound of it, I figured a good amount of time." He stood. "Get the ice and beer out of the truck. Then let's talk. I've got to take a piss." With that, the old man disappeared through the door.

Cody strode outside to where Amber and Jenna huddled in the back of the truck bed rifling through the bags of clothes.

"Cody, do you see how much is here?" Amber said, her mouth hanging open after she spoke.

"That's Grandpa for ya. Never does anything half-ass." Cody lifted the bags of ice.

"This was just so thoughtful. I can't ever repay him."

Cody shot her a mischievous look, imagining her in the sexy shirt she held up. "He meant what he said. No need to pay him back. Grandpa doesn't do anything he doesn't want to do. *Ever*. But I, on the other hand, will be open for suggestions should you feel the need to show your thankfulness."

She smiled so sweetly, the look in her eyes warned him of good things to come. "I may have some ideas to show you what I think of you protecting us, Cody. I'll have to take a rain check and get back to you."

His breath hitched with the promise in her voice. "Of course." He lifted the six-pack of beer from the back seat and shut the door as they climbed from the back of the truck.

"Now if you'll excuse us, we have some things to try on," she said, lightly skimming her fingers over his cheek and jaw before sashaying in front of him.

"That was so not fair, darling. Payback will be swift."

Her laugh carried on the warm breeze. Watching her curvy ass sway side to side in front of him killed him. It was a good thing his jeans were fairly tight and would only let his hard-on grow so big, painful though it was. How he managed to walk he didn't know.

He hauled his bundles into the cabin, catching just a glimpse of Amber and Jenna as they disappeared into their bedroom with their bags of clothes. Grandpa had already returned from the woods and sat in the kitchen.

Cody placed the ice in the large bucket in the kitchen and joined Grandpa at the table with a cold beer. Some of his earliest memories were at this cabin, sitting with his grandfather while the old man kicked back with a cold beer and told stories of his law enforcement days. The inspiration from those tales had encouraged Cody to follow in Grandpa's steps and join the police force. Even though he did a great job as a Boston police detective, Cody would never expect to excel as much as his grandfather had during his brilliant forty-year career.

"Hot damn, boy. Never thought I'd see the day you fell in love," Grandpa said after taking a long swallow from the beer can.

Cody frowned. *Was it that friggin' obvious?* "What are you talking about, you crazy old man? I'm working here. I'm protecting them from hit men."

"I wasn't shitting when I said it's all over the news. Bostonians are going nuts trying to figure out where the Blue

Diamond is. It's like a friggin' treasure hunt broke out all over the city."

"Afraid that bit of knowledge died with Amber's ex. So far, it appears only he held the answer to the question on everyone's mind."

"I read the reports. Had them sent to me after you disappeared. You have your hands full, boy. What can I do to help?" he asked, finishing his beer. "Damn, that hit the spot. Was a long damn ride. Had to make sure no one followed me."

Cody didn't even have to question whether his grandfather would make sure he wasn't followed to the cabin. Being a retired F.B.I. agent, Grandpa would never have risked a ride here without making damn sure no one followed to pay a surprise visit.

"Guess it won't hurt having some backup with me. So you brought extra ammo?"

"Back up my ass, son. You've seen my medals. Get me another beer. What kind of host are you?" Yeah, he was in one of his joking moods. Everyone knew it was how the old man dealt with stress, especially when it involved his family or those who were dear to him.

"Host *my* ass," Cody rebutted but stood to get another beer. "This is your cabin."

"And you were occupying it before I got here so that makes you the host. Now what can I do? Any sign of trouble around here?"

"So far no and I hope it stays that way because my options run out if we lose this hiding spot. Nowhere else could be half as safe as here." Cody pushed his beer away. "But I can't shake the feeling we're being watched."

"I always said a man's got to trust his gut, his instincts."

"Yeah, but I find nothing when I investigate unusual

noises. It's always wildlife. But then I feel like there are eyes boring into my back. I don't want to alarm the girls but I've done checks around the premises every morning to see if I can find signs that someone's gotten close. But there's been nothing. No cigarette butts. No trash. Nothing."

Amber and Jenna emerged from their room dressed in their new clothes. Jenna wore a light green sundress and sandals while Amber had on a pink pair of shorts and matching low-cut shirt. Cody made a mental note that he owed his sister-in-law a kiss for the outfit. His cock stirred in his jeans and he resisted the urge to pin Amber to the counter and kiss her senseless. Only thing making him think twice was Grandpa and Jenna.

"We're going to catch supper," Jenna announced, waltzing through the kitchen and out the door. Over her shoulder, she yelled, "Hope you brought your appetite, Grandpa. You're gonna need it. I catch the biggest fish."

"I've got to keep up with her," Amber said, passing by the table. "Thank you again for the clothes. They're wonderful. We'll be back." She hurried out the door after her daughter.

"You're more than welcome," Grandpa said, his smile the same as when he was surrounded by his own kin.

"Girl ain't lying, Grandpa. Catches some mighty big fish for such little arms." Pride surged through him at how well his little protégé had done these past few days.

Grandpa leaned back in his chair. "All the more reason to stay on your guard with two lovely ladies to distract you, but trust your gut, son. May just be that someone is watching you and is as trained as you, maybe better. Knows how to stay hidden until he no longer wants to found."

"There's absolutely no way for anyone to have found us here."

"A wise man knows never to say never."

Cody shook his head. "I wasn't followed when we got back on the road. I made damn sure of it. Hell, I tagged on an extra hour traveling here by taking a longer route. You know those roads. I would've seen someone following me."

"That's true."

Cody chugged his beer before speaking again. "And just a handful of us know of this place or how to even drive here. You know it's impossible to give directions for this place."

"I also have seen, in my career, the desperate lengths a man will go when his back is against the wall. All I'm saying is trust your gut feelings and keep your guard up. Just because it's isolated here doesn't mean shit. The men chasing you are pros. They won't stop until they find you, the woman, and the child. Remember that."

Cody sighed. "How can I forget it? That's all I think about. How Amber and Jenna will always be on the run until the jewel is found. And how I've got absolutely shit to go on."

Grandpa took a deep swallow of beer and wiped his mouth. "Then let's hear what you have so far. See if we can't piece this damn puzzle together and get your life back to normal."

That was just it. Cody didn't want his old life back, not if it didn't include Amber.

Cody started from the time he entered Amber's apartment to question her and filled the older man in on every detail since then, leaving nothing out. Thirty minutes later, he had given Grandpa the best picture he could of the investigation.

"Case like this and you'll find out people searched way too far and wide for that damn Blue Diamond. That fool Derek would've kept it close to him. Somewhere he could retrieve it at a moment's notice. Some place he trusted no one would look," Grandpa said, more thinking out loud than talking to Cody.

"The Mob hit men turned Amber's house inside out and upside down and still haven't found it or they would've stopped chasing her by now." Cody rubbed his temples where a headache threatened to form. "Amber and I have been over every detail of this case and she made a good point. The only person Derek ever seemed to trust was Bones, the Boston Mob boss."

"I know of him. Real mean bastard. Trouble is that his foolish men end up serving the time he should in jail because they're stupid enough, or fearful enough, to take the rap for him."

"Like Derek Norris did for the armed robbery stint. Since Derek worked for Bones and practically idolized him, Amber thinks Derek may have given the Blue Diamond to Bones and that Derek going into hiding was some kind of ploy to throw everyone off of Bones' trail. If people think Derek double-crossed Bones and never gave him the Blue Diamond, then no one's going to look at Bones as having it. They'll continue to chase Amber and it'll give Bones the time he needs to sell it."

Cody stood to keep an eye on Amber and Jenna through the parlor window. He could see the dock where they sat. A quick scan of the surrounding woods showed nothing out of the ordinary.

Grandpa sat back in his chair at the table and remained quiet. His expression showed him deep in thought as he stared at his beer can. Finally, he spoke. "Sounds like a hell of a theory, but I don't see Derek being stupid enough to turn over a fifty-million dollar diamond to a guy with Bones' history of killing people he had no use for. Derek may not have been the brightest bulb in the package, but he still managed to steal a valuable diamond from a prince with one of the most elite security teams in the world." He shook his head. "No. Derek had possession of the Blue Diamond. He would've known that all he had to do was hide out long enough to make the right connections."

"Then why the hell would he resurface in Boston if he truly did fuck over Bones? It's the one place he would end up dead faster than anywhere else."

Grandpa shrugged. "Never said the jackass was a genius. That's why you've got your work cut out for you, boy. Put those brains that your mama gave you to work and figure this shit out. I'm retired. My days of working are over."

Cody laughed, keeping his attention between the dock and Grandpa. "Yeah right, old man. You didn't haul your ass all the way up here for nothing. This case has all the markings of a classic. You want a piece of it. Admit it. You want to be in the middle of the action. You said yourself that you studied the file. Now with what I've shared with you to fill in some of the blanks, you've got to be itching to solve it."

Grandpa chuckled, tapping his empty beer can on the table. His pale blue eyes twinkled. "I'll admit the adrenaline kicks up knowing all of the details of this investigation now. And you're damn right, I want to solve it to ensure my grandson and those two pretty ladies are kept safe. But my gut still says Derek hid the diamond close by. Somewhere he could get to it at anytime. Maybe even in Amber's house."

"Impossible."

Grandpa waved his finger. "Uh uh. Never say never I told you."

Cody cracked a grin. "Listen, you crazy old man, Amber kept Derek at the doorway. She never let him into the house."

"Maybe he hid it outside then."

Cody considered that. Interesting insight. "That's always a possibility since everyone's been concentrating on searching the inside and coming up empty handed. But Amber has a nosy landlord and she would definitely have noticed if Derek lurked around the outside trying to hide it."

"Think about it, Cody, for a minute. These hit men chasing Amber are not only mobsters but also hired professional guns for the prince. Do you honestly think they are just chasing their tails by chasing Amber? Of course not. They must have reasonable proof she has the stone. Maybe Derek's assassins got info out of him after all before killing him."

Cody felt his blood pressure rise. He fucking hated criminals. For once, he was at a loss for words, his mind swirling with all the possible scenarios his very experienced grandfather had presented. During the last hour of their intense conversation, Cody had been given more angles to his investigation than he wanted. Proving how complicated a case it was, Grandpa just kept offering the 'what ifs' and Cody had to consider some of them. His grandfather wasn't a decorated agent for nothing.

"You have to consider that maybe she doesn't know she has the Blue Diamond," Grandpa said matter-of-factly. "I know if she did, she would've admitted it to you by now. She's too smart a lady not to and her reputation as a law-abiding citizen is remarkable, considering the criminal element she was exposed to. She never walked down that path of crime, never took the easy way out."

"Of course she didn't. Amber's not like that at all."

"And what the hell would she do with a fifty-million dollar diamond anyway?" Grandpa continued without acknowledging Cody's words. "You need serious connections on the Black Market to cash in on that baby. Word from the Bureau is that a rival of Prince Al-Hussein's has made a public statement and bid for the gem."

"Shit. That must've pissed off Prince Al-Hussein."

"More than you can believe. He's threatened war and violent retaliation for anyone who dares to purchase his family's heirloom and reward the thieves who stole it."

Cody shook his head still watching the girls on the dock. Amber appeared to be more relaxed since their arrival. New clothes probably dramatically improved her comfort-ableness.

Every hair on the back of Cody's neck stood in eerie acknowledgement of Grandpa's last comments. He had to agree with Grandpa that Derek wouldn't have been stupid enough to just hand over the gem to Bones. So that put Cody back to the belief Derek double-crossed Bones by stealing the diamond and then disappearing. Coming out of hiding was plain stupid since he was killed only days after doing so.

Of course, the bastard Derek had to have mentioned Amber and the Blue Diamond together or the Mob wouldn't be so damn adamant it was in her possession. "That fucking slime bag is still controlling Amber's life from the grave. How could he put his family's lives in danger like that? Hell, he would've known the brutality he would bring down on their heads should it even be *suspected* she had, or knew where, the Blue Diamond was stashed. Fuck!"

"Keep your temper in check. You'll need it when those assholes come calling. You know they will, too. They're hunters and they don't give a rat's ass who the hell the prey is as long as they get what they believe is theirs," Grandpa said, his voice calm but laced with the anger Cody felt.

Jenna ran inside and both men bolted upright, ready to

attack and defend. "Cody, Mommy says she caught dinner, so you get to clean it," the little girl repeated, probably verbatim.

"Not a problem, honey. I'll be right out." Jenna ran back outside and Cody faced the old man. "I'm sure glad you're here, Grandpa. Ain't no one I'd rather have watching my back."

"Takes a strong man to admit when he can use a little help. I'm proud of you, boy. I figure I won't have much to do if you get to the stupid bastards who might dare to hurt either one of them ladies. They've stolen your heart, Cody. Better stop wearing it on your sleeve before you're a whipped bastard taking out the trash and watching sappy love stories." The old man roared with laughter as they walked outside to take care of dinner at the fire pit.

CHAPTER 17

If Cody was a whipped bastard, then that made Grandpa a wrapped bastard—wrapped around a seven-year-old girl's finger who chatted non-stop about anything that came to her mind. Grandpa gave her his undivided attention, even going as far as ignoring Cody when he asked if he needed anything.

"Okay, Jenna, I think it's time for bed. Say goodnight," Amber instructed.

"Good night. I've got to tuck Sarah in first," Jenna said running ahead of Amber into the cabin.

"Who the hell is Sarah?" Grandpa demanded, looking around as if he expected another little girl to run out.

Cody smiled and stabbed at the smoldering wood in the fire pit with a long branch. "It's a doll her father, well... Derek, brought her a few days before he was murdered. It pissed Amber off since she believed he only gave the girl the doll in hopes of crashing at her place. A lot of trouble for a wanted man to go through, if you ask me, when he should've been watching his ass. Jenna hasn't let go of the damn thing. And I mean we've had to run through woods and thick brush, and still she holds onto the thing like it is priceless."

Grandpa's chuckle resonated into the quiet night air. "Dolls are always priceless to little girls. Us men don't have a clue what the value of a doll is to girls but—"

"Holy fucking shit!" Cody yelled and jumped up.

Grandpa jumped as well, defensive, ready to respond to an attack. "What is it?"

"The doll. The Blue Diamond. It's got to be in the doll. That's why Derek gave her the damn thing. He hid it with his daughter. Come on," Cody said, sprinting into the cabin. "Amber! Amber!"

He fumbled to light the lantern on the table. A strong flame erupted in the glass candle and illuminated the small room.

"What's wrong?" she asked from the bedroom doorway, her face pale, her voice shaking, frightened, using her body to shield Jenna.

"The doll. I need the doll. He must've hidden the diamond in the doll." Cody blurted out the words, hoping he made sense.

If she got any whiter, she'd hit the floor. She was speechless.

Cody stepped toward them. "Jenna, honey. I need the doll. Just to look at her for a moment," he said, looking around Amber to where Jenna sat on the bed, the doll clutched protectively in her little hands.

"Be careful with her, Cody," she said softly as she walked to the door and handed Sarah over.

Grandpa stood patiently in the kitchen.

"Cody, I already thought of that," Amber said, her

expression relaxing. "I checked that doll over head-to-toe and there's nothing."

"Let me try. It's the only thing that makes sense." Cody inspected the doll, hoping to find any telltale rips that would've been sewn. Nothing. The doll looked perfectly normal. "Damnit. I'm sorry, Amber, but a guy who doesn't want to spring for medicine for his daughter isn't about to spend squat on a toy."

Behind him, Grandpa cursed under his breath about Derek.

"I know that. But you see, there's nothing in it." Amber sounded disappointed.

"Does the head come off?" Grandpa spoke quietly.

Cody desperately wanted to find the gem. Then he could lay this nightmare to rest for Amber and Jenna. "No. And I don't feel anything inside her. A fifty-million dollar diamond would be quite large and the bulge noticeable if he hid it in the doll. There's nothing here," Cody said, defeated. He handed the doll back to Jenna. "Thank you, Jenna. She's really pretty."

"Just like her necklace."

"Necklace?" Cody asked.

"Yeah. I found it under her dress. It comes off and I can wear it, too. See." Jenna pointed to the small silver necklace with a key charm she wore around her neck.

Cody swung around and looked at his grandfather who froze. Cody faced the little girl and spoke softly. "Jenna, what does that key go to?"

"To Sarah's backpack."

"Backpack? But she's not wearing a backpack," Cody said, confused.

"That's because I took it off when we got here. It was silly looking."

"Oh my God," Amber whispered. "With everything that's been going on, I never noticed her wearing the necklace."

"That's because I only wear it to bed. I don't want to lose it outside," Jenna said with all the innocence of her seven-year-old wisdom.

Cody swallowed hard. "Jenna, where is the backpack now? Can you get it for me?"

"Sure can." The child ran to the bed and back to Cody. "Here you go." She placed a small faux backpack into his palm, the thing weighing more than it should have. Cody's eyes caught Amber's wide golden ones.

Without a word, she removed the necklace from Jenna and handed the key to Cody with shaking hands.

"All that's in there is an ice cube," Jenna said. "It's pretty ugly if you ask me. Whoever heard of a blue ice cube?"

The three adults stood in awe as Cody unlocked the backpack with the tiny key and the solid, huge Blue Diamond fell into his palm.

Holy. Mother. Of. God. In. Heaven.

The sheer weight of the gem was enough to burn a hole in his palm knowing what its value was, not just monetary but also its worth to save the lives of Amber and Jenna, the loves of his life.

"Can I have my necklace back?" Jenna asked before yawning.

"Of course, sweetheart." Cody passed her the necklace, without taking his eyes off his hand.

"Good night, Cody. Good night, Grandpa," Jenna said and disappeared into her room clutching Sarah.

Cody glanced up and caught Amber's stare fixated on his palm. "Amber, join us when you get her settled," Cody said, curling his fingers around the gem and clutching it tighter.

"Be right out." Her eyes were wide like golden saucers but at least the color had returned to her face.

In the kitchen, Cody placed the stone in the middle of the table and he and Grandpa just sat and stared at it for a long moment.

"Jenna's right, Cody. Damn thing sure is ugly."

Cody would've laughed if he weren't so preoccupied with saving Amber and Jenna. "We have to come up with a plan to get this back to the Saudis without pissing off the Mob."

Grandpa shook his head. "That you won't avoid. The Mob will be pissed to lose this fortune. Best you can hope for is to say publicly that Amber never had the Blue Diamond, and after extensive investigation, it was found with some of Derek Norris' personal affects."

Cody stared at his grandfather. "Damn, you're good, Grandpa."

"You're pretty good yourself, Detective Maguire," Amber said, coming behind him to wrap her arms around his neck and plant a loud kiss on his cheek. When she didn't move away, Cody knew he had earned her trust, not only with her and her daughter's life but with her heart.

"Get that thing out of here, Cody. You'll have to get it back to Boston," Grandpa said, removing ammunition from the bags on the counter. He removed a lock box and opened it to take out his favorite handgun. "I'll cover the home front until you return."

"Sounds like a damn fine plan," Cody said, smiling, relief swarming through him with the knowledge the case was almost over. Amber and Jenna would soon be safe. "Amber, you and Jenna will stay here with Grandpa while I get back to Boston and get this diamond returned to Prince Jamal Al-Hussein. I'm going to make damn sure there's no longer a price on your head then I'll return for you and take you home." With him, but that particular discussion could wait until this matter was settled. One thing at a time.

"Oh, Cody, please be careful. When will you leave?" Amber asked, her arms still around his neck.

"Right now. Grandpa, I need to borrow your truck since that heap of shit I stole isn't dependable."

The old man tossed him the keys when he stood. Cody pocketed the diamond. Having fifty-million in the pocket of his fifty-dollar jeans was pretty funny.

Cody lifted Amber to her toes and kissed her lips hard and fast before placing her back onto the floor. There'd be plenty of time for kissing when this was over. "You're in good hands, Amber. I wouldn't trust you ladies with just anyone."

"I know that, Cody—truly I do. Come back quickly, okay? And please be careful. I couldn't live with myself if anything ever happened to you because of me."

"She's right," Grandpa said, dressing in his shoulder holster. "There's bound to be a lot of people looking for you in Boston. Better not make any stops. Just get to your station and have them go into lock-down mode."

"That will draw attention that I'm not sure we want right now. I should be able to sneak inside my precinct with very few noticing, since it's so late." There was always the concern that a mole may exist amongst the rank and file but there was nothing he could do about that now. He had to return to the precinct to finish this business. "Don't worry, Amber. I'll be making calls along the way to ensure this goes as fast as possible."

"But what about your cell phone. You said the hit men could trace it."

"Only if I'm on the line long enough. And I just didn't want to be traced here. But I'm headed back to headquarters, so anyone listening now can meet me there for all I care. As long as they stay away from you."

"I brought along one of those throw away cell phones," Grandpa interrupted. "But the darn thing gets no signal around here. Pretty useless. I'm sorry."

"Oh, God. I don't like any of this," Amber said.

"I know, baby. It's almost over. You'll have the hardest part waiting here without me being able to call you. But my captain will handle things on his end. He'll know without me saying it that I wouldn't return if I didn't have the diamond or know its whereabouts," Cody explained, his knuckles caressing her cheeks.

"And that goes for everyone else. If you're spotted, word's going to fly on the street that you're back. Then all hell will break lose," Grandpa said, his tactical skills and thinking still sharp.

"Grandpa, you're not helping the matter," Cody pleaded.

The old man just shrugged. "Just want you to be careful. Worst mistake after finding that thing would be to get comfortable and let your guard down. Remember what you're up against. And watch your back."

Cody heard something in his grandfather's voice that he'd never heard before. Fear. "Definitely plan on doing that, Grandpa."

"I don't want what happened to Derek to happen to you, Cody. I'm scared. Promise you'll be careful. Promise me." Amber's pleading was all he needed to ensure he'd stay safe. He could never hurt her.

"Believe me, darling, neither do I. I promise you. I'd like to stay breathing, thank you. Don't worry. I'm a trained police officer and had the best teacher," he said and slapped his grandfather's back. "I'll be back as fast as I can."

Without another word, Cody was out the door, in the

truck and driving away, praying he made it back to Boston in time to save the lives of Amber and Jenna.

CHAPTER 18

ody arrived in Boston in less than two hours. Speeding down the highway was the least of his worries. He wouldn't feel better until he was back at Amber's side and keeping her safe.

When he walked into the precinct through a side access door, as expected he received stares from fellow officers working the night shift. It was almost eleven and shift change was in an hour. Best to get this taken care of before more officers arrived for work or before the mole had time to tip off his Mob boss. Cody wasn't too concerned since he knew almost every Boston Police Officer and he could only peg three of them to possibly be greedy enough to be moles. None of them were working tonight's shift so Cody relaxed knowing that if all hell did break loose his fellow officers at the station, and on their beats, would have his back.

Captain Ferron walked into his office where Cody waited, the minutes seemed like hours before his boss arrived. Captain Ferron wasn't in uniform but had a shoulder harness to carry his weapon. "Maguire, you said it was urgent. Start talking. Tell me what the hell you're doing out of hiding. And you better have damn good news for me."

Cody didn't have to talk. He opened his palm to showcase the Blue Diamond and thought he had witnessed a heart attack when the captain clutched his chest and sank into the chair behind his desk.

"I'll be damned. That's what fifty-million big ones looks like, huh?" Captain Ferron asked, his eyes wide and fixed on the gem.

"Schedule a press conference ASAP and get SWAT in here. I want this place protected until Prince Jamal Al-Hussein arrives in about an hour." Cody issued orders like he was the superior officer. He didn't care one bit if he offended his boss. All he wanted was to get back to Amber. If only they had cell phone reception at the cabin, he could at least call and check on them.

It wasn't that Cody believed Grandpa couldn't keep them safe, especially since the man was trained better than he was, he just wanted to be the one to do it. It didn't help matters that his gut warned him of danger, an uneasiness had settled deep in his bones. Dismissing the feeling as nerves and stress, Cody concentrated on his plan.

"The Saudi prince is coming here?" He stared at Cody.

"Yes, sir. Within the hour." Cody placed the diamond back into his pocket. It was not leaving his possession until he personally handed it to Prince Al-Hussein.

"How the hell did you manage that?" Captain Ferron asked, the color finally coming back into his face.

"Not me. Douglas Maguire, my grandfather, former F.B.I. Agent In Charge. He gave me a name at the Bureau to contact while I drove here. The agent got in touch with the prince's people and he's on his way. He's been in Boston for over a week searching leads."

"I knew that."

Cody paced the worn carpet. "Once I give him back the Blue Diamond, we'll do a press conference immediately. Then the bounty will be off Amber's head because no one will know how we found the Blue Diamond. Everyone will believe she really had nothing to do with it after all and she and her daughter can return to their lives."

"How did you find it, Maguire?" The captain sat back in his chair and pinned Cody with a stern glare.

"Derek lived up to his scumbag status to the end. He used his daughter to hide the damn thing. He brought her a doll when he paid a visit to Amber to crash at her house. He stuffed the diamond in a small backpack accessory on the doll. Who would've guessed we had it with us the entire time." Grandpa guessed, Cody remembered. "My grandfather is still sharp as a tack and said Derek would've kept it close by. But we thought in Amber's house or something. And Amber had already thought of the doll, but when she had checked it, she found nothing just like I did. But then the daughter had a small necklace from the doll that held a key. The key went to a backpack that the girl had removed because she thought it was ugly."

Cody smiled. Yeah, fifty-million dollars had sat in the old rustic fishing cabin with them and they didn't even know it.

"You're telling me a child solved this case?" Captain Ferron cracked a grin.

"Yes, sir. Kind of. Grandpa and I were brainstorming possible scenarios of where Derek had hidden the diamond. When we got to talking it, dawned on me about the doll."

Captain Ferron picked up his phone and hollered orders for SWAT to secure the building immediately. "I'll also arrange for all bookings to go to other precincts until we get this taken care of." He picked up the phone again. "Dispatch, this is Captain Ferron. Be advised that Precinct Four is in lock-down mode until further notice. Divert bookings to other stations. SWAT will control access to and from this building. A perimeter of a two-block radius will also be secured. Notify the other precinct captains STAT." He hung up the phone and stood to shake Cody's hand. "Don't think I have to say it, but what the hell? Great detective work, Maguire. Never seen a case like this one. You did exceptional work."

"Thank you, sir. But as soon as the prince has this damn thing in his hands, I'm headed back to Amber and Jenna. Grandpa's watching them for now. And I'm taking a vacation."

The captain laughed but the sweat forming on his brow proved he was as nervous as Cody. "Understood."

"Now we just wait for the prince." Cody said and peaked out the window. Operational measures were being deployed three stories down on the street. SWAT members were already in place securing the perimeter. Police vehicles moved to the outskirts of the yellow and white police metal barriers blocking street access. The dark cover of night was broken with the headlights of multiple vehicles participating in the lock-down.

"We'll wait but not in here. This is the first place people would look for you."

"I have faith in SWAT to keep the place secure, Captain." Cody heard his grandfather's words whisper in his head. *Never say never.* "On second thought, you're right. Police officers are only human and there's a possibility of a security breach—no matter how hard we try to contain this. Where do you want me to go?"

"Weapons room. It's the most secure place in the building. And here, put this on," Captain Ferron ordered, tossing him a bulletproof vest and donning one himself before picking up the phone. "Get four from the SWAT team up to my office to secure Maguire."

Opening his door cautiously, Captain Ferron surveyed the outside room. All non-police personnel had been evacuated. Cody looked over the captain's shoulder, only a few officers remained. Within seconds, four members of the SWAT team, dressed in black protection gear and fully armed, stormed into the room, walked to Captain Ferron's office, and ushered the two of them out, swarming in a protective circle around them. Every other officer in the room stood on guard, weapon in hand assisting the SWAT team with securing the scene, watching for any intrusions.

The team hustled Cody into a stairway that led to the fourth floor where they entered the weapon's room. Steel bars secured the area. Once inside, Cody breathed a sigh of relief but realized this was hardly over. Every minute he remained away from Amber broke his heart. He could only imagine the terror she felt not knowing how he was doing.

His arms craved to hold her. His lips begged for the taste of her kisses. Shaking his head, he pushed the thoughts from his mind. Thinking of them now just wouldn't make the time fly by any faster. A quick glance at his watch and the hour had indeed sped by, even if it didn't feel like it did. The prince should arrive any time now.

As if on cue, the SWAT leader's phone jiggled. He answered and immediately hung up. "Sir, the prince is on his way up. Men get into formation." The other three men took places on the sides and aimed their weapons at the front of the room, the only entrance.

The elevator door opened. Cody held his breath. All hell could break loose right now if one person made the wrong move. Then he may never see Amber again. He swallowed, his throat desperate for a cool drink.

Armed men dressed in tan battle fatigues and some dressed in black suits poured out of the elevator. All had weapons and spread out around the hallway. Where the hell was the prince?

"Who's in charge?" a man in a suit yelled through the bars covering the window at the front desk.

Captain Ferron stepped up. "Captain Ferron, Boston P.D. And you are?"

"Gerald Wiley, U.S. Secret Service. We're providing assistance to Prince Jamal Al-Hussein's security team." He spoke into an earpiece. "All clear."

Considering a meager thug like Derek Norris fucked up the last security team, it didn't surprise Cody that the prince and the U.S. government would take extreme measures now. "Sir, where is the prince?" Cody asked, standing beside the captain.

"On the way up," Wiley said. "You can understand the need for us to first secure the floor."

"Yeah, good thing you're here. SWAT couldn't have done it without you." Cody rolled his eyes, not caring about his sarcasm.

"Maguire," Captain Ferron warned beside him.

The elevator door opened again and a man dressed in white robes with gold tassels stepped into the hallway with another entourage of armed men.

"Gentlemen," another man spoke in a thick accent. "Prince Jamal Al-Hussein."

Yeah. Yeah. Yeah. Let's get this over with.

The prince stepped forward, his men remaining by his side. The forty-ish something man was tall and thin, dark eyes, dark hair, stern face. "I believe you have something that belongs to me."

Captain Ferron motioned for the SWAT team to open the door and everyone converged slowly into the hallway.

Cody stood in front of the prince and looked up at him speaking calmly. "I certainly do, but first you must promise me something."

The prince's face reddened and Cody swore he heard his captain curse under his breath. "I had no idea I was arriving here for a negotiation. My patience is very limited when it comes to the Blue Diamond. You should be aware of that now before you make any demands...whoever you are." The prince's voice brooked no argument.

Cody was man enough to admit he was treading a fine line here. The prince indeed owed him nothing and could just take back the Blue Diamond without the blink of an eye. But, hell. If Cody wouldn't fight for the woman he loved, he wasn't much of a man. He made a promise to Amber and Jenna to keep them safe, and by God, he planned to do just that, even if it meant pissing off a very powerful Saudi prince.

"Name's Detective Cody Maguire, Boston P.D."

"Pardon me, Detective," the prince said, drawing out the last word. "But I don't really give a fuck who you are."

"Maguire," Captain Ferron said through gritted teeth beside Cody as the SWAT team members tensed.

The prince raised his voice, the thunderous sound echoed in the halls. "I was informed by the F.B.I. I could recover my family's heirloom here and I'm not leaving without it. And, for that matter, no one else is leaving either." The man folded his arms, his white robes flowing around him.

Cody swallowed hard. "Well, then we're both even,

Prince. You see, I don't really give a fuck about holding your Blue Diamond a second longer than necessary, but all I ask, in return for finding it, is your assistance in removing any bounty from Amber and Jenna Norris' heads. They were innocent victims of Derek Norris just the same as you were."

The prince didn't flinch, just continued his hard stare. "I don't have any idea what you are referring to, Detective Maguire. But I will assure you I will look into the matter and promise to rectify any misunderstanding. For this, I give my word." The prince spoke in a calmer voice, but anger still blazed in his eyes.

Of course, the prince was too smart to admit to ordering a hit on Amber and Jenna. But Cody interpreted the simple promise as the prince fulfilling his request. It was the best Cody would get and his gut said it was trustworthy.

Cody opened his hand and held his palm out, displaying the Blue Diamond. Gasps filled the hallway and the prince quickly grabbed it, studying it intensely.

"Yes, this is it. I would recognize an imposture immediately. My deepest gratitude, Detective Maguire. Where was it found?"

"You won't believe it if I told you," Cody said, avoiding the topic, not wanting any connection to Jenna.

"Try me. I'm not leaving until I hear the truth from you. I do not want to be publicly shamed on television any more. These damn news reporters managed to find out information before me. Now talk."

Cody sighed, the truth would hopefully make the prince realize, without a doubt, that Amber wasn't involved with Derek's scheme and get him off her back. "To make a long story short, Amber Norris was victimized by her husband while married to him. When she divorced him, she still found it hard to escape his violent wrath. Before he died, he arrived at her house and threatened her. It was then that he gave their daughter, Jenna, a doll. He had hidden the gem in the doll, unbeknownst to Amber or anyone. Somehow after his death everyone, from the Mob to you, believed Amber had the Blue Diamond. Truth is, she never even heard about it until they were kidnapped by the Mob's hit men. They were innocent and almost killed because of Derek Norris' lies. As soon as we discovered the diamond hidden in the doll, I headed straight back here and had the F.B.I. get in touch with you."

Cody breathed deeply before continuing. "All I want is for Amber and Jenna Norris to be safe. They've done absolutely nothing wrong and, yet, their lives have been turned upside down. They've been hiding in fear these past few days and I'll do anything to keep them safe. You, Prince Al-Hussein, should know that." Cody knew issuing a veiled warning to a prince was probably suicidal but a promise is a promise and he'd protect Amber and Jenna at all costs.

The prince grinned, the gesture friendly, not evil like he'd expect. "I understand, Detective Maguire. You should know that," the prince said with a slight smile putting Cody further at ease.

When the prince laughed loudly, it stunned all present, their mouths opened with no words coming out.

"Imagine the absurdity of such an expensive diamond being held by an unknowing child," the prince said. "Please. This Jenna. You must give her my deepest gratitude. Now I believe I owe you a press conference so that you may return to the woman and child."

SWAT escorted everyone down the stairwell to the pressroom on the first floor where a group of reporters sat quietly. When Captain Ferron stood at the podium, the room erupted with reporters flinging questions at him.

Cody had always hated being in the spotlight. But standing beside Prince Jamal Al-Hussein while he announced the safe recovery of the Blue Diamond was worth it. For security purposes, he stated the jewel was secured at another location. Cody basked in the glory of a job well done and the thrill of knowing he'd be holding Amber in his arms in just a few hours.

"Where was the Blue Diamond found?" a reporter asked.

The prince glanced at Cody. "Detective Maguire can answer that."

Cody stepped to the podium, grateful for the opportunity to publicly state Amber's innocence and stop all hit men and mobsters from chasing her. "After extensive search of Derek Norris' personal belongings, the Blue Diamond was found hidden amongst them. No one else ever had possession of the Blue Diamond or knowledge of its whereabouts."

Cody answered no more questions, relieved that peace and quiet could return to Amber's life. Well, at least until they filled their house with lots of babies.

Cody wasted no time after the press conference ended. He wanted to get back to Amber and his new life immediately. Living a normal life with Amber and Jenna would be much welcomed after these past few crazy days. He hurried through the police station but didn't get far when the prince stopped him again.

"Thank you, Detective Maguire," Prince Al-Hussein said, shaking his hand.

"It's no problem at all. Just doing my job." The Missing Persons poster on the wall behind the prince caught Cody's eye. He ignored what the prince continued to say and tore the paper from the bulletin board and stared at it.

The man on the Missing Persons poster was Derek Norris, but his name was different. "What the hell?" Cody said to no one in particular.

"Something wrong?" the prince asked, following his stare.

"I don't know." Cody took out his cell phone and dialed the New Jersey number on the flyer. "Yes, Detective Maguire, Boston Police. There's a man missing from your precinct. Name's Gary Donahue. Can you give me details?"

Cody felt all the blood drain from his face as he listened to the man. "Gary Donahue has been missing about a week. No reason to believe he was involved in any criminal activity. Guy worked, had a family, paid his taxes on time, no marital or financial problems. Just disappeared without a trace. No activity on his credit cards or phone. No reported sightings. Very strange case. We usually have some kind of lead."

Cody's mind swirled with this information. *What the hell?* "There's a guy, Derek Norris. He looks identical to Gary. How can that be?"

The man on the other end spoke sluggishly. "Well, he should. It's his twin brother. Gary's wife said Gary had just discovered a month ago that he was adopted and had a twin brother. She said he was excited about meeting him."

Poor bastard didn't even know what Derek was about. "I think Gary Donahue has been the victim of a homicide. Can you call the Medical Examiner's Office in Boston? They'll assist you. Tell them Derek Norris is actually Gary Donahue so they can begin testing. I have to go."

"Appreciate the information. But wait—"

Cody disconnected. "Son of a bitch! Captain Ferron!"

The captain ran out of his office as all staff stared at Cody. "What now?"

"Derek Norris is alive. It's a long story, but Amber's in

danger now that this press conference says the diamond has been found." Derek would be furious to know she outsmarted him, found the diamond and turned it in. *Shit!* "I've got to get back to the cabin."

The prince said something to Cody, but he didn't hear a word as he raced out of the precinct through a side door and jumped into Grandpa's truck. SWAT members dragged the barriers open for him to drive away.

Derek staged his own fucking death with his twin brother's body. Never would he have guessed that without the Missing Person's flyer. *Fuck!*

Trust your gut. Cody *knew* someone had been watching them at the cabin. Damnit! *He knew it.* But how did Derek find them? Certainly not by following their truck enroute to the cabin. No way. But then how?

There was no way to warn Amber or Grandpa that Derek was alive. No modern amenities at the cabin meant no contact with the outside world unless the outside world came to make contact with them. Cody promised any god who would listen that if Derek harmed even one hair on Amber, or Jenna, or Grandpa's heads, Cody would personally tear him limb from limb.

Driving onto the deserted highway, Cody pressed the gas pedal to the floor and watched as the odometer climbed.

Please let me make it there on time. Please.

CHAPTER 19

mber peaked in on Jenna again. She couldn't
shake the uneasy feeling settling deep in her
bones. She prayed Cody was safe. He had to be in
Boston by now and, hopefully, on his way back to her. It had
been over five hours since he had left. How long would it
take him to return the Blue Diamond to the prince and end
this mess? Would the hit men find him before he could
arrive in Boston?

Amber shook her head. She mustn't think bad thoughts.
Only good thoughts would get her through this long waiting
period. She forced her mind to think about when Cody
returned and wrapped his strong arms around her.

Jenna slept soundly. Amber headed back to the kitchen
to join Grandpa in their never-ending cup of coffee and
stories to help them stay awake for Cody's arrival. Grandpa
refused to sleep while he was in charge of protecting Amber
and Jenna. Amber wouldn't have slept even if the caffeine
didn't lace her veins. She'd do so when Cody came back and
could hold her all night long.

What would it feel like to be held in his muscular arms,

just held for hours on end until the sun awakened them? Would he still want to continue what their attraction had started? She wanted forever but that might not be possible with their different backgrounds. She would just settle for his safe return and worry about everything else once she regained some energy.

Walking back into the kitchen, Amber froze when she saw a sight she believed she'd never see again.

Derek.

"Surprise, surprise, *bitch*. Thought you'd never fucking see me again, did you?" Derek snarled, holding a gun to Grandpa's temple.

Grandpa's gun was lodged in Derek's waistband. The old man was calm as he sat in the chair, his palms flat on the table, his lip bloodied. He watched Amber, his eyes serious. How did Derek ambush him when she didn't hear a peep?

"D-Derek? But how? They said you were dead." Her voice cracked just getting the words out.

"Bet that made your fucking day, didn't it, bitch?" He had lost considerable weight since she last saw him, but his eyes still glared dangerously, the same look which was usually her warning that his fists were about to use her as a punching bag.

She ignored his taunts. Confusion fueled her fears. He was declared dead. The police had *told* her he was dead. It's not possible for him to be here.

Please let me wake up from this nightmare.

"Grandpa, are you okay?" Amber asked, quickly scanning him for any other injuries but not daring to move closer and risk setting off Derek's temper.

Grandpa only winked.

"Relax," Derek snarled. "I only bitch slapped him for being stupid enough to think he was a match for me. He won't forget that piss in the woods." He laughed. "I've been specially trained. I know how to take care of myself now."

Yeah, it looked like it. With hollow eyes and pale skin, his face resembled the living dead. Whatever training he received certainly didn't keep him from appearing so sickly and weak. No matter what physical state he was in, Amber knew his mental health was just as severely flawed and that was a danger to all of them.

She swallowed the lump that formed in her dry throat. "How did you find us, Derek? Cody made sure we weren't followed and this is too secluded."

Derek laughed, a sinister snarl. "Technology, bitch. Doll has a tracking device. Wasn't about to take a chance on you giving the damn thing away because you hate me. It's not you I give a shit about or the brat. Get me the fucking doll."

Oh no! He had come for the Blue Diamond. And it wasn't here. *Oh no! Jenna.*

Stall. Stall. Stall.

"What would you want with a doll? Jenna loves that thing."

"Just get it," he screamed, his eyes bulging.

She needed more time to figure out a plan. "Okay. Sure. But Derek, I don't understand. Why did the police lie to me that you were dead? I was ready to tell Jenna. She'd be heartbroken," she lied.

"Like hell she would be. She don't even remember me. You made sure of that, bitch. Couldn't even bring the brat to visit me in jail." He pressed the gun harder into Grandpa's temple, but the old man didn't even flinch. His lip, fattened on one side, didn't distract from his handsome features and cool attitude. It was clear from whom Cody inherited his looks and strengths.

"Amber, get the man a drink. There's whiskey in the

cabinet there. Man with his problems deserves to have a stiff drink," Grandpa said, authority lacing his tone.

"Now you're talking, old man. Glad I haven't blown your head off yet."

"Me too," Grandpa agreed sarcastically.

Amber did as told but made a point to move as slowly as possible to stall for time to think of what to do. She poured a deep glass of the light brown liquid knowing it would take a lot to get Derek drunk enough where she might have a chance to overpower him long enough to get the gun off Grandpa's temple and then Grandpa could take over. "Are you hungry, Derek? I-I could make you something to eat. We have some supplies and—"

"Just get the doll." His thin body couldn't stop moving, his feet constantly taking a step then another but never straying more than inches from his hostage.

She placed the glass of whiskey on the table in front of Derek and quickly stepped back. "Please, Derek. Jenna's sleeping."

"Aww, really?" He pointed the gun at the ceiling and fired, shards of splintered wood rained down on them, the smell of acrid smoke filling the tiny room. "Guess that was her wake up call."

"Mommy!" Jenna ran from the room and into Amber's arms. When she saw Derek, her eyes widened. "Daddy? What are you doing here?"

"Yeah, kid. Go get me the doll I gave you or I'll shoot your mother." Derek aimed the gun at Amber who gasped.

"Noooo." Jenna yelled and clung to Amber even as she tried to shove her daughter behind her.

"Honey, go to your room and do as Daddy said. Go." Amber's voice shook.

She needed a damn plan. Grandpa still remained calm.

How could he when this maniac held a gun to his head? There wasn't any room in the small cabin to make a run for it. They'd only be a running target.

Amber crossed her arms and held her chin up. She'd get him to use his fists on her and give Grandpa a chance to jump in once the gun was off of his head. "How are you alive, Derek? Why would the police lie to me and tell me some tale about a stolen diamond?"

Stall. Cody, please hurry back. Stall.

Derek's sinister laugh made her skin crawl. His eyes were black like he had no soul. "Turns out you had another brother-in-law. One you never met. My twin brother."

"What? You've got to be kidding." There was another despicable person like Derek walking around?

Derek took the glass and swigged the whiskey, swiping the back of his hand over his mouth before slamming the glass back onto the table. "Yup. You see, I didn't know about him since I didn't even know I was adopted. Found out when my loser father needed a blood transfusion and my blood was too rare for me to have come from his loins. Mom confessed that they adopted me when I was three or something. Doesn't matter. Didn't give a shit really until I needed to clone myself."

Amber kept her body between him and Jenna to shield her while she was in the bedroom getting the doll. If Cody didn't hurry up back, they'd all be dead. "I don't understand. What do you mean clone yourself, Derek?"

He shrugged. "Awful lot of questions for a bitch about to get her friggin' head blown off."

There was no way they could get out of this alive. Amber needed to at least give Jenna a chance to run. If Jenna survived, that's all that would matter. "I'm just trying to understand what you're going through, Derek. The last few days have been a blur."

Amber dared a look at Grandpa who was calm, like a man studying something. Would he try to tackle Derek? Amber didn't doubt that in his day Grandpa was a tough man, but Derek was crazy and probably a good match for the old man. Amber would run with Jenna if she got the chance with a distraction from Grandpa. Her heart immediately overflowed with affection for Grandpa, willing to sacrifice his life for their safety. He may have had to do that in his career, but there was nothing forcing him to do it now. Except the love for his grandson. Amber bit back tears to concentrate on the situation. Tears would be useless. Derek fueled off of her tears.

Derek's voice was sadistic, no emotion whatsoever. "Let's say I have some really mean, pissed off people looking for me. So when I remembered I had a twin, well, it really was a blessing." His laugh was pure evil making her skin crawl like she was covered in slime. "So I paid my dear brother a visit. Turns out I was even the older one."

"But how did he help you?" Oh, God, did his family's bad blood ever cease?

"He didn't know he was helping me," he spoke, never leaving Grandpa's side and continuing to keep the gun at his temple.

Amber worried Derek shook so much that he'd accidentally shoot the gun. Grandpa's steady eyes remained focused on hers. If he attempted to clue her in on any plan of attack, then she missed it. She needed Cody.

"I'll pour you more whiskey, Derek. If you'd like."

He stared at her, his eyes perusing her body not hiding his stare on her chest. She resisted the urge to gag and waited for his permission to move, wanting to set off his rage as a diversion but frightened to bring on his wrath. "Sure. It's the old man's dime, huh?" he asked, elbowing Grandpa.

Again he didn't flinch, but spoke calmly. "You're welcome to as much as you'd like. Just be careful. Shit's potent as hell. Never knew a man who could handle drinking that crap."

Derek rose to the challenge. "Fill 'er up, bitch. Guess you never met anyone like me then old man."

Amber filled the glass to the rim. When she placed it on the table, she caught Grandpa's wink. It reassured her more than a hug would right now. He had some kind of plan.

Without warning, Derek's hand swung out and caught her across the face, leaving a stinging, hot mark on her cheek and sending her falling back onto the counter. The gun still rested on Grandpa. *Shit!*

"No need to do that, Derek," Grandpa said, his voice serious. "Woman did what you told her. Now don't waste energy beating her. Just enjoy your drink."

Amber moved away from the table and out of hitting range. She wouldn't give the asshole the satisfaction of rubbing her sore cheek. At least, she had the chance to see Jenna hiding at her bedroom door, peeking out. *God, please let her stay right there.*

"She had that coming. Right, you whore?" Derek asked before swigging half the whiskey, keeping the glass in his hand.

"Y-you were telling me about your brother, Derek," Amber said, softly.

"I had chatted with him a few times. You would've liked him, Ambs." The use of the cutesy nickname he'd once given her made her nauseous. "He was educated and had manners and all the fancy shit that you tried to do with your life."

She remained silent just waiting for the chance to get Jenna to safety.

He swigged the other half of the whiskey and placed the empty glass on the table. The effects of the alcohol became apparent when his speech slurred. "I had him meet me for dinner one night. But I didn't show up. You see...the twin came in handy to help me stage my own death. I set him up. Made a few phone calls to those mean pricks chasing after me and gave them a tip that I'd be there for dinner. But, of course, it wasn't me. It was long-lost baby brother. The Mob got him that night in the parking lot."

"Oh my God," Amber whispered, finally realizing the extent Derek would go through, not only to save his own hide but also to keep the money from the Blue Diamond all to himself. She couldn't stop trembling when her eyes met Grandpa's solemn ones.

Derek continued, his smile so sinister Amber was afraid of puking. "Poor bastard was tortured before they put a few bullets in his head."

So Cody had spared her the details.

"Funny thing was he really knew nothing about the Blue Diamond. *My Blue Diamond*. That fucker is worth more than you'll ever see in a lifetime. Jenna, where's the fucking doll?" he hollered.

Jenna ran out of the bedroom with her doll and Derek snatched it from her. Jenna clung to Amber crying silent tears.

"You see, I've been following you, bitch. I had to wait until the perfect time to snatch my diamond back. When the hero cop went for a ride, well, this is as good a time as any to finally claim what's mine."

"It's not yours, Derek. You stole it."

"Shut up," Derek screamed at Amber. He put the gun in

his waist and shredded the doll and the backpack with a knife.

No Blue Diamond.

Oh God. Where the hell is Cody?

Derek whipped the doll across the room and lunged at Jenna. "Where's my diamond?" When he attempted to grab her, she screamed and jumped behind Amber.

Amber's fist swung out and caught Derek in the eye. "You stay the hell away from my daughter."

Still Derek leapt for the child.

Grandpa exploded from the chair. "Don't you hurt her, you asshole."

Derek turned in time to be tackled by Grandpa. The men struggled on the floor in front of Amber and Jenna.

"Grandpa," Jenna cried.

"Derek! Stop! Get out of here," Amber screamed when she saw the gun in his hand again.

Both men held onto the gun, rolling on the floor, kicking, grunting, swearing. Suddenly, the gun went off. Grandpa rolled onto the floor, blood flowing from his side.

"Cody will shred you to pieces, asshole," Grandpa spoke softly, trying to grab Derek's leg when he stood.

Derek punched Amber in the stomach and grabbed Jenna. When he held the gun to Jenna's head, Amber jumped at him, gasping for air, visions of clawing his eyes out floated in her mind. How dare he lay a hand on her innocent, precious little girl. Death would be too good for him. "Leave her alone, Derek. She's only a child. Let her go."

"Stay back or she's dead," he yelled, saliva pooling at the edges of his mouth, the image of a rabid dog.

"No! Let her go, goddamn you!" Amber screamed. She couldn't risk Jenna's safety so she stayed back; every ounce of her being wanted to peal Derek's skin from his body.

Think. Think. Think.

Jenna struggled. She screamed, cried, kicked, tried to bite. It broke Amber's heart to see her daughter in the fight for her life and she was helpless to do anything about it.

"Give me the diamond. That's all I want. Then you can have the brat back," Derek yelled, his arm under Jenna's throat and swinging her like she was a rag doll.

"The diamond isn't here. Cody has it. Go get it." Amber edged closer.

"Yeah, come get it, Derek," Cody said from the doorway, his eyes as dark and menacing as Amber had ever seen them, pointing a gun at Derek's head. "You have no way out."

Derek held the gun to Jenna's temple. Amber gasped, ready to lunge.

"Well, well, well. If it ain't Mr. Hero Cop. Give me the diamond or you can watch me blow their heads off and finish the old man, too." For emphasis, Derek kicked Grandpa's leg.

"Asshole," Grandpa muttered, trying to pull himself up but too weak to do anything but lie on the floor.

"Not a chance. Amber, take Jenna," Cody said calmly.

Amber didn't hesitate, knowing he had a plan. When Amber leapt forward and grabbed for Jenna, Derek didn't know who to fight, her or the man with the gun. When Derek flung Jenna toward Amber and pointed his gun at Cody, Cody launched his body at Derek taking him by surprise.

Amber pushed Jenna behind her, grateful for Cody. She leaned down and grabbed Grandpa's hand and pulled him backward into the parlor, feeling strength she had never possessed before.

Cody and Derek struggled, fists punching faces, heads

butting, grunts and groans. Amber couldn't escape with Jenna since the men blocked the only door. Keeping Jenna behind her, Amber held her hand over Grandpa's bleeding wound. If they were stuck inside, then she could at least attempt to save Grandpa's life, like he had theirs.

A gunshot sliced the air. Then silence. Amber's head whipped up.

"Cody!" she screamed, her eyes searching desperately over the entwined bodies to see if he was shot. He was under Derek's body lying on the floor.

Strange men entered the kitchen and Amber gasped.

Oh no. The hit men had found them. Now they were all dead.

"Detective Maguire, we are Prince Al-Hussein's Royal Soldiers. Was that the only gunman?" a man dressed in tan fatigues asked from the doorway, rifle aimed at Derek's lifeless body as Cody pushed him off.

"Yeah. That's the only one," Cody said. "Amber. Jenna. Are you okay?"

Amber and Jenna ran to Cody. "Grandpa. He's shot. Cody, help Grandpa," Amber said.

"Nah. The old man has seen worse. Ain't that right, Grandpa?"

"You know, you could help an old man out here and let me enjoy the attentions of a beautiful woman for a few minutes before I die."

Cody laughed. "You won't ever die. You have too much fun busting my balls. Ambulance will be here shortly. Stay still. I don't want to clean up any more of your blood than I have to."

"You're welcome," Grandpa said and rested.

"Thank you, Grandpa," Cody whispered into Amber's hair.

"And who are you?" Cody asked the soldier standing silently behind them.

"I'm sent by Prince Al-Hussein. He was with you at the policia station when you ran out to save the woman and child. He ordered us to follow and help you. I'll be going now. You have it under control." And as quietly as the man and his team appeared, they disappeared into the night's shadows. Cody was glad he hadn't had to fight them.

Captain Ferron arrived moments later.

"Captain, how do foreigners find me before you do?" Cody teased, keeping Amber and Jenna close.

"Shut up, Maguire."

CHAPTER 20

C ody walked through the white hallways of the hospital to the ICU waiting room in search of Amber.

"Just got an update from the doctors. Grandpa's surgery went great and he'll be pleased to know he'll need constant care and attention for at least the next month," Cody reported to Amber as Jenna sat beside her sniffling. "He's giving them hell in the Recovery Room so they'll be bringing him up soon. Don't worry—he's being his regular stubborn self. Grandpa always said a bullet was no match for him."

"He deserves to be taken care of. He took care of me and Jenna. I'll be forever grateful to both of you, Cody." Amber said, tears welling in her eyes. "I'll never forget you."

Never forget him? What the hell did that mean?

"I hope not since I plan to be a part of your life, Amber," he said, sitting next to her, brushing his knuckles over her tear-stained cheeks.

"You don't owe me anything, Cody. I never expected there to be an 'us'."

He stared at her wondering where this was coming from. "Well, I sure as heck did." The way her eyes studied his shook him to the core. Did she not want him? His heart pounded at the thought.

"But there can't be. You're a police officer and I'm...well, I have a past. I wouldn't be good for you."

"Says who?" His fingers gently grasped her chin, turning her head so she faced him. "And what past are you talking about? I clearly remember not finding much of anything on your background check when I took this case on."

Her sigh echoed her sadness. "My past with Derek. Police still look at me like I'm some sort of criminal. How can I date a police officer when I have that kind of reputation?"

"Listen, Amber. This case will go a long way in proving you're a decent woman, not a criminal. And for the record, I don't give a crap what anyone thinks. I love you, Amber."

Her golden eyes widened and her breath hitched. "You do? But how? We've only known each other a few days and the circumstances were far from the best."

"True. But I know my life will be boring without you and this princess in it," he said, tweaking Jenna's nose and earning a smile.

"Oh, Cody, my emotions are all scrambled. I can't think straight. I'm just eternally grateful to you and your grandpa for saving us."

"As am I," Prince Al-Hussein said, stepping into the private ICU waiting room. Cody stood, shook his hand before he stepped aside. "Jenna, my dear, I heard you lost your favorite doll," the prince said gently, a far cry from the mean tone he invoked earlier with Cody. "I know some things cannot be replaced, but I was hoping you could give this new doll a good home," he said softly, handing a blond doll to Jenna.

"She's so pretty. Daddy shredded Sarah," Jenna said, a small pout forming on her pretty face.

"Well, maybe you could give this one a special name, too, and take good care of her," the prince said, his friendliness putting the child at ease.

"I guess so. I think I'll call her Allie. Kind of like your name Al." Jenna smiled brightly at the man leaning over her.

The prince laughed a deep, roaring sound. "You are a remarkable child, my dear Jenna." He straightened and faced Amber. "I am so grateful to you for returning the Blue Diamond. You know, it's a family heirloom and means almost as much as the monetary value since it's been passed down through generations. The stone is believed to possess special powers that protect the owner from harm, which may explain why you and your daughter survived this ordeal."

Amber stood and crossed the floor to Cody, circling her arms around Cody's waist. "Nope, Prince Al-Hussein. You see, Detective Maguire promised me that Jenna and I would be safe and he's yet to break a promise."

Cody spoke softly, as if they were the only ones in the room. He held Amber in front of him, his eyes watching hers. "I promise to love you and Jenna forever, Amber. I don't give a damn about your past. All I care about is the future. Will you marry me?"

"Really?" Her mouth dropped.

He kissed her forehead before studying her beautiful face. "A man only has his promise and his last name in this world, or so my grandfather claims. I'd like to give both to you, Amber. I'd like to adopt Jenna as my daughter and have many more babies with you."

Her eyes softened, and for the first time since he had met her, her shoulders relaxed and her expression lightened, all worries gone. "Then you have my word, Cody, to uphold your last name in the most honorable way and bless us with as many children as we desire."

"Is that a yes?" He held his breath hoping he had heard her right.

The huge smile said it all. She beamed as she yelled, "Yes, Cody Maguire. I'll marry you."

Cody kissed her possessively, mindful of the company in the room but too thrilled to care who witnessed him kissing his future wife.

"Oh no!" Jenna complained. Amber and Cody immediately separated and stared at the girl. "Another doll with something hidden in it."

Amber took the piece of paper hidden in the zipper on the back of the doll. When she unfolded it, she almost fainted and would have collapsed if Cody weren't attached to her like glue.

"It's a check for one million dollars payable to Jenna from Prince Al-Hussein," Amber stated, stunned.

"My sincere gratitude," the prince said, offering a slight bow, his white robes flowing around him.

"Oh...I'm sorry, Your Highness, but we can't accept this." Amber handed the paper back to the prince who didn't make a move to accept it.

"What? Of course you can," the prince insisted.

"No. We didn't return the Blue Diamond to you for any reward monies. It was just the proper thing to do. I said from the beginning I had nothing to do with the diamond nor did I want anything to do with it. Taking this money just doesn't feel right. We were both victims of my ex-husband but there's no way I should profit from it." For emphasis, she shook the paper at him and still he refused to take it.

"Such an admirable woman, Detective Maguire," the prince said to Cody before facing Amber again. "But, my dear Amber, this is not reward money. I had refused to offer a reward for the return of something that was mine to begin with." He folded his hands in front of him and continued speaking softly. "You see, my family is eternally grateful to you. Had we known the real truth behind the Blue Diamond's loss, my men wouldn't have added to your troubles. Please accept my sincere apology for any grief we caused you. You will always have a friend in me. The money is a token of appreciation so that darling Jenna can have anything she wants in life."

Jenna jumped from her seat and ran to Cody, grasping his hand. "I got what I want. I have a new daddy."

Tears ran down Amber's cheek when Cody picked up Jenna and hugged her like she was his own. Now she really would be.

"The child is wise beyond her years," the prince said, bowing. "Goodbye. I do expect an invitation to the wedding and, of course, notice of all babies when they're born. The Maguire and Al-Hussein families will be life-long friends." The prince and his security entourage left quickly and quietly.

Cody spoke into Amber's ear, still holding Jenna and her doll in his arms. "Jenna is indeed the smartest little girl I've ever met, but her mom's much wiser."

"Oh, yeah?" Amber asked.

"Yup."

"Why?"

"Because you agreed to marry me. I think it's the best

decision you've ever made," Cody said simply. Her heart swelled with more love than she ever imagined being able to possess.

"Best question you've ever asked me," she said, leaning up on her toes and kissing his cheek.

"Let's go tell Grandpa he better get his butt out of bed soon because I'm marrying you as soon as possible. I need a vacation and what better way to take one than to spend it on a honeymoon." He led the way out of the waiting room.

"Can I come on the honeymoon?" Jenna asked.

Amber laughed. "I think you'll have more fun staying at Grandma and Grandpa's for a week."

"We'll take another vacation as a family soon, peanut," Cody said, kissing her cheek and placing her on her feet at Grandpa's hospital room door.

Jenna walked slowly into the room. "Grandpa, are you okay?"

Grandpa lay propped up on pillows like he hadn't just been gunned down and had surgery. He struggled to sit up more as Cody and Amber watched from the hall. "Me? Of course I am. Trying to talk them into letting me go home now that they've stitched me up."

"Grandpa, guess what?" Jenna asked, excitement flowing from her while she sat on the side of his bed. "I'm gonna be your granddaughter."

Grandpa's usual strong voice was softer, but his face showed his determination as he kept his attention on Jenna. "Is that so?"

"Yup."

"Does that mean I need to buy you lots of presents?"

Jenna giggled. "Only if you want to, but I can give you a list if you like."

Grandpa laughed so hard, he winced in pain. "So tell me what I missed while they got me cooped up in here."

"Well, Cody asked Mommy to marry him. And then she said yes. So he gets to be my daddy now." Jenna rambled on quickly, excitement etched in her voice. Amber was happy to finally give the child the happiness she deserved.

"Want to know a secret?" Grandpa asked in a whisper. Jenna nodded and leaned closer. Grandpa held her pinky finger. "You already have Cody wrapped around this little finger of yours. That means he loves you. You've been through a lot, Jenna. More than any child deserves. I promise you that, from now on, things will only get better. Cody is a good man and comes from a good family. You're part of the Maguires now, sunshine. You and your mother will always be loved and cared for. You're both special. Never forget that, understand?"

"Yes, Grandpa."

From the hallway, Amber and Cody continued to watch the old man and little girl converse like they were long lost friends, or conspirators. "Cody, I've never seen Jenna so relaxed and happy. After everything she's been through and witnessed, I can't believe she's not scarred for life. Emotionally. Mentally. It's incredible how fast she bounced back from this nightmare." Cody held her hand, his fingers caressing her knuckles while he stared into her eyes.

"She'll have the bad memories forever, Amber, but now it's up to us to fill her life with so many good memories that the bad ones just remain in the past. I love her like she was my own. Believe me, I will treat her that way. We're going to show her what a family is supposed to be like, okay?"

Tears welled in Amber's eyes and for once they were happy tears. "Okay. Thank you, Cody. For just being you... wonderful you."

"I love you, Amber."

"I love you, too, Cody. I never thought I'd ever be this lucky. I love you so much." Three simple words, but never had she felt them profoundly. He was branded on her heart forever.

"Oh, yeah? Then prove it. Kiss me, Amber."

With her arms circling the neck of the man she loved, Amber placed her lips on Cody's, not regretting one moment of her past as it led her to where she was meant to be. In Cody Maguire's arms. Forever.

No jewel in the world was more priceless than her love for this man who showed her things really do happen for a reason.

Chapter One

Mitch drifted off to sleep, warring with the visions behind his eyelids when the dream took hold.

Transported back to that horrible day, terror gripped him by the throat, defying his attempts to suck in air with desperate breaths. Fear's icy fingers crawled along his sweat-dampened skin like a slimy worm slithering across a rain-slicked ground. But Mitch couldn't let fear win. If he did, death would surely follow. He could only fight his way out of the nightmare.

Moving quietly along the liquor store's dark hallway to the backroom where the girls were held captive, Mitch relied totally on his specialized police training to guide him to the hostages. His eyes scanned the darkness, adjusting to the lack of light. His ears strained for any sound but found only silence. The ominous scent of death—the smell of spilled blood—made his heart pound painfully within his chest.

Mitch's mind filtered a thousand vicious curses as he

inched forward, desperate to reach the girls who depended on him for their lives.

Time passed too slowly as he ignored his own pain and crept onward into the darkness, maybe to his death.

His gun steady in his hand, his senses on high alert. The second he viewed the figure lying on the ground, motionless in a dark pool of liquid, his world changed forever. And not for the better.

Mitch woke abruptly in a cold sweat, his skin chilled and clammy. The way his heart pounded, he felt like he had just run a marathon. He pinched the bridge of his nose and shook the sleep from his foggy mind. Sitting behind the steering wheel in his truck while using the seat's headrest as a pillow only cramped his muscles. Taking a nap on the side of the road wasn't conducive to a decent rest. A quick glance at the clock showed he'd been asleep for just under an hour. And he felt worse now than when he pulled over to rest his bleary eyes.

Turning the ignition, the engine roared to life and Mitch pulled his truck back onto the rural highway. He was tired, hungry, and lost somewhere in the damn Smoky Mountains. Running from a past that haunted him to a future he couldn't see would have been better with a direction in mind. Small drops of water splattered on his windshield, just a hint of the storm brewing in the east.

He had driven with no particular destination. But for the first ten hours on the road, he had an idea of where the hell he was. Not now. Now, huge green fields dotted with grazing cows and horses seemed never ending. Deep forests with tall, leafy trees and ragged undergrowth abutted the fields. And still there was no sign of civilization. The two-lane backcountry route was an infinite winding road. Like being stuck in a maze with no way out. Similar to what his memories did to him, keeping him stuck in the past, stuck on one day with no way out.

The once deep blue skies held dark gray puffy clouds and threatened rain. His six-foot-two inch frame ached from being cramped behind the wheel for so many hours. His fault really for driving with no purpose. A glance in the rearview mirror confirmed that he looked as bad as he felt. His eyes were bloodshot, the tiny red lines making the whiskey color of his eyes dark and menacing. Gray half-moons had set in under his eyes, causing him to look old and withered. Scratchy dark stubble covered an angular jaw that gave his chin an angle of defiance, jutting out just enough to square his face. His thick, light brown hair cried out for a haircut.

The "ding ding" alarm sounded just as big fat raindrops hit the windshield. The tiny picture of a red gasoline pump on his dashboard warned of low fuel. He burst out laughing, laughing so hard that it hurt. It was either laugh or punch the windshield and that would just let in the heavy rain now lashing out from mean skies.

Ding, ding.

"All right, for Christ's sakes. I'll get you some go-go juice as soon as I find some sign of life around here," he complained, while straining his head to look into the distance through the rain-spotted windshield.

Slowly, Mitch drove through the downpour. Scanning the distance, there was no sign of people anywhere. The mountains were a huge mass of land and he cursed himself for not paying attention to his whereabouts.

His arms tensed, holding the steering wheel, while his thoughts wandered to the recent events that had left him in this current predicament. He still couldn't believe that he had really left his home, his life, his job. Everything. Just ran. There was nothing left for him now in Boston. Only haunting memories and a job with the police force that was out of reach. His conscience weighed heavier and heavier each day. He only hoped the distance from Massachusetts would help ease the pain. Wherever the steering wheel turned, he'd go but not for long without some gas and sleep.

There might be enough gas for another few miles... maybe. He smirked when he saw the old green and white sign on the side of the road indicating the Town of Courtsville two miles ahead. With the rain pelting the windshield, he sure was glad to find civilization again.

Lightening streaked across the sky, spotlighting the distant mountains. Thunder crackled with deafening roars. The wind shook his truck, blowing through the trees and slanting them toward the roadway. No way in hell did he want to get stranded in a friggin' thunderstorm with no food or water and no damn aspirin. He didn't know what hurt more, the pain between his eyes or his knee.

"Just like in the movies," Mitch complained, squinting to see through the stream of water pouring over the windshield. Small hailstones bounced off the glass like ping pong balls. On the roof, it sounded like drums.

He slowed, squinted, and almost drove right by the one-island gas station. There were no lights on. No sign of anyone working. What the fuck? To his relief, when he pulled up to the pump, he glimpsed a dim light in the window of the small shack. The front door opened as a tall, white-haired elderly man in overalls holding an umbrella stepped out.

Mitch rolled down his window. "Fill 'er up, please," he directed, unfastening his seatbelt to get his wallet.

"You ain't from around here, are ya?"

"No, sir." Mitch caught bright blue eyes watching him. He wasn't looking for conversation. Just some fuel.

The man started to pump the gas. Mitch was rolling up his window when the guy reappeared.

Mitch stared at him in bafflement. "What?"

"Can't very well talk to the hose while she fills ya up, so thought I'd talk to you."

"About what?"

"Don't know."

Small towns. Is this what people did? Make idle conversation just to hear themselves? "Well, I don't have much to talk about. Been on the road too long." As proof, he yawned, unable to stop himself.

"You got far to go?" the man asked, holding the umbrella as the rain slowed to a light drizzle. Thunder still echoed in the distance. At least the storm had passed.

"Not sure. But I could use dinner and a night's sleep. Can you tell me if I'm anywhere near either?"

"Not gonna get far in this truck," the man announced, angling his head toward the hood. "Nope. Not more than two miles I'd say."

Now he had Mitch's attention. "Why?" Mitch followed the man's glance. A large plume of white smoke bellowed from under the hood. "Son of a bitch!"

Before Mitch finished another line of curses and managed to get out of the truck, the old man was already standing in front of the hood.

"Pop it," the man commanded.

Mitch complied, reaching under the steering column and pulling the black lever until he heard a pop. He walked slowly to stand by the old man who used his hand to brush away the smoke.

"Yup. Just as I thought. You cracked the radiator. Ain't no

antifreeze or water left in 'er." He shut the hood. "It'll get you about two miles but not more without stalling or worse, blowing the engine."

"Shit!" Mitch stood with his hands on his hips and studied the shack. There was no sign of a garage, but he had to ask. "Can you fix it?"

"Wish I could help you there, my friend, but I only sell gas. There's a good mechanic in town."

"Can I get to him without causing more damage?"

"Sure, I guess. But won't do you any good. He's closed up shop by now. It's poker night."

Mitch wasn't even going to ask. "What do you suggest then? What if I filled the radiator with some water?"

"Won't do any good. It'll just piss out of the hole. Your engine's so hot, probably been on the road some time now. You'd stall or blow your engine after two miles. That's my guess."

Mitch wanted to kick the truck. But he just stared at the ground trying to think of something. Every situation had a way out. Or at least he once thought so. Had once been trained to think so.

The old man left Mitch's side to take the hose out and replace the cap. "That'll be thirty three even," he said, returning to Mitch.

Mitch pulled out his wallet for the cash.

"You a cop?" the man asked when he noticed his badge in his wallet.

Mitch didn't know why he kept the thing. How many times had he thought about chucking it out the window the last ten hours, but could never bring himself to do it? No. That badge had been earned with his blood and guts. He may no longer be a cop, but he'd hold onto it.

"Not anymore, sir."

The man pointed to his leg. "Got injured on the job?"

"Yeah."

"Too bad. We could use a new sheriff in these parts."

Mitch smirked. "Sorry. Not interested."

"Now that's a damn shame," the old man said, the hopeful smile he held a moment ago now gone. "Tell you what. You look like an honest man. For a cop, that is."

"Ex-cop," Mitch reaffirmed.

The man waved his hand in the air. "Okay, ex-cop. Anyway, why don't you come home with me? The missus will take good care of you, give you a meal, fix up a bed for you for the weekend, until you get your truck fixed."

Mitch stared, not use to such hospitality. "That's very kind of you, sir."

"Name's Joe McFadden. Folks around here call me Ol' Joe. Not because of my age. Hell, I've still got a lot of years left. But because I've been in town for generations. Well, not me, but my family."

Mitch laughed. "I get the picture. I do appreciate the offer, but I have to decline. Can you give me directions to the mechanic? I'd like to see if I can catch him."

"I'm telling you it's pointless. He's closed up by now. But suit yourself. I doubt you'll even make it to town. You'll only end up having to sleep in this cramped truck all night. Probably wouldn't be a smart thing to do with that bum leg of yours. But get a pen and right down these directions."

Mitch did as instructed.

"You sure you want to risk driving instead of coming home with me? Your truck can be fixed first thing Monday morning when Maddy opens his shop."

"I'll be fine. Thanks again."

Mitch pulled out onto the road and followed Ol' Joe's directions. He'd beg the mechanic to fix his truck and offer him extra money if need be. But no way was Mitch bunking down with strangers, especially someone who would offer him food and comfort. He'd just left that behind with his family for Christ's sakes.

Per the instructions, he'd watch for the yellow tower and follow the road into town. Once his truck was repaired, he'd get directions to the nearest motel. In the morning, he'd drive again until he figured out what he wanted to do with his life now that his career was over.

ABOUT THE AUTHOR

Christina James is an award-winning romance author of contemporary, erotic, romantic suspense, and sweet romance. Her books offer witty banter, a dose of sarcasm sprinkled throughout, and lots of love. The happy ever after never fails to touch the heart and need a box of tissues. She is a fan of books that involve family and friends and her stories involve more than just the romantic relationship.

Living in a Boston suburb with her golden retriever and two ragdoll cats, Christina enjoys creating stories where her readers fall in love with her characters as much as she does.

Christina enjoys binge watching Netflix, spending time with friends and family, romantic walks on the beach, or just listening to the rain fall.

ALSO BY CHRISTINA JAMES

A Place to Call Home

Christmas at Snowfall Lodge

Falling for the Firefighter

For the Love of a Woman

Harvest Hideaway

Saving Christmas

Seasons of Sweet Romance: Sweet Romance Collection Box Set

Erotic Romance:

Make A Wish and Blow

Operation: Spank Me

Operation: Tell Me More

Operation: Tempt Me

Operation: Desire Me

Operation: Seduce Me

Operation: Persuade Me